MW01130658

Contents

Language

Please note that this book is written by an English author about British characters. It's therefore written in UK English, which differs slightly from US English. Examples of their differences are:

Realize is Realise

Organize is Organise

Behavior is Behaviour

Spelled can be Spelt

Dreamed can be Dreamt

Jewelry is Jewellery

Anemia is Anaemia

Traveled is Travelled

License can be Licence

Whiskey is Whisky

There are obviously too many examples to catalogue (that's another one) them all here, but just to make you aware ahead of time.

Trigger Warnings

What triggers are not in the book?

There is no mention or depiction of animal abuse, child death, eating disorders, fatphobia, homophobia, incest, misgendering, racism, terminal illness, or transphobia.

Why provide a list of triggers that aren't in the book?

Some readers have asked why I include this—it's to allow people with specific triggers to quickly scan the list, ensuring their trigger isn't present, so they can enjoy the story without spoilers. Everyone deserves a safe and enjoyable reading experience, and this method lets readers make an informed decision without revealing key plot points.

MAJOR SPOILERS ON THE NEXT PAGE

What triggers are in the book?

Heart of Stone is a dark romance, and it contains several triggers. These include: abortion, being framed for a crime, cancer (non-terminal), car accidents, child sexual abuse (CSA), depression, drug addiction, explicit sexual content, false imprisonment, foul language, gambling addiction, human trafficking, knife play, loss of limbs, murder, physical violence, poverty, pregnancy, prison, rape, revenge porn, spanking, suicidal actions, suicidal thoughts, and torture.

1

"**D**ad," Kate whispered, horrified. The misery budded in her heart threatened to bloom. "I don't understand—you've *lost* your club?"

He took her hand, perhaps to stop the shaking in his own. The acrid notes of cheap alcohol and cigarette smoke hung heavy on his breath, as they always did when he returned from his club. *Charlton's Gentlemen's Club*. Club. A word fragranced with memories of aristocratic gentlemen's establishments in St James's, where the nobility would hide from nagging wives and share a tipple over the newest copy of *The Times*.

Her dad's business was little more than a seedy casino-turned-strip club, where only the most desperate would be found on any given day. Or the most dangerous.

Dad's eyes remained glued to their intertwined hands, as though he were too afraid to look her in the eye. "I made a bet," he admitted.

Kate's shoulders sunk in horror. She wrenched her hand from his. "You promised you wouldn't gamble again. You *promised*."

"I know," he nodded, letting loose a cider-infused sigh. "I'm sorry, but you should have seen—"

Her anger exploded from her in a fierce strike as his excuses began. She'd heard them all before. "I've spent all evening on the phone to the debt management people!" She picked up the enormous stack of invoices she'd had to compile, brandishing them in his direction. "Do you know how long it took to sort out? I had to detail every single asset—"

Her airway was almost cut off by the realisation.

The house.

The house that Dad had bought under the name of the club as a way of finagling his way out of paying tax, as suggested by his dodgy accountant.

"Dad, please tell me you didn't."

Her father, who she'd always accepted regardless of his many faults, couldn't even meet her gaze. He glared at his hands like a naughty schoolboy sitting outside his headteacher's office, waiting for a bollocking. "I'm sorry, Katie."

"Don't *Katie* me," she hissed, storming to her feet. "I have spent the last decade of my life trying to get the club back on its feet financially, working day and night to solve every single mess you've made, consolidating loans and pleading with companies to help you get back on your feet." All while her friends from school had been moving on with their lives, marrying and multiplying without a care in the world. Not that they kept in touch with her anymore, given that she spend her every waking hour attempting to manage Dad's finances and doing admin for the club. The only contact she had with any of them was social media, seeing their perfect lives plastered across her shattered phone screen.

Kate shook her head, holding her arms across her chest. *What am I doing with my life?*

Living in a one-bedroom terrace house with her father. The only sacrifice he'd ever made for her was to give her the bedroom and sleep on a futon in the living room. The pale green carpet beneath her feet was threadbare, whilst her father's smoking had long since stained the walls a sickening yellow.

"I can't do this anymore." Her voice was soft. *I can't do anything anymore.*

At that, he looked up. Finally. "What does that mean?"

"It means I can't sit here and watch you throw your life away! In addition to the club and this fucking house, apparently." She gestured to the photo on the coffee table next to the futon; the only photograph Dad would allow in the house. "Ever since Aaron died, you've been *destroying* yourself, Dad." Her voice cracked. "And in the process you're destroying me."

"Do you not think I've had enough to put up with?" he responded, his backbone suddenly appearing at the barest hint of criticism.

"You were supposed to be the adult. No one forced you to get into that car." The disappointment in her expression said the rest. *No one forced you to let a drunken teenager drive your car.*

It had been the morning of Aaron's eighteenth birthday when she'd been woken by a kindly social worker telling her that her father, brother, and brother's best friend had been in a car accident, and that her brother hadn't survived. She'd been taken into care for the two months that her father was in the hospital, having had no one else to care for her.

There's still no one to care for me.

The world fell away beneath her feet at the realisation that she was totally and utterly alone in the world. Dad had used her as nothing more than a workhorse to keep his business afloat, gambling away years of her work whenever the need struck him, whilst his drug addiction took care of the rest.

"Don't you *dare,*" Dad hissed, pointing a yellow-nailed finger at her. His face had turned an alarming shade of pink, as it always did when he drank too much. They never spoke of Aaron's death, nor the circumstances surrounding it.

Or, more specifically, the fault surrounding it.

Kate blinked slowly, her anger deflating like a popped balloon. Dad was failing her just as much as he failed Aaron, just at a tenth of the speed. "I'm going to bed," she announced colourlessly, heading towards the narrow set of spiral stairs in the corner.

Her father nodded, flicking on the TV and finding a boxing match to watch. "I think that would be best. Perhaps… perhaps things will look better in the morning. We have a few days before the club and its assets change hands. We'll sort something out."

Tears burnt the back of her eyes, but she managed to conjure a final smile at him as she ascended the stairs.

No, we won't.

The layout of the upstairs of the house was a perfect match to the downstairs, with the kitchen being downstairs and the bathroom up. The yellowing walls pervaded here too, her father's cigarette smoke drifting up through the stairs. Kate glared at it as it invaded her space. What she wouldn't give to have a door. Instead, the curved staircase came right through the floor of her bedroom, crashing through any privacy she might have wanted.

Silently, she packed her things into an old weekend bag she'd bought at a charity shop. The musty scent of disuse wrinkled her nose. The fake leather was peeling off in flaky chunks, but it would have to do. Tears attempted to escape down her cheeks when she found the single item she kept in the bag, but Kate furiously swatted them away. She ran her thumb over the little heart-shaped locket; the only thing she had left of her mother.

She clipped it on, hiding it underneath her collar with a clenched jaw. Dad didn't deserve it. Not after everything he put her through.

A commotion outside pricked her ears. Dogs barking. Her neighbour's staffies, she guessed. Kate poked her head out of the window. Her neighbour—Peter—worked the night shift down at a local hotel. To stop his dogs destroying his house, Peter usually left them in his garden whilst he worked, but they were making quick work of his lacklustre fencing. They'd escaped last week. Again.

She exhaled a sigh of relief when she saw they were still in the garden. In fact, judging from the plumes of weed smoke rising from beneath the front door's awning, Peter himself was home.

Good. The last thing she needed tonight was to be a dog wrangler.

When the few belongings she had were packed, Kate sat on her bedroom floor. The metal railings of her bedframe pressed uncomfortably into her spine, but she remained where she was.

The cold reality of her situation hit home when there was nothing left to do. No physical task to take her mind off things.

Kate scrolled through the job listings with a growing heaviness in her chest—not to mention the price of studio flats. Even the smallest, grottiest of flats neared a grand a month. A grand a month to live in a flat so small she could touch the kitchen sink whilst lying in bed.

Her father's business was largely illegal. True, the strip club and casino elements were legal, but the prostitution was not. The drugs changing hands were not. What would her CV even say?

Kate Charlton

Employment history:

After working at Charlton's Gentlemen's Club since leaving school four years ago, my attempts to save my father from his many vices have finally failed. Consequently, I'm looking for a new challenge. Experienced in balancing (probably) dodgy books, general administration, payroll, social media, organising illegal fights, completing tax returns, communicating with bailiffs, and not voicing my many concerns about the way the business is handled.

Uncomfortable around people in general, but skilled in Microsoft Excel and catching badly trained dogs. Still annoyed about the last season of *Game of Thrones.*

She let her head fall back against the foot of the bed and closed her eyes.

At the same time, a heavy thump rocked the front door.

Kate heard her father moving slowly towards the porch and scowled. Had he phoned his dealer? *Like he usually does whenever something goes wrong.* It was what he'd done after Aaron had died. Spend money they didn't have on a habit he couldn't fucking afford. Even when he'd said he had nothing, what he meant was *nothing for you.*

A decade after Aaron's death, his title as the *favourite* child still stung. The favourite of two. It would have been easier to handle if she had other siblings to commiserate with, but to play favourites with two children? All it did was separate them. Kate had never had a *brother.* She had had a competitor. A challenger for her father's love and affection.

The title of *favourite* still reigned even now. Aaron was barely cold before his sanctification began.

Kate loved her brother, deep down, but she hated who her father made him out to be. Aaron had grown up in Dad's club and had fallen in with a bad crowd at an early age. He'd not been long out of Borstal at the time of his death, sentenced for theft.

She sighed as she heard her father unlock the deadbolts she'd inexpertly drilled into the front door. The photograph of Aaron on the coffee table was a far better child than she would ever be, at least in her father's eyes.

"Talbot," Dad's voice drifted upstairs. The sound put Kate on edge—the false cheeriness laced within. "You all right?"

Where Kate had been expecting Talbot to make a reply, the only response was the quivering *bang* as the front door bounced off the wall behind it, closing shortly after. It was only then that Talbot deigned to make a reply, whoever he was.

"Paul," Talbot said curtly.

"Gents!" Dad laughed gratingly over the sound of movement. Heavy bangs reverberated through the floorboards. How many of them were there? "Gents," he said again, sounding slightly more strangled. Kate knew her father too well not to recognise desperation when she heard it. "Perhaps I can be of assistance."

"You're right," a second voice said. A deep, heavy growl that sounded as if it belonged to a bear of a man. "Sign this."

Paper rustled. "No. I have a week before the company needs to be signed over. It's barely been two hours. Tell your employer that I need tim—"

The sick crunch of a fist crashing into flesh made her jump, closely followed by her father's pained grunt and shattering glass. "I'll take no orders from you," the bear replied.

Kate gasped as the stairs began to rattle; the tell-tale sign that someone was climbing them. There was nowhere to hide. Not even a cupboard.

A bald head came into view as she scrambled to her feet, closely followed by a pair of angry, glaring eyes.

"There's a woman up here," the bear told the others, raising his growly voice as the odd noises and bangs continued downstairs. A hairless bear, then. He took the last few steps, towering above her. "Is this your latest tart?" He inspected her from head to toe in a long, lingering look that made her skin crawl. "I thought your deal with Graves would have scratched this particular itch for you."

Kate held her hands up, flinching as something shattered downstairs. "I don't want any trouble."

The bear snatched her unlocked phone out of her hands. "I'll be having this." He grabbed her arm in a punishing grip and began to yank her back towards the stairs. "Get down."

An enormous hand landed in the middle of her back, propelling her down the first few steps until she came crashing into the metal railings. They dug deep into her ribs, but she kept her complaints silent. "I'm going, I'm going."

Devastation met her eyes as she reached the ground floor. The television was smashed. Her neat pile of paper for the debt management people had been scattered on the ground. The curtains had been ripped from their poles. A man was even tearing the couch cushions to shreds, turfing white fluff onto the threadbare carpet.

She jumped. Another man was sweeping their porcelain tableware onto the floor. Dinner plates and cereal bowls hit the ground, exploding into razor sharp shards.

Kate yelped when the bear grabbed her by the hair, brandishing her like a weapon in front of her father. "Talk," he hissed, whilst Kate scrambled to hang onto him, attempting to minimise the pain.

Dad's eyes were on the man destroying the couch cushions. Blood dripped from his nose. "Please, there's no need for this. Just tell me what you're looking for."

The redheaded man now emptying out their cutlery draw answered. "Ah," he said. Talbot's voice. He sauntered towards Kate. "I'm impressed, Paul. Or are you paying her?"

Too close. He was too close.

Kate attempted to move backwards, but the bear held her firm by the hair. Talbot's hands trailed up to the curve in her hips, and he nodded appreciatively, even as Kate attempted to wiggle away.

"Fuck you," she hissed, trying to kick at him.

Talbot's sneer creased his nose. "Do you not like it when the shoe is on the other foot?"

Dad said nothing, refusing to meet her eyes. *Like always.* "What are you looking for?"

"What makes you think we're looking for anything?" the bear said from behind her, his hand still knotted in her hair.

"Is that what *your employer* wants, whoever he is?" Dad spread his arms wide. "Has he not taken everything already? Even the house is his now."

Talbot glared at her father, his eyes narrowed. "And whose fault is that?" he said softly. He bent to pick up the photograph of Aaron that her father had been standing in front of.

"No!" Dad attempted to snatch it back in a ferocious swipe, but Talbot shoved him away. Thrown off balance, Dad tripped over the pouffe, landing on his arse in an untidy heap.

"This is your boy, is it?" Talbot's lips twisted in disgust. He stared down at her father with nothing less than utter revulsion. "His whole life ahead of him too. Aaron, wasn't it?"

"Aaron," Dad confirmed, his grief as sharply illustrated as it had been a decade ago.

"Well," Talbot made himself comfortable on the leather pouffe, "we have a few questions for you, Charlton. And my friend here—" he pointed to the bear still holding Kate in his grasp "—is going to take *her* somewhere safe. In the meantime, you and I are going to have a little chat."

Kate spoke up, just about managing to hide the fear slinking its way into her veins. "And what exactly are you going to do with me?"

A cruel smile lit Talbot's face. "That's entirely up to Charlton here," he nodded towards her father. "But know this, if he fails to comply with our instructions, you'll suffer for it." He threw Aaron's photograph back onto the coffee table. The glass cracked over Aaron's smile.

Kate's eyes were wide with horror.

Dad got to his feet, his jaw clenching as the third man finished ripping the couch cushions to shreds. "What are your questions?"

Kate cried out in pain as Brax—the name of the bear-like, hair-pulling bastard—yanked the bag off her head, removing some of her hair in the process. For the first time in an hour, light flooded her vision. Too much light. She gave a pained squint, holding her hand up in front of her face to shield her gaze.

"This is where you'll be staying," Brax rumbled. In his fist, a few strands of brown hair fell from the bag to the floor.

The world's worst hairdresser. Kate scowled at him, blinking away her sensitivity to the light to take her first glance of the room—the bedroom. Her lips parted. She had expected to be squirreled away to a dirty warehouse, or even taken to her father's club to await a sharp questioning.

But this bedroom was… *magnificent.*

Where her bedroom at home was a plain creation of poverty, providing only the bare essentials, this room had been designed by a master craftsman. Dark blue panelling covered the walls, contrasting against the stark white decorative coving. The ceiling hadn't been spared, with a rose medallion stretching out to all four corners of the room. At its centre hung an elegant chandelier, scattering light over the king size bed draped in a foliate-themed bedspread in a dangerously dark midnight blue. A matching sofa was positioned in front of the bed, upholstered in a lustrous fabric that Kate knew would be silky to the touch. She pulled in an endlessly satisfying lungful of the scent pervading the room. It was intoxicating; she wanted to bathe in its warmth.

There were matching elements everywhere; the cream leather headboard matched the bedside tables, the sofa matched the bed, the cushions on the sofa matched the enormous circular rug under the bed, all reflected in an enormous mirror running along the length of the wall opposite the curtains.

The curtains themselves were no less luxurious. Floor to ceiling windows peeked out behind the kind of sweeping drapes Kate had only seen in films; heavy pleated fabric topped by matching cornices. The faded blue curtains she had in her bedroom looked like rags in comparison.

The thought hit her like a ton of bricks. A reminder of her constant poverty. A reminder that by twenty-two she should have had her life in gear. Instead, she lived in her father's ratty house filled with the cheapest of possessions and a sparsely populated fridge that was only ever visited by food from the reduced section.

Here, though…

Even the lamps screamed *money*.

I hate poverty. The constant feeling of it bearing down on her shoulders whilst she desperately tried to clamber out from underneath it, compounded by her father digging deeper beneath their feet.

Kate looked up to Brax, hating him and the room in equal measure. The only emotion she could bring herself to feel. "How long for? Hours? Days?"

"Until Stone decides you can leave." Brax walked to the door, dipping his head slightly to get through it. A long corridor could be seen behind his bulk, with furnishings of gold running along its length.

"Who is Stone? And what about my father? What's going to happen to him?"

"Stone is my employer." Brax looked down at her with something like pity. Or disgust. "But I would be more worried about yourself, Ms Charlton."

"Why?" she asked, panicking. The disgusting luxury of her bedroom had lulled her away from the tied-to-a-chair torture she had been envisaging. "I haven't done anything wrong."

Before he locked the door, Brax left her with a single question. "Haven't you?"

In the silence that remained, Kate's attention swirled around the room. She sat on the bed. Or, rather, she sat on the silken cloud masquerading as a bed. *How can something be this soft?*

Money.

Kate ran over to the window, desperate to find any indication of where she was being imprisoned. She almost laughed at the view in front of her. The open window let in still, warm air perfumed with the sound of crickets and summer insects. The rising moon was full and bright, casting soft, silvery rays on the garden. The garden—if she could call it that—was enormous. If she squinted, she could make out a stone path winding through the flowers and shrubs, leading to a picturesque pond.

Where the fuck am I?

Brax's question stayed with her, prodding at her brain. Kate locked onto the bedroom door, dreading what—or who—was behind it. *Had* she done something wrong? Her teeth worried at her bottom lip as she pondered the question.

She had enabled her father for far too long, that was for sure. Charlton's Gentlemen's Club would have gone under years ago had it not been for her, but was that a crime? She thought of all the times she'd overlooked some of the Club's transactions. The stolen goods. The money laundering. The tax evasion. She pressed her lips together. But no one was being *hurt* by it. There was no victim there. The stolen goods were taken from massive companies whose insurance would cover everything.

Kate hugged her arms around herself. What was happening to Dad at this very moment? Were those men hurting him? Were they going to hurt her? Was this entire bedroom-fit-for-a-king situation a way to lull her into a false sense of security?

She flinched as a door somewhere in the house slammed with such force it rattled the mirror on the wall.

The unknown pecked at her brain with all the delicacy of a sledgehammer. Leaping to her feet, Kate traced the perimeters of the room. Her lips parted when she entered the en-suite. The shower alone was enormous enough to need two showerheads and six downlights—something she found ridiculous.

The sharp sound of the bedroom door closing behind her had Kate jumping up in fright.

A man cleared his throat; a gravelly noise that put her on edge. Had Brax returned to pull the rest of her hair out? The drive here had given her plenty of time to enjoy his company, after he'd shoved a bag on her head and thrust her into what she assumed was a van.

Kate inched around the corner. Relief loomed large when she saw it wasn't Brax but—

"Warren?" she breathed, unable to believe her eyes.

He was so like the teenager she'd once trailed after like a lovesick puppy, recognisable underneath the sinister guise of a tall, scowling man. Not even his locks of jet black hair could shadow his glittering emerald eyes. Black stubble grazed his cheeks. Where the Warren she'd known had been lanky, a wiry boy not yet having grown into a man, *this* Warren stood proudly. A man in his prime, with the wide shoulders, dark beard, and tattoos to match.

A smile broke through her worry, shattering it into a thousand pieces. Kate crossed the room on wobbly legs to throw herself into his arms. "Warren," she hit his unexpectedly solid chest, clinging to him like he was the only thing keeping her afloat in a sea of misery. "I thought you were still in prison," she choked, pulling his once-familiar scent into her lungs.

Warren's arms remained at his side.

She reared back. "You're taller than the last time I saw you." *Aaron's death.* Her lips tightened at that. Kate had been so relieved to see a friendly face she'd forgotten what he'd done.

He'd driven whilst drunk and high and killed her brother.

His face remained expressionless, but his eyes were raging infernos.

Kate attempted to take a step back, but Warren grabbed her chin with a hand that dwarfed her own. His touch was rough, far from the calm, protective manner in which he'd used to care for her. Her brother's closest friend, who was more gentle than her brother had ever been. "Warren…" she whispered, trying to push him away. "What's wrong with you?"

"With me?" His brow cocked up as a cruel glint lit his face. Kate wriggled in discomfort as his eyes traced her body, riding her curves. Just like Talbot had done.

Except she *knew* Warren. Warren had taught her how to tie her shoelaces and how to ride a bike. He had been with her through so much of her childhood, a comforting, nurturing figure she could always rely on. More than she'd ever relied on Aaron or her father.

"You're angry," Kate stated, just as Warren forced her back against the wall.

"I was." His eyes shone bright with hate; an emotion he'd never before directed at her. "But now I'm just disappointed in you, kitten."

Kate's sharp inhale nearly choked her. *Kitten.* A name she hadn't heard in years. A treasured relic that had nearly been forgotten amongst her memories.

"You're not quite grown up to be a Kate," Warren had said not long after they'd met. The two had been at the local park next to the children's home in which Warren had grown up. It had been an early spring day, drowning in butterflies and bumblebees and laughter.

"I am so," Kate giggled, squealing as Warren pushed her higher and higher on the swings. She swooped her legs, flying through the air.

Warren had kept a close watch on her, even from the beginning. "You're not a Kat either."

Kate leant back, her long plait dangling behind her. "Definitely not a Kat."

He'd darted round to the front of the swings. "Jump," he dared her. Warren braced as Kate leapt into his embrace without hesitation, but he caught her with ease. Giggling with joy, she wrapped her arms around Warren's neck and squeezed him tightly.

Warren's face had slackened in shock at her touch, as though it was something he'd never experienced before. But then he'd hugged her in turn, holding her close with an expression of fierce joy. A boy of 10, Warren was a giant to her then. As they stood, surrounded by the bright sunshine and the sounds of laughter and play, Kate had felt the connection between them growing. Even then.

He'd ruffled her hair, his face alight with pride. "Not a Kat, but perhaps a kitten."

Kate leant against him, treasuring the feeling of being cared for—for once in her life. A small grumble of acquiescence left her as she accepted Warren's name for her.

"Come on then, kitten. We should be getting you home." Warren announced, treading the path towards Kate's house. "But first let's get you an ice cream cone."

A small giggle left her. A nickname. Kate smiled gleefully; someone liked her enough to give her a nickname!

The eighteen years since then had wrought changes in them both, but Kate still reacted to her old nickname. *Kitten.* "What exactly have I done to disappoint you, Warren?" she asked pointedly. "Given the fact that you were imprisoned for causing Aaron's death, I think the disappointment should be the other way round."

Warren loomed over her, pressing her further against the wall. His hand still held her chin in a punishing grip. A jolt shuddered through her as his thumb caressed her lips. Nothing more than a gentle whisper following their contours. His nostrils flared, his eyes fixed to her mouth.

"Warren, I…"

"Shh," he urged her quietly, his free hand beginning to outline the curve in her hip. Warren pushed his body against hers, his wide shoulders engulfing her completely. She squeaked as he reached the bottom of her breast.

A strange sensation came over her, plunging beyond the pit of her stomach. A hot, fiery warmth that called out for more. She wriggled, opening her mouth to speak—

Only to have Warren roughly cover it with his hand. "What did I say?" he said carefully.

Her attention was called to something pressing into her stomach. A long, thick length that seemed both eager and firm. *Oh god.* She let out a muffled squawk of alarm. He was aroused. He was *very* aroused.

"Quiet." Warren pressed his nose into her neck, deeply inhaling. "*Kitten*," he growled savagely.

Her breath sawed in and out of her lungs, the sound magnified by Warren's hand partially covering her nose. Was this really happening? Kate was mesmerised by his eyes—as she always had been. Their green depths seemed to sink into her very soul, laying her bare for his examination.

Something that he apparently seemed keen to explore.

An inch from her face, Warren removed his hand. His thumb trailed behind, pulling her bottom lip downwards slightly as it left. He dipped his head. Kate could feel his breath against her face. The atmosphere between them hummed with energy and unspoken emotions. Kate tipped her chin upwards, reaching towards his lips. She was going to kiss *Warren*, the boy she'd always yearned for, even at the young age of twelve. She closed her—

"Stone."

Stone?

The word cut through them both, severing the connection.

Brax stood near the doorway, his muscular build and scowling face giving him an immediate air of harsh authority. "You're needed in the cellar."

Warren nodded, his gaze never leaving Kate. He waited until Brax left before speaking. "Who would have thought you'd turn out to be as much of a scheming cunt as your father, kitten?"

Kate frowned in confusion, but Warren had already pulled away. "Wait," Kate stammered, following him. "*You're* Stone? The Stone that ruined my father and kidnapped me?" The emotional turmoil heaved through her. "I thought we were friends, Warren." Even if he was partly responsible for Aaron's death, she wouldn't have thought he'd be capable of wilful maliciousness towards her.

He turned to her at the last moment with those burning eyes of hatred. "I thought so too, kitten."

2

Warren

Water tinged red with blood seeped into the shower drain. He'd lost his temper with Paul Charlton. *Deservedly so.*

The first rays of dawn were splashed across the landscape as Warren stumbled out of the shower. He swiped a hand through the condensation fogging up the mirror, grumbling at the bloodshot eyes looking back at him. Attempting to blink away the grittiness, Warren dressed himself slowly. It wouldn't be the first night he'd gone without sleep. It wouldn't even be the first night he'd gone without sleep because of Paul Charlton.

The nights in the hospital had been the worst. After he'd been pulled out of Paul's car in pieces and rushed to hospital in a screaming ambulance, protesting his innocence all the way. The next time he'd woken was to find his room guarded by a police officer, who told him he was under arrest for causing death by careless driving under the influence of drink or drugs. Aaron's death, no less. His best friend. The words that ruined his life.

When Warren should have been focusing on the long process of grieving and trying to regain his independence, he'd instead been imprisoned. He'd spent the first year of his sentence in the prison's healthcare wing, surrounded by dying criminals and the repetitive noises of unceasing equipment.

He'd been 18, still half a boy.

Through the two-sided mirror, Warren watched Kate with keen eyes. She'd curled herself into a tight little ball in her sleep.

He shouldn't have gone in to see her last night. *That* had been a mistake.

The bookkeeper. She was the fucking bookkeeper.

There hadn't been a whisper of Kate when Warren had been investigating Charlton's Gentlemen's Club. She was never seen there, nor was there any sign of her on the security cameras. The employees had no knowledge of her. Warren had assumed that—given the trainwreck her father had turned into—Kate had simply bailed and found happiness elsewhere. He hadn't expected her to be as dirty as Paul himself.

Please, Paul. Don't do this! Please!

Warren's pitiful voice echoed in his mind, as clear as the day he'd said the words, trying to drag himself out of the crumpled car.

The day he'd been released, Warren had sworn he'd never be that weak again.

He stepped out into the bedroom corridor, almost running headfirst into Linda. His housekeeper was a short, rotund woman, ruling the house with an iron fist.

"You need to get those seen to," Linda said with a frown, pointing at his hands. "They'll be black and blue by this evening."

Warren casually glanced down at his split knuckles. She was right, of course, but he shrugged. "I'll be fine."

Linda shoved a hand on her hip. "Dare I ask?"

"It was in the cellars." Braxton was likely readying the pressure washer as they spoke. "Nothing you have to worry about."

"I'd better not," she warned him. "Will that girl in your bedroom need feeding?"

Kate. His nostrils flared when he thought of how he'd acted with her last night… The moment she'd pressed her body against his, clutching him tightly, he'd lost his mind. His kitten. Where was the sweet girl he'd always known? Lost somewhere in the body of a wildcat.

"No." After what she'd done, she could starve.

Warren didn't bother knocking on the bedroom door. He wrenched it open, powering against the chair she'd wedged under the door handle in the night. The chair legs screeched against the floor, setting his teeth on edge.

Kate was on her feet in an instant, standing before him in the same creased clothes she'd worn last night. "Warren," she said, her lips tightening.

Not troubling himself with a greeting, he tightly clasped her wrist and dragged her from the room, ignoring his body's response to her. Ignoring the urge to lock the door behind them and lick every inch of her skin.

"Wait," she begged. "Please, Warren. You're hurting me."

He didn't spare her a look as he wrenched her down the back stairwell. A clean, white shaft that would allow them to directly descend two storeys to the cellars.

"Where are you taking me?" Her question echoed around the cavernous space. "Warren," she panted, struggling to keep up as he rounded yet another set of stairs. "I can't walk this fast."

And yet she did.

Finally, he pressed his thumb to the scanner on the cellar door and hauled her inside. They met a long corridor dotted with heavy doors, each with its own fingerprint scanner. With a macabre smirk, he steered her into the room from which her father had so recently departed. A sizeable pool of blood remained on the floor, congealing where it lay into a thick red soup. Red handprints could be seen around the space, as well as great red droplets scattered like seeds in the wind.

"Whose blood is that?" Kate's voice was high as she stepped away from him, cradling her wrist.

"Sit." He gestured to the small table and chairs in the corner. A command, not a request.

Kate edged around the room, avoiding her father's blood with every step, arriving at the table with the whites of her eyes on full view around her pupil.

Warren's grin was a lazy one. "Are you scared, kitten?"

"Why are you doing this, Warren?" She finally pulled her focus away from the ocean of blood on the floor, curling her arms around herself as she sat.

He took the seat opposite her, leaning across the table. To his left was a box file full of the same documents he'd shown to Paul. "Because I can."

Because I deserve to.

"Where is William Graves?" he asked her, pinning her to the chair with a heavy glare.

"I don't know who that is." Her eyes widened when her gaze finally fell on his knuckles. "What happened to your hands?"

He kept his face neutral. A simple thing. "What do you think happened to my hands?"

"Have you killed my father?" she whispered, nothing more than a hushed exhale. Her voice rose with every word. "Is that his blood? Is he dead?"

"Your father is alive," he told her. *Just.*

Relief swamped her face.

"For now."

It disappeared just as quickly beneath the fierce knotting of her brows. "What?"

"If you answer my questions, we can keep it that way. At present, he has all his fingers and toes—amongst other things I'm sure he is rather attached to. If you lie to me, I will begin removing them. I will make you watch. And then I'll start on you. Do you understand?"

"Yes," she squeaked, pale as a ghost.

"Good," he tilted his head to the side. "William Graves. Where is he?"

"I don't know! I don't know who that is."

For fuck's sake. Paul hadn't known the man's whereabouts either. "What is your precise role as part of your father's club?"

"I'm the bookkeeper," Kate flashed a glance at the bloodied room. "I pay and send out invoices. I make sure the employees' salaries are paid. I sort out the social media. I pay Dad's debts. Or try to. I pay out winnings. I handle the company's ledgers. Umm..." she exhaled a panicked breath. "Um, I... I file the company's tax returns! Just g-general bookkeeping duties."

"Where are the company's ledgers kept?"

"On my laptop. On the desktop."

Warren nodded. That's what Paul had said too. "Is it password protected?"

"Yes," she confirmed shakily. "The password is Aaron01121989 in brackets. With a capital A."

Good. Paul hadn't been able to tell him that. Brax's team had gotten into it anyway, but it was nice to think she was starting off by being truthful. "And where is the laptop?"

"In the leather pouffe in the living room."

Another truth. Warren pulled out his phone as it buzzed. He flicked through a message from Rhys concerning an upcoming board meeting. *That* was something he could deal with later. Afterwards, he pulled the box file towards him, ready to lay out what he'd compiled. He took the first photograph out. A grainy image taken from the security cameras inside Charlton's Gentlemen's Club. The cheap, shitty cameras courtesy of Paul Charlton. "Tell me about this man."

Kate slid the photograph towards her, peering closely. "I don't know him."

He tried another—to the same result. A different man, albeit one guilty of the same crime as the first.

"I don't know him. I'm sorry, Warren."

The third photograph was of a woman wearing nothing except a terrified expression. Black boxes had been strategically placed to conceal her modesty.

"She looks petrified," his kitten observed, her brows drawing together in sympathy. "Is that a bruise on her cheek?"

"You tell me," Warren replied softly. She was the one who'd handled the transaction. Or did she prefer not to see the evidence of her *bookkeeping*? He pulled out the next three photos. All nude women. All dishevelled.

Kate's eyes were as round as saucers. "These were all taken at my father's club?"

He didn't answer her. They both knew the truth. Instead, he pulled out photocopies of four pages in the club's ledger and placed each above the photographs of the corresponding women. "What was it you said? You handle the company's ledgers, and yet you've no idea who these women are."

"Why would the two things be connected?"

Feeling his eyebrow quirk, he began setting out the worst photographs. One after another, he laid them out, ignoring Kate's fake gasps of horror. They overlapped by the time he'd finished. "Look," he commanded her, standing to grab her by the back of the neck and force her face forwards. "Don't you *dare* look away."

She turned her anguished eyes on the photographs, her lips twisting in revulsion. "Why are you showing me these?"

"Because I want you to look at what you facilitated. Do they look like consenting women to you?"

Kate shook her head. A choke came out of her as she recognised a familiar face. "Is that my *father*?"

"Yes, kitten. That's your father." He'd hidden the identities of the women, but he hadn't bothered with the men.

She shoved the photograph away as if it burned her. "I didn't know he…" she trailed off.

"What? Partook of the goods?" Warren suggested.

"The *goods*?"

"Was that not what you recorded them as on the ledgers?" he bit out, feeling a palpable sense of satisfaction as he watched her throat moving uncomfortably, her skin a distinct shade of grey. "Perhaps you'd like me to chec—"

Kate lurched to her feet unsteadily, spraying vomit across the cold, soulless room. It splattered wetly onto the congealed blood left behind by her father. Each heave wracked her body, until she finally sank to her knees and wept.

Warren was hit with an uncomfortable thought. During his interrogation, Paul had painted Kate as a co-conspirator. A partner in crime. She'd been there at every turn, he'd said. As his bookkeeper, Kate knew more about the business than he did. Every woman trafficked. Every crime committed.

What if he's trying to pin the human trafficking on Kate like he tried to pin Aaron's death on me?

No one had listened to Warren when he'd protested his innocence. And Kate…

What if I'm making the same mistake they did?

Fuck.

Warren shrugged his jacket off his shoulders and tucked it over hers. "Come on," he said softly, scooping her into his arms.

"What are y—?" she twisted when he lifted her, grabbing onto his neck as though she expected him to launch her into the puddle of gruel in the middle of the room. "No, no, no!"

"Shh. It's okay. I've got you."

Her body shook with another sob, but she remained quiet on their way back upstairs. She eyed him closely when they entered the lift, no doubt wondering where they were going, but the surprise was evident on her face when the doors pinged open to reveal the bedroom corridor.

Walking in the opposite direction, Brax stopped in his tracks when the two of them came into view, a thick folder under his arm. "Stone?" he grumbled uncertainly, his head tilting.

"Tell Linda to send breakfast up to my bedroom. A proper one."

He left with a curt nod, side-eyeing Kate as he went.

Sighing, Warren entered his bedroom with Kate sniffling in his arms, heading straight into the en-suite he rarely used. He set her onto the marble counter in the bathroom, turning on the shower and hanging a fluffy midnight blue towel on the hook next to it.

His old instincts nagged at him when he faced a despondent Kate, tears still falling freely down her cheeks, her legs dangling off the counter. The instinct to take her into his arms and protect her from the world returned then, as strong as it had ever been. Warren ground his teeth. Except her problems could no longer be solved with a trip to the park or a visit to the ice cream van.

"You didn't know." Warren wiped her tears away, as he'd once done so often. Nostalgia pumped through his veins when he thought of all the times he'd dried her tears in the week he'd taught her how to ride a bike. She flinched back from him, staring at the floor.

It wasn't a question, but Kate shook her head anyway. "I didn't know."

"Shower," he told her, picking at the shoulder of the ragged shirt she wore. "I'll get you a fresh pair of clothes. There's spare toiletries in here." He opened the cupboard under the sink and pulled out a wicker basket brimming with products. "Take what you need. All right? You'll feel better after a shower and some food."

The slight movement of her head might have been a nod.

He was closing the bathroom door when her small voice called to him. "Warren?"

"Mm?"

"Are you going to kill my father?"

He answered truthfully. "Eventually."

Kate stared in front of her, unseeing. "Okay."

Rhys Stone leant on the doorway to Warren's office, his dark hair artfully falling over his brow. "I'm assuming your original plan of keeping Charlton locked in the cellar for the rest of his life and throwing Kate in prison for the rest of hers has gone out of the window somewhat."

"Somewhat." Warren leant back in his chair. He'd let Kate go back to sleep after her breakfast, curled up under the covers, her chestnut hair streaming across the pillow. It had been more difficult than he'd expected—to drag his body away from hers.

Rhys lifted his chin. "Has she pleaded for mercy for her father?"

"Not at all."

"Ah, a woman after my own heart," Rhys wiggled an eyebrow suggestively, approaching the computer monitor to get a closer look. "Now I know she's not running a human trafficking ring, I wouldn't mind trying my luck."

Warren pinned him against the wall in an instant. "Don't you fucking dare," he snarled.

A sly smile crept onto Rhys's face. "A joke, my friend." He raised his hands, displaying the jagged scar across his palm—one that he'd received back when the two of them were cellmates in prison.

"Fuck you, and fuck your jokes." Warren collapsed back into the office chair, swivelling around to face the computer monitor in front of him. It felt like an invasion of her privacy, to watch her on the security camera, but he couldn't bring himself to stop.

"Stone?"

Both Warren and Rhys turned to see Brax enter the room, taking up far too much of the doorway. Brax cleared his throat. "I didn't realise you were busy. Shall I come back later?"

"No need to leave. I'm not here for company business," Rhys waved a hand, his expression hardening.

Warren nodded, an eye on the monitor. "Have you heard from your contact at the police?"

"I've just got off the phone with him. Nothing we haven't heard before. Graves was a decorated officer whose speciality was in undercover operations," Brax announced. "According to his records, he received the Queen's Commendation for Bravery just before you were imprisoned. The following week he resigned from his post."

Prick. "And his current whereabouts?" Warren prompted.

"No one has seen him since."

Warren's mind drifted to the night of the crash. To begin with, he hadn't realised what was happening when Graves arrived on the scene, the blue lights of his police car flashing. He'd just been relieved to see a police officer, reassured that the emergency services were beginning to arrive.

He'd weaved in and out of consciousness. At that point, he hadn't even realised that Aaron was dead, flung through the windscreen in a spray of glass and blood. Warren had seen the distant figure lying in the road but, in his confusion, had assumed they'd hit a deer.

"Let me know if anything changes," Warren said, his mind a decade away.

Brax took his leave with a short, "Will do."

Eventually, Rhys spoke up. His arms crossed over his chest. "What's your plan for Graves?"

"I intend to take from him what they took from me." A simple answer for a simple question.

"Do you not think your plan is a *tad* gruesome?"

Warren countered his friend with a derisive laugh. "Did they not earn it? They took *years* from me, Rhys. What should have been some of the best years of my life. Instead, I spent it rotting in a prison cell. I'm not surprised you don't understand—you actually committed the crime you were imprisoned for. As did Jensen." He raised his hands as Rhys opened his mouth. "I do not blame you. Fuck, if I'd have been there I'd have helped you do it, but neither of you understand what it feels like to see your life slipping away before your very eyes, knowing there's nothing you can do about it."

Rhys gave him a long, unwavering look. "Given the friends you made in prison, I'd say it hasn't turned out too badly."

"No." This time, his laugh was genuine. "No, it hasn't." The four of them—Warren, Rhys, Jensen, and Aldous—had all been dealt shitty hands by life, one way or another. "If someone had said to me on the day I entered prison that a decade later the four of us would own a company worth billions, I'd have laughed in their face."

"True," Rhys's smirk was crooked. "I was nothing but a mouthy little prick from a council estate and yet," he spread his hands, "here we are."

"*Was* a mouthy little prick?"

"Don't give me that shit," Rhys aimed a kick at Warren's good leg. "I'm a reformed man compared to what I used to be."

"Mm," Warren threw a pen in Rhys's direction, snorting when it hit him right between the eyes. "What not living in poverty does to a man."

Rhys was picking up the pen to launch it back in his direction when his face fell, his eyes focused on a point over Warren's shoulder. "Are those tablets?"

Warren swivelled round on the office chair, sucking in a panicked breath. Kate sat on one of the armchairs in his bedroom. Small boxes were strewn across the floor next to her. He recognised the packaging as the painkillers he'd received after his last surgery.

The boxes weren't what had him panicking, however.

What had his heart stopping was the pile of tablets on the table in front of her.

He leapt to his feet, stumbling as he raced from his office, skidding around the corner slightly too quickly and smashing into a framed photograph on the opposite wall. Glass shattered behind him, but Warren didn't stop. Rhys wasn't far behind him as he leapt up the stairs, taking them two at a time in his desperation to reach his kitten.

The look of despondency on her face this morning had cut him deeply, knowing it had been inflicted by him. Knowing he'd shown her those fucking photographs. *He'd* taken her into the room in which he'd beaten her father black and blue.

Warren shouldered into his bedroom, barely bothering to use the handle.

Kate jumped a foot in the air as he burst through the door, the glass of water in her hand slopping over her lap.

Skidding to his knees before her, Warren shoved the table away. The tablets scattered across the floor. "How many have you taken?" he croaked, taking her face in his trembling hands.

She looked away with red-rimmed eyes. "Go away." Her voice cracked.

"How many?" he shouted, hearing Rhys moving behind him. "*Tell me!*"

"It's all right," Rhys whispered softly, a balm to Warren's bite. "We're not angry at you. We just need to know how many you've taken."

Kate shook her head as much as she was able to within his grasp. "I haven't." Tears ran down her cheeks, tracking salty paths underneath her chin.

The relief was so heady that Warren felt light-headed. He pulled her into his lap, holding her with a vice-like grip as she wept into his suit. Blood pounded through him, furious and relentless. "I have you, kitten," he chanted into her hair. "Everything will be okay. I have you."

"But it won't be!" she pushed away from him. "I enabled my father for *years*. I took out credit card after credit card to keep his stupid fucking club open. I saved every penny I could to help him, to allow him to invest in his business. I sacrificed a decade of my life to help him, and he was using it all to…" She choked in a breath, unable to finish. "I facilitated the abuse that went on in his club. I've wasted my life, Warren. I thought I was helping him through his grief. Instead, I allowed him to…"

He attempted to soothe her as she hyperventilated. "You didn't know."

"Ignorance is not an excuse." Her cheeks were shiny with tears. "Even before this morning, there was no point to my life, Warren. The debt was *burying* me. My father has never cared about me. Aaron was always his favourite. Even when Talbot was touching me, Dad was more concerned about them damaging Aaron's stupid fucking photograph than he was about me."

Warren didn't say anything, letting her get everything out. He simply stroked her hair, letting her know he was listening.

"I have no one. There isn't a single person that gives a shit about me. The only people that contact me are from fucking debt companies about missed payments and defaults. The only people that ever visit the house are bailiffs or Dad's dealer. And Dad digs me deeper with every move he makes. I just… I don't see the point of it anymore, Warren. The best apology I can give those women—those *girls*—is to… to…"

Kill herself, Warren realised.

"Just let me go," she begged tearfully. "Let me have some peace."

Rhys's expression was tortured as he looked on, as white as Warren had ever seen him. Had it been anyone other than Kate in his arms, he would have checked to see if his friend was all right, given Rhys's history with suicide. But all Warren could spare him was a grim look, devoting his attention to the weeping woman in his arms, murmuring platitudes into her hair and making affectionate passes over her skin.

This was his fault. He'd treated her as a suspect from the get-go. He'd given Talbot and Braxton free reign in collecting Paul and his anonymous bookkeeper. Even when he'd discovered the bookkeeper was Kate, he hadn't stop for a minute to wonder at her guilt, to wonder if she might be innocent.

To wonder if it might be the straw that broke the kitten's back.

3

Kate

It had taken Kate an age to remove all the tablets from their blister packaging, cracking each one open only to carefully arrange it in a mandala-like formation. She'd fiddled with her little piece of art, shuffling it around like a picky child playing with their food.

Only to come to the conclusion that she didn't want to kill herself. She just didn't want to continue living.

No, that wasn't true. What she wanted was to never have existed at all.

Perhaps her own personal fairy godmother could come and take her life and give it to someone who needed it. An equitable compromise. Kate would cease to exist, and someone else would get to live.

"I need to take a Zoom call," Warren said, looking up over his laptop screen. He sat at the desk in his bedroom as she rested on the armchair in the corner, gazing listlessly out of the window.

Kate nodded, uncaring. He'd barely left the room since finding her little art project laid out across the coffee table, working at the desk in the corner and sleeping on the sofa. From what she'd been able to ascertain, Warren owned a company. Or part of it, anyway.

She recognised one of the voices on the call as the man who'd flushed her ex-mandala down the toilet. Rhys. The kind, regal-looking man with high cheekbones and striking amber eyes. The other two were strangers, distinguishable only by their accents; one Scottish, the other from the Home Counties, just like her and Warren.

The figures they discussed were insane. Throwing around so many millions that she was sick of hearing the word. Sick with jealousy. Sick with hate.

Had she sunk so low that she apparently hated anyone doing better than her?

Yes. Yes, she had.

Exhaustion swamped her thoughts. Kate closed her eyes, curling up against the stupidly expensive armchair and letting out a long sigh. The photographs of those poor women flashed through her mind like awful, horrifying fireworks. She grimaced, trying to shake away the thought.

She flinched as Warren's broad hand encased her shoulder, coming out of her reverie.

"Are you all right?" he asked. On the desk, his laptop was closed, his business meeting clearly over.

"Fine," she said dully.

Warren checked his watch. A heavy, expensive watch with a black leather band and an emerald green face to match his eyes. "Come outside with me. I want to show you something."

Kate felt like a spectre walking through Warren's house. With the exception of her trip down to the cellars the morning after her arrival, she hadn't bothered to leave the bedroom. Warren led her down the pale golden corridor, taking her down a set of curved marble stairs that ran alongside a row of arched windows looking out over the garden.

If it could be called a garden—it resembled a golf course, with islands of mature trees and a striped lawn that some poor gardener must have spent hours creating. Come to think of it, he probably wasn't that poor if he had this much work.

It was the kind of house that she'd only ever seen when scrolling through houses for sale online, the ones that were so far out of her budget it was laughable. It would only ever depress her, but she did it anyway. A moment's reprieve from her misery.

When Warren opened the front door, Kate died a little inside when she saw columns proudly adorning the front porch. Because of course they did.

Her brow furrowed when she looked past the columns. A pink and white ice cream van was parked in Warren's driveway, complete with childlike illustrations and photographs of the different ice creams available. "Why is there a Mr Whippy van here?"

Warren's grin was a thing of beauty. A crooked reminder of the adoring crush she'd had on him as a twelve-year-old girl. "It's here for you."

The middle-aged ice cream man leant his elbow on the window. "What'll it be?"

"A double ninety-nine for me." Warren turned to Kate expectantly. "With two flakes."

"A ninety-nine for me, please. Just a single one," she said, a sense of shyness coming over her.

"With a flake?" the ice cream man asked.

Kate nodded, remaining silent as Warren's hand slipped into hers.

"Just like old times?" he murmured.

"When you used to pick me up from school," she played along, pretending that his touch wasn't jumpstarting her heart. Warren would wait for her at her school's back gate; come rain or shine, he would be there. Aaron would usually be bunking off somewhere, up to no good, but she could always count on Warren. "And in summer we'd stop at the ice cream van on our walk back home."

Warren took their ice creams, passing hers over. Their fingers touched again for a moment, and she couldn't help her breath quickening, thinking of how he'd touched her on the first night. The feelings he'd elicited when he'd pressed her up against the wall, his erection grinding into her stomach.

That Warren had seemingly disappeared after he'd realised she hadn't been involved in her father's activities. Instead, she'd fallen back into the platonic 'best friend's younger sister' territory.

They followed the stone path she'd seen from the window, walking past the picturesque pond full of orange-and-white koi. The fish clustered to the side of the pond when they approached, their mouths bobbing open in the search for food.

"Have they been fed?" she asked Warren, walking past the tall hedge circling the pond. "They look ravenous."

"They're lying bastards," he assured her, making quick work of his enormous ice cream. "Don't trust a word they say." Warren walked through an archway built into the hedge, leading into deeper woodland, down a winding path where the scent of earthy moss pervaded and pine needles littered the soft ground.

After a few minutes of silent walking, a large tree came into view, and Kate realised why Warren had brought her here.

A swing hung from one of its branches, swaying gently in the summer breeze.

Warren took hold of the frayed ropes attached to the thick block of wood acting as a seat, darkened splotches scattered across his knuckles. "One push. For old time's sake."

Too spiritless to argue with him, Kate sat. "Cone?" she offered him, holding it up.

"Do you still not eat them?"

Kate mumbled vaguely about *sugar-scented cardboard*. It was a hill she would die on.

His eyes creased, but he took it without a word, consuming it in three quick bites. "You're a philistine," he chided her, placing his first push on the small of her back.

The ropes were harsh against her palm, but Kate held on as she began to swing. The tips of her faded trainers disturbed the fine layer of soil beneath the swing, but all she could focus on was the intermittent pressure of Warren's hands on her back.

"Didn't you say one push?" she chided him softly.

"Mm, one push for old time's sake," he agreed. "I didn't say what the rest would be for."

She almost had the energy required to roll her eyes. A businessman through and through. "I'm surprised you didn't go into politics with that attitude."

"A boy who went straight from foster care into prison for manslaughter. Yes, I'm sure I'd do well rubbing shoulders with the Old Etonians who've barely had to lift a finger to wipe their own arses."

She thought back to the call he'd been on earlier. "Were you not discussing buying a company for £120 million only this morning?"

Warren's pushes stopped coming, and Kate let her feet drag her to an untidy stop. "I didn't think you were listening." He came around the swing to lean against the tree's thick trunk.

She shrugged. "I wasn't. Not really." Kate pressed her lips together with a sigh. "How did you get so much money?"

"Luck, coupled with meeting Rhys Stone and his brother Aldous, in addition to their cousin, Jensen."

Kate finally released the question that had been rattling around her brain like a sharp stone in her shoe. "What happened to those women in the photos?"

His emerald eyes flickered. "We're looking for them. We've been questioning your father since he arrived."

He was still alive then. "We being… you and Brax?"

"Mostly." Warren crossed his arms over his chest, frowning down at her.

"So you're Warren Stone now?" Had Warren Harper died entirely?

"Warren Harper died with Aaron, kitten."

The thought was like a knife in her heart. "Why?"

"When I was in prison, I was more alone than I'd ever been before." He looked away with a frown, a tattoo creeping above his collar. "I was lucky enough to have Rhys as my cellmate. His mother, Alison… She did more for me than any foster family or social worker ever had. Eighteen months into my sentence, they offered me their name, and I took it."

Kate pressed her feet to the ground, propelling the swing slightly. "When did you get out of prison?"

"Four years ago."

Her lips parted in shock. "How did you go from being in prison to owning—" She gestured in the direction of the house "—Buckingham fucking Palace in *four* years?"

"Rhys, Jensen, and I were in prison. Aldous was on the outside managing the holding company."

She blinked. "That doesn't even remotely answer my question." Just as she heard distant voices, movement turned her head to the left.

Two men were walking nonchalantly up the path. One had a pair of binoculars hanging around his neck, whilst the other bore twin walking poles in his hands. Ramblers. Kate had sometimes seen them out and about in the forest that bordered their estate, walking at a brisk pace and avoiding teenagers on mountain bikes like the plague.

Warren lifted his body off the tree trunk, wearing an unfriendly expression. "Gentleman. This is private property."

The two men shared a look. "Our apologies," the one wearing binoculars said, pulling a map out of his pocket. "We are a bit lost, however. We've gotten slightly turned around. I don't suppose you'd be able to point us in the right direction?"

"Back the way you came," Warren said grumpily. "Where are you headed?"

"Broadwood's Tower near Box Hill."

"Then you're on the wrong side of the A24." He pointed at a spot on the map. "You're here, on this path. If you follow it to the North Downs Way—"

Kate looked up in time to see the other man drop his walking poles and pull a wicked-sharp knife from his jacket. She shouted out a garbled warning, but Warren was already moving. He spun to the left, avoiding the bite of the blade, before wrenching the attacker's arm down and twisting hard.

But whilst Warren was gaining the upper hand, the second moved in for the kill, drawing his own blade.

She had barely seen the bright sunlight flicker off the second attacker's knife before she jumped into action.

Her father may be a neglectful addict, but he had also been a keen boxer back in the day, and was still an avid follower of the sport now.

Curling her hand into a fist, just like her father taught her, Kate took advantage of the attackers' focus on Warren. With all her strength, she launched herself at the second one. Or, more specifically, at his liver.

Kate grunted as her shoddy, untrained punch connected. The impact sent a jolt up her elbow, but she ignored the pain, readying herself for another punch.

But the second attacker collapsed where he stood, his knees caving in and his arms coming around his waist. He hit the forest floor with an agonised groan.

A smile flashed onto her face momentarily. Had that actually worked? But there was no time to contemplate her victory. Warren, distracted by the sound of her grunt, turned.

A mistake.

The man he'd been fighting, his nose bloodied, took the opportunity as soon as it presented itself, aiming a lethal kick at Warren's right leg, sending an awful, *terrible* crack through the air. Despite his trousers covering the skin beneath, the sight of his broken calf, bent at almost a right angle, nearly had her retching.

Somehow, Warren barely reacted, clearly running on nothing but adrenaline. As soon as he hit the ground, he snapped up the knife the second attacker had dropped and plunged it into the incapacitated man's throat.

And then Kate made a mistake of her own. She cried out at the sight of Warren murdering the second man, realising too late that the first attacker's attention was no longer on Warren, but on *her.*

"*Run!*" Warren bellowed, attempting to get back onto his feet—his *foot*, his snapped calf *swaying* as he moved.

Filled with adrenaline and terror, Kate ran with every ounce of energy she possessed. Tree branches whipped past her, occasionally snatching at her hair. Chancing a look back, Kate was propelled forward with a start of fear at the sight of the man racing behind her, getting closer with every step. Her chest heaved, a stitch carving its way into her side.

A whimper left her when she broke through the treeline, faced with a gentle meadow—and nowhere to hide. Without pausing, she—

Kate cried out as the man tackled her to the ground, forcing the air from her lungs. She gasped, trying to scream for help, but he wrenched her onto her back, wrapping his hands around her neck, pressing into her with such pressure that she was afraid he'd snap her spine. His knee compounded the pain, digging into her ribs.

Her legs kicked uselessly, achieving nothing but thudding her heels into the earth. Her eyes watered, tears streaming into her hairline. Kate desperately tried to suck in air, a thin, reedy sound escaping from her throat.

Fading. Everything was fading, from the pain to her fear. The nothingness grew, lulling her towards the darkness that would never end. Hadn't she wanted this?

Just as her eyes began to dim, the man's body shuddered, his eyes widening, his pupils dilating. Blood began to drip from his open mouth. Slowly at first, but then the flow gathered speed, until a continuous stream landed on her chest. Was he... drooling blood?

Inside his mouth, something sparkled silver in the sunlight. Something beautiful.

The crushing grip around her throat loosened in minute increments. Kate pulled a deep, painful breath into her lungs, and then another. With every inhale, her surroundings began to return. Sunlight. The meadow. The trees. The pain around her neck.

Warren, standing behind the attacker with a grim, satisfied smile. The attacker's lips sagged open. The flow of blood had turned into a river, and on top of his tongue sat the tip of the blade that Warren had plunged through the back of his head.

"If you had given both the Charltons and the evidence to the police, this would have never happened!" Aldous bellowed, shooting Kate a furious glance. She shrunk into the sofa, not having the energy to fight back. Not today. Every word was a painful rasp, so she settled for a glare in his direction.

"The same police with a history of accepting bribes from Paul Charlton?" Warren went to stand in front of her, resting his hand on her shoulder as it butted up against his leg. A barrier from Aldous. She resisted the temptation to lean into his side, her brain whirring back into action.

Where had her father gotten the money to bribe the police from?

Aldous laughed at that. "Yes! It's what Charlton deserves." He glared down at Kate as though expecting her to defend her father.

"And what I deserve is to have Paul Charlton and William Graves locked in my cellar," Warren rasped furiously, "screaming for fucking mercy."

"Sadistic prick," Aldous shook his head with a grimace.

Kate's head turned when Braxton entered the room, as formidable as ever, having been given the task of moving her father—and the two corpses—to some nameless location. It had been the second thing Warren had shouted on carrying her back into the house—the first being to get her medical attention.

She had been looked over, poked and prodded by a doctor. A private one, she assumed, given that he'd been summoned to the house with nothing but a phone call and made no suggestion of calling the police. Broken blood vessels hid underneath her eyelids, whilst her neck was a network of bruises and scratches, the latter being self-inflicted in her desperate attempt to get the attacker off of her. Not that Kate remembered that bit.

"Can you blame me?" Warren retorted, his tone dripping with sarcasm.

Aldous's nostrils flared as he delved his hand into his hair. "I blame you for being a prick. The rest is excusable."

Leaning against the doorjamb, Rhys snorted at his younger brother. "Are we ready? I want to get going before rush hour."

Warren nodded, lending Kate an encouraging smile. "We're going to stay with Rhys for a bit." He touched her shoulder kindly. "For safety reasons."

Kate nodded, perplexed by the fact that Warren was *walking*. Had she simply imagined his snapped leg? She *had* been deprived of oxygen, after all.

Rhys pursed his lips to the side. "And I won't dress you up like a roadman."

Jensen's dark eyebrow quirked up. "A *what*?"

Rhys shared a private smirk with Kate, helping her to her feet. "Jensen's exceedingly old," Rhys muttered into her ear, slinking an arm around her shoulders in a surprisingly brotherly embrace. He steered her towards the front door, gently supporting her across the smooth tiles. A third pair of footsteps shadowed them. Familiar ones. "You'll have to excuse him."

"I heard that, you prick," Jensen's Scottish accent rang out after them.

"I'm not surprised. Did you know ears tend to get bigger as you age?"

Soon, Kate and Warren were being shepherded across the countryside in Rhys's sleek grand tourer, a Range Rover full of security guards shadowing their every move.

Warren sat next to her, as still as stone. A ticking muscle in his jaw was his only sign of life.

"Are you sure this is a good idea?" Kate rasped, when the silence grew too great, wincing.

"Is what a good idea?" Warren murmured, finally looking at her.

She caught Rhys's eye in the rear-view mirror. "Taking the targets of an assassination attempt to your home."

"I don't have a house in the middle of nowhere, Kate. It's far safer. I live in a penthouse overlooking Regent's Park," Rhys explained, his face illuminated by the mood lighting around the dashboard. "There's security on the ground floor, with private lifts to each of the flats. I have my own private security working in the building, as do several of the other residents. Warren's guards will be joining them. You'll be safe there, Kate. I promise. And better dressed."

"May I ask why you seem to have women's clothing on-hand at the drop of a hat?" Warren pondered.

"I sent my assistant to Peter Jones to find some clothing for Kate. Hadn't had a chance to send it down yet." Rhys turned round momentarily. "Fair warning. She bought more lingerie than expected."

Her face flamed red, but she managed to mutter a meek, "Thank you."

The impressive beige façade of Rhys's apartment building came into view just as the last of the day's light fell below the horizon. Kate squinted at the bright lights as she was ushered straight towards the correct lift, feeling overly conspicuous in Warren's overlarge clothing, complete with extensive bruising around her neck.

"Kitchen," Rhys announced when they entered his vast, airy flat, the white walls stark against the blooming plant life. "Dining room. Living room. Bathroom. Cinema room. The bedrooms are upstairs. Do you want dinner?"

Kate stared at the dining table. That thing alone was bigger than her bedroom. An enormous mahogany monstrosity. "Um…"

"Order a curry," Warren bit out a curt command, dragging her along with him as he walked. "We're going upstairs."

"I… Thank you, Rhys," she whispered, her throat scraping against itself.

"Clothes are on the bed in the spare room," he smiled, tapping away at his phone.

Warren led her straight to the bedroom she'd be staying in, clearly knowing his way around Rhys's lavish apartment.

"Warren, what's th—?"

He slammed the door shut behind her and threw the lock.

Suddenly, Kate found herself entombed in Warren's grasp, his body pressed against hers. Placing his nose under her ear, he groaned, letting out a deep exhale that sent sparks travelling down her spine. He leant back, catching her gaze in an iron grip. "You nearly died today."

Warren closed his eyes with a shudder, as if the thought was too painful to bear. "I nearly lost you again, kitten." His hand played around her jawline, sinking down to the painful bruising that bloomed on her throat. His nostrils flared in anger, but she lay her hands against his chest, ignoring his jolt.

Going up on tiptoes, Kate brought her hands up to massage the back of his head, revelling in the soft touch of his dark hair, gently scraping her nails against his scalp.

Warren's lip curled in a blissful, nostalgic smile. "You remember?"

Her grin joined his. She gave him a silent nod, recalling the endless head massages he'd given to her after a stressful day at school. Despite his protests, Kate would always reciprocate, meaning the both of them would come away looking like they'd been in a fight with an electricity pylon.

Chest heaving, he stared at her with heavy-lidded eyes. "You're not a child anymore."

Kate shook her head, pulling him closer. Her body egged her on all the way, dazzled by his firm figure against hers. She pressed her hips into his, wanting more.

"My kitten," he whispered. Warren's gaze flicked down to her lips, but he yanked himself away with a small shake, going over to the enormous bag on the bed and shuffling through the clothing within it. "Come on. Let me get you settled."

The first tinges of something rolled through her. Was it hope?

Perhaps that first night wasn't such a one-off after all.

4

Warren

The three of them had had far too many Cobras.

He'd sent Kate to bed after her fourth beer, but he and Rhys had stayed up, drinking and talking into the early hours of the morning.

A morning Kate might never have seen if he had taken thirty seconds longer to reach her.

Ignoring that murderous thought, Warren scaled the stairs in the darkness. He'd lived here too, at one point. It had been a shock to the system; to go from a prison cell to a multimillion pound penthouse flat, but he'd provided the start-up funds for Aldous to work with. Rhys and Jensen had been released from prison eighteen months before Warren, meaning by the time he was a free man he was richer than he'd ever dreamt of.

The four of them had made a good team.

Even if his method of obtaining their start-up funds had not been entirely in-keeping with the law.

Except now he had more than Paul Charlton to consider.

It hadn't been a concern before, when he'd assumed Kate had made her own way in the world. Perhaps with a partner and children.

Since the night Braxton had brought her to his house, however, the guilt had begun to seep into his very marrow.

Warren crept into the bedroom on silent feet, not wanting to wake his kitten. He savoured the sound of her soft breathing, unable to shake off the feeling of *possession* that intoxicated him whenever she was near. Everything from her scent to her voice drove him mad, turning him from a reasonable, albeit bad-tempered, businessman into a sex-crazed monster whose only relief would come from the heaven between her thighs.

And then she'd do something that reminded him that she wasn't just a woman. She was his kitten.

Even if she was a woman in her twenties, Warren couldn't get past the fact that this was the same girl he'd cared for as a boy. He'd loved her then, but that love had been familial in nature. There had been nothing sexual about it. The thought of it made him ill.

Lying on the couch cushions he'd stolen from downstairs, he tossed and turned, trying to get to sleep. Up on the bed, Kate became just as restless as him, muttering incoherently, her voice high and raspy from the attack.

Warren couldn't help the sly smirk growing on his face. Even in her sleep, she wouldn't rest her voice, the little hoyden.

"Warren," she mumbled. "Warren."

He got up, perching on the side of the bed that had once been his. "Kitten?" he said softly, taking her hand. "I'm here."

"Mmm." Her voice was crackly, a sobering reminder that the day could have gone *very* differently.

He reached out into the darkness to find her cheek. "Do you need a drink?"

"I dreamt of you," she slurred. "Like the first night I arrived, when you nearly kissed me. Except you didn't stop."

His cock hardened, recognising the need reinforcing her voice, but he shook his head. Not that she would see it. "I shouldn't have done that." Even in his drunken haze, he knew that.

"I dreamt that you stayed. My ex left me after he slept with me, but in my dream you stayed."

Jealousy plunged into him like a dagger. The mere mention of someone else touching her slayed him. *Mine*, the angry voice in his chest hissed. "You're damn right I'd stay," Warren sunk lower into the bed. "Who was he?"

Kate's hand found his hair, and he purred with pleasure. "Just some guy I met on a dating app. He was sweet—up until I had sex with him. Then he ghosted me." She let out a sigh that tickled his chest hair. "Like it meant nothing."

"Give me a name. I'll have him in a shallow grave by sunrise."

She giggled then, clearly thinking he was joking. "Daniel. He kissed like a washing machine."

"You know I'm going to have to kiss a lot of Daniels before I find the right one."

She palmed his cheek clumsily, but her voice was a low murmur. "Can I watch?"

"Naughty kitten," he chided her.

Kate offered an alternative, throwing it to the darkness between them. "Needy kitten."

Warren growled into her neck, entirely too drunk for this conversation. "Tell me what you need."

"Touch me," she panted into his ear. "Please."

Fuck. "Touch yourself for me, kitten." Warren clung to his last shred of decency like it was a life ring, steadfastly ignoring the way his cock roared for attention. When her hand disappeared from his face, he sighed into her skin. "That's it. Do you like to tease your nipples when you touch yourself?"

"Yes."

"Good, then do it. Slowly flick your finger across your nipple, nothing more." The covers rustled as Kate moved beneath them. Her breath hitched. "Tell me where your hands are, kitten."

"One on my breast. The other between my legs."

Warren's cock jumped in his boxers. "Spread your legs wide for me. Circle your clit for me, darling. No touching, just teasing." A dark grin grew across his face when Kate whimpered, her legs pressing against his beneath the duck down. "Now trail your hand down from your clit, right down to the entrance to your pussy. Trace your entrance, kitten, around and around."

"Warren!"

"Do you want to go deeper?"

"Yes!"

"Use two fingers then. Gather up as much wetness as you possibly can." Satisfaction coursed through him at the slick sounds coupled with Kate's rapturous gasps. "Now bring your fingers up out of the covers." He grasped her arm as soon as it emerged, feeling his way in the darkness until he located her wet, sticky fingers.

Warren sucked her fingers into his mouth, snarling in pleasure at the copious wetness adorning her skin, the evidence of her pleasure. He swallowed, as drunk on her as he was on alcohol. "Again," he ordered. "Touch your clit for me, kitten, until I say you can stop."

Again, Warren listened carefully, until her exhales turned into sighs of pleasure. "Stop."

Kate let out an unhappy groan.

"Put your fingers inside yourself again. As wet as possible." Her hand had barely emerged from under the covers before he descended once more, licking her fingers clean. "More," he instructed her, eagerly swallowing her honey. "Play with your clit. Pinch your nipples."

His cock was painfully hard as he listened to Kate coming to the edge far quicker than she had before.

"Stop."

Kate's raspy cry of frustration shouldn't have been anywhere near as satisfying as it was.

"I'll let you come this time," he promised, licking her arousal off her skin, delving his tongue in between her fingers. "Again."

His kitten sighed with pleasure as the rhythmic movements resumed. Slick sounds reached his ears. "That's it. Chase it for me, Kate." He snarled victoriously as she choked on an orgasmic cry, her limbs stiffening with pleasure.

"Warren," she moaned, throwing her head back onto the pillow, riding out her pleasure in endless waves.

When she sighed in exhaustion, Warren gave her his final request. "Feed me your orgasm, kitten."

Even after she'd found relief, Kate dipped her fingers inside herself, offering them up to him.

Warren *feasted* on her, finding every drop she had to give, swallowing until there was nothing left.

Despite the layer of the covers separating them, Kate nuzzled into him. Her hand played over his ribs, dipping lower with each pass. "Let me touch you."

He took her hand in his, ignoring the protests of his aching cock. "Not tonight. Sleep."

For once, she listened to him.

"You coming back to the flat tonight?" Rhys asked, glaring at Warren through the video call.

His hair still dripping from the shower, Warren flicked through the report put out by one of the organisations owned by their holding company. "Have you seen this month's management accounts?"

"Don't answer my question with a question." Rhys's eyebrows lowered into a disappointed line. "And yes, they've markedly improved compared to this time last year. Now stop being a prick and come back to the flat. Apologise for whatever you've done."

His phone buzzed. Brax still hadn't managed to pull the whereabouts of William Graves from Paul Charlton. The man was a ghost.

Hopefully not a literal one. Warren had far too much to say to the man.

"I can't be around her, Rhys."

"Do you think I abandoned Aldous like this after his suicide attempt?"

Glaring at his screen, Warren straightened his spine. "It's not even remotely the same thing." He scrubbed a hand over his face, his sharp stubble digging into his palm. "I knew her when she was a child, Rhys. I feel…" Warren placed his cards on the table, glancing out of the window towards the koi pond in his garden. "Whenever I look at her, I feel like a predator."

Rhys crossed his arms. "We've met predators; you aren't one. You're an adult male attracted to an adult female. There's nothing predatory there."

"I did things that I shouldn't have done." Things that tasted *fantastic*.

"Let her be the judge of that." Buzzing came through Warren's headphones as Rhys's phone began to ring. "She's been asking after you for days. I can see the hurt on her face. Come back. Stop being a fucking coward."

With that, Rhys ended the call, leaving Warren alone in his living room.

Indecision warred within him. He looked out of the window again—past the koi pond, down the path where Kate had nearly been strangled.

God, the image of her doe eyes, hurt and abandoned…

Swearing under his breath, he closed his laptop

An hour later, he stepped into Rhys's flat. His heart pounded with the knowledge that Kate lurked in here somewhere. He searched through each room, practising the speech he'd been preparing on the drive over.

He found her where he'd left her; in his old bedroom. The sweet, hypnotising tones of her scent hit him.

Kate lay on the bed, her legs stretched out in front of her, her nose deep in a book. She paused when she caught sight of Warren, her gaze hardening whilst a rosy blush reached her cheeks. "What do you want?"

"To take you out to dinner." The words left him before he could think them over.

"Why?" she croaked, instantly suspicious. The bruises around her throat had faded over the last few days, he was pleased to see. Her voice was better too.

Warren exhaled a huff, his chest sinking. "Because I'm an arsehole."

"You are. You left me," she said hatefully, but Warren could see the insecurity lurking beneath the surface. "You said you wouldn't."

"I know. You deserve more than a drunken fumble."

She closed the book and placed it on the bed next to her. "Why did you leave?"

"Because I'm a fucking idiot." Warren let his thoughts out. They erupted from him like a shockwave. "Because I feel like a predator whenever I look at you," he shrugged, slowly approaching the bed and taking a seat. "I never expected to see you again, let alone…" His eyes trailed down to her lips, his heart beating faster. *Let alone feel like this around you.* "Come to dinner. Please."

She sunk her teeth into her bottom lip. "What about the attempt on your life?"

"We'll have security, and Brax has been questioning your father about Graves's whereabouts."

"Questioning… You mean torturing?" she whispered.

"I mean doing whatever is necessary to ensure your safety. If he needs *incentivising*, then yes."

Kate fell silent, twisting her hands in the bedsheets.

"He isn't an innocent, kitten. You saw the photos. He's the furthest fucking thing from it."

"I know." With a deep breath, she nodded. "Fine. I'll come."

Warren couldn't help the dirty grin that stretched across his face. "Yes, you will."

"Warren, this isn't going out to dinner. It's renting out an entire restaurant." Kate glanced around her in the restaurant's private dining room. The walls were inlaid with refrigerated wine racks, displayed to advantage around the single table at which they sat.

He shrugged, utterly unapologetic. True, he could have rented a private room, but it made it so much easier for the security he'd installed downstairs not to have to watch the entire restaurant. Warren took her hand. "The measures are necessary for your safety, kitten."

Pressing her lips together, she gave him a little smile. "It's nice though. I commend you on your taste."

"I'm glad I didn't disappoint."

"Not this time," she said threateningly.

"Ouch," he winked. "How are you feeling?" It didn't escape him that a fortnight ago he'd found her with enough tablets to kill an elephant. "Not… not with the attack. With everything before it."

Kate closed her eyes, and he instantly felt like a prick for bringing it up. "The reasons are still there."

"Tell me."

"Debt. Guilt." She took a careful bite of her steak. "The feelings have always been there, and I think they always will be. Since I was a teenager, it's felt like this malignant presence on my shoulder, whispering into my ear wherever I go."

"What does it say?" Warren asked delicately.

"It's not a voice so much as a feeling. I'll never be good enough for my father."

He brushed his thumb over hers. "Your father is the one who isn't good enough for you."

"My brain doesn't agree, but it's not just that. Debt has been like a pall over my life. Endless debt, endless worry, endless depression."

Warren's insides burnt with guilt. "Your father's debt?"

"Debt that I took out to try to help him. I don't know if some part of me thought that maybe if I destroyed myself enough, he'd finally love me."

He let his head fall. *You could have stopped this*, the little voice in his head taunted. *She would have been happy if not for you.*

"How much debt are you in, kitten?"

A snort left her as she pulled her hand from his. "A pittance to you, I imagine, given the figures you were throwing around."

Lips tightening, he nodded. He'd send a note to Brax to investigate when they were on their way home—and an order to clear them immediately.

"But when you miss a payment, the interest rate skyrockets. Suddenly you're missing payments left, right, and centre, and you're drowning. Each bill is another concrete block pulling you down."

"I'm sorry."

She took a sip of her drink. "How long will you torture my father for?"

"Why?" Holding his fork in mid-air, he paused. "Does it bother you?"

Kate's eyes widened. "How can it not bother me?"

"He deserves this, Kate."

Placing her knife and fork on her plate, she narrowed her eyes in his direction. "Why do you care?"

"About the fact he's involved in human trafficking? Letting his scum clientele rape girls forced into modern slavery? And then taking *money* for it? I should think it's fairly obvious."

"I mean why my father. Regardless of what he's done in the years since Aaron died, he was always kind to you. Why even begin to investigate him in the first place?"

Warren let silence fall between them. It was a fair question, because Paul *had* been kind to him. Whenever he'd needed a place to relax from the chaos of the children's home, Paul's house was always open to him. Whenever he'd needed a meal, Paul would be there. Paul had even given Warren his first job, delivering leaflets around the neighbourhood back when Charlton's Gentlemen's Club was a viable business.

It had all made his betrayal so much worse.

"What did he tell you of the night Aaron died?" Warren's voice was soft.

She lifted her shoulders. "Not much. You'd been drinking and lost control of the car. You and him were the only ones to walk away."

Walk away? Despite himself, he laughed. "Did he now? Funny that."

"Why is that funny?"

"Because, kitten," he began, pushing his chair back from the table and bending to undo his laces, "*part* of that story is true. The car hit a tree. Aaron died. But your father was driving the car, not me."

"*What?*" Kate's eyes were wide. "But the police..."

"The officer that was first on the scene accepted a bribe from your father. A man called William Graves. The bribe was some £50,000, if the statements from the Club are anything to go by. Your father took out a loan to cover it rather than go to prison."

Kate's eyes were fixed to his. "That was the loan that nearly bankrupted him. It sent our finances into freefall. He said it had been a big gambling win for one of his punters."

"Just like he said I *walked* away from the accident."

She looked at him questioningly, but he rolled up his trouser leg rather than explain it to her. A choked gasp left her as she went to her knees in front of him. Fabric tore somewhere in her dress, but she ignored it. "Your leg," she cradled the prosthetic attached to what remained of his right leg. "Warren..."

"Your father drove drunk and killed his only son, leaving me a below-knee amputee, kitten." Warren tried to ignore his body's reaction to her kneeling at his feet in a tight lavender dress, the slits on her legs showing far too much. And somehow not nearly enough. "He bribed the police officer to say I was the one who was driving. I lost everything. My health. My future. My best friend. My kitten," he stroked her cheek with a faint smile. "After I was released from prison, I started investigating your father. That was when I found out about the human trafficking."

"I'm sorry, Warren." Her eyes sparkled with tears as she stood.

"I'm not his only victim, kitten." He pulled her up to stand between his spread thighs, their breath mingling. "I hate that he dragged you into this."

"I worked for years to pay off the debt that put you in prison," she choked. Her eyes were heavy with remembrance, taking on a glazed look. "Can I ask you something?"

He nodded. "Anything."

"Did Aaron die instantly? Dad always said he did, but in light of..."

"He did," Warren confirmed. "He was passed out before we hit the tree. He never woke up." Aaron had been lying on the backseat, hurtling through the windscreen at the sudden impact.

Buzzing prompted him to take his phone out of his pocket. His heart jumped when he saw who was calling.

"Brax? Tell me you have something."

Brax got straight to the point. "Charlton last saw Graves at a location in East London a month ago. I've texted you the location. Charlton reported that it was where he sourced some of the girls from."

Sourced. He shared a disgusted look with Kate, who was near enough to hear Braxton's every word.

"A brothel?"

"Seems to be," Braxton replied.

"Was Graves running the brothel or was he merely a customer?" Warren put it on loudspeaker, opening up the address Braxton had sent.

"Neither. Apparently Graves takes a bribe from the brothel's owner to ensure the police look the other way. Meaning he's still got contacts in the Met."

Warren's brain whirred into action. "The frequency of the bribe being?"

"Charlton wasn't sure. There was also a mention of a warehouse in Ruislip. He visited it on occasion."

"I'm heading over to the brothel to investigate. I'll take the security detail with me, but I want one of them stationed outside at all times.

Hopefully Graves pays them another visit. Can you send some of Rhys's back-up to check out the Ruislip warehouse?"

Brax ended the call with a brief, "Will do."

Warren stood, taking Kate's hand in his. "I'll have one of the security team take you back to Rhys's flat."

The incredulous look she gave him was an immediate red flag. "No, you bloody well won't. I'm coming with you."

"Kate, these people a—"

"I'll stay in the car," she bargained with him fiercely. "I'll wait outside for you with the rest of your security team. I'll be as safe as can be." She took his hand, her sweet doe eyes burning away his resistance. "Don't shut me out again, Warren. Please."

"Fine," he gripped her chin. "But you'll do as I say. Understood?"

A breathy sigh escaped from her lips. "Understood."

Pulling his focus away from the double meaning—and Kate's reaction—Warren escorted her from the restaurant and bundled her into the car. Plugging the postcode into the car's satnav, they set off.

They pulled up on a dirty street just past midnight, sheltering under a graffiti-laden bridge next to an overflowing bin. Paint was peeling from the shopfronts, and litter dotted the kerbs. "Is this it?" Kate asked.

He nodded his head towards something on the pavement, grimacing in revulsion. "What do you reckon?"

"Ew," she muttered, her face scrunching up at the sight of the discarded condom slapped onto the pavement.

Taking the keys from the ignition, he placed them in her hand. "Lock the door whilst I'm gone." He checked in the rear-view mirror to ensure his security team were close enough for his liking. "The others will keep an eye on you from their vehicle. Okay?"

"Okay."

He paused, suddenly remembering something. He took a small box out of his pocket. "I was going to give this to you at the restaurant."

Frowning, she accepted it. "Oh," a small smile curved her face. "My mother's locket."

"I found it on the ground after your attack. It must have been broken…"

Kate picked up where he left off. "When the attacker was strangling me."

"I had a jeweller put a new chain on it." A proper chain, not the cheap tat she had been using.

"Will you put it on me?" She handed it back to him, turning around and pulling her hair over one shoulder.

Unable to resist a bit of teasing, Warren trailed his fingers across her neck, enjoying the shivering of her shoulders as he did so. After clasping the two ends of the chain together, he pressed a soft kiss to the back of her neck. "Perfect," he whispered, breathing in her intoxicating scent before sliding out of the SUV and bracing himself to shut the door.

"Warren?" Kate gave him a small grin, fingering the repaired locket and nodding towards the brothel. "This is the worst apology dinner I've ever been on."

5

Kate

Kate spent the first fifteen minutes fiddling with the little tablet built into the car's dashboard, amazed by all the different functions. Until she switched to the different cameras the car had and found herself staring at a close-up of the discarded condom.

Ugh.

She sighed. She'd watched Warren go into one of the blocks of flats that dominated the landscape, smothered in jealousy that she wasn't quite sure she was entitled to feel.

His leg.

She hadn't imagined it. His leg *had* been bent at a right angle that day those men tried to kill them in the woods, but it hadn't been bone that was broken. His prosthetic had simply been kicked off.

And, *god*, her father…

Just when she thought he couldn't disgust her any more than he already had. The image of an eighteen-year-old Warren pleading for help, and instead getting framed for a crime he hadn't committed.

Warren could do whatever he wanted to Paul fucking Charlton. He'd earned it.

Kate took a closer look at her surroundings before she thought too hard about what horrors her father was currently enduring. Depressing wasn't the word—in both instances.

At least she'd had some greenery surrounding her growing up. The only green she'd seen around here were the traffic lights. The shops all spoke of poverty too. Some were boarded up, whilst others were low-end discount shops or bookies.

Her father had *sourced* women from here, Braxton had said.

Movement in the corner of her eye made her look up. A woman wobbled on the pavement, her tight dress restricting her steps. Her long blonde hair swayed as she walked down the street, eyeing the dark, expensive car in which Kate sat.

The blonde woman approached slowly, swinging her hips as she walked. A few feet away, however, her high-heeled shoes caught on the uneven pavement, and she went flying, landing on the ground in a heap of scraped knees and elbows.

"Oh my god," Kate flung the door open, wincing as the woman's head bounced off the kerb. "Are you hurt?" The doors of the security car behind them opened too, with two men quickly approaching. Kate bent down, her lavender dress tightening at even that small movement.

The woman looked up slowly, her cheeks flushed pink. Her eyes roved up and down Kate's figure. "Aren't you a pretty thing?" she smirked lazily.

"Miss," one of the security guards said. Kate hadn't ever been told his name, but she recognised him as one of the men who'd been tailing Warren at the restaurant. The other stood like a sentinel a few feet in front of the car, glaring in her direction. She couldn't help but feel that *that one* didn't like her very much. "We strongly advise that you get back in the car."

"I'll just be a moment." She held out a hand to help the woman up, bracing herself when she weighed far more than Kate expected. "What's your nam—?" Kate let out a yelp as she slipped on the discarded condom.

A ripping noise was the cost of regaining her footing, and Kate gasped at the feeling of her dress sagging open—and the touch of cool night air hitting places that she definitely wasn't comfortable revealing in the middle of the dodgiest-looking street in London. A city *full* of dodgy-looking streets.

"I'm Adina," the woman said, standing far too close. Her eyes caught on Kate's lips.

"Kate," she gave an awkward smile. Kate took half a step back, hoping Adina would take the hint and retreat from her personal space. She clasped her torn dress to herself uncomfortably. "Your head… Do you want to sit down for a moment?"

Nodding, Adina opened the car door and jumped up into Kate's seat. *Right then.*

When Kate got into the back, one of the guards climbed in next to her. Thankfully the one that didn't have resting bitch face. Giving him an odd look—and feeling much more secure now that her arse wasn't hanging out in the middle of the street—she leant over to see Adina. Past the screen in the back of the headrest in front of her. Because obviously the car had TVs in the headrests. The reminder of her poverty and endless debt was an unnerving one, knotting her stomach. She swallowed. "How are you feeling?"

"Fine," Adina said, smiling back at her. "Are we not leaving?"

She tried to remember what she knew about concussions and drew a blank. "I don't know how to drive, but my… friend will be out in a moment. Sorry." *And I also don't want to go back into the street half naked.* "We'll give you a lift home. Or do you want to go to the hospital?"

Adina turned to face Kate head on. "I don't do more than two customers at a time." Her eyes flicked between Kate and the security guard. "If you want your other friend to join us, I'll have to go in and get a second girl."

Oh. An uncomfortable feeling settled in her stomach as the penny dropped. "Are you… are you a prostitute?"

Adina stilled. "What did you think I was?"

She lifted her shoulders. "A woman who'd fallen on the street?" After a brief pause, "Well, I suppose you can be both."

"A fallen woman on the street." Adina let out a harsh laugh. "So you're not wanting me to do anything for you?"

Kate opened her mouth. "I mean I think you should sit down for a moment at least. You might be concussed. When my friend comes out, he can take you to the nearest hospital. Are you in pain?"

"No," Adina let out a long, disappointed breath. "I need to get back."

"Actually…" Kate asked slowly. "I don't suppose you know someone called William Graves?"

Narrowed eyes stared back at her in the rear-view mirror. "Why?"

Oh god. She'd never been a very good actor. "He's a friend and he's missing." Kate offered up her most sincere smile. "I'm very worried about him."

Adina began to open the car door.

"Wait!" Kate cried. She faced the security guard. "Do you have a pen and paper?"

Reluctantly, he delved a hand into his pocket and handed her a business card. "No pen."

"Adina, if you see him, will you call this number and let me know?"

Just as reluctantly, Adina took it, surreptitiously tucking it into her dress.

"Thank you," Kate called after her. The slam of the door left her alone in the car with the security guard. "Did you know she was a prostitute the entire time?" she asked him quietly, tightly holding her sagging dress.

"Yep."

Twiddling her thumbs awkwardly, Kate nodded, feeling more like an idiot with every second that passed. She watched Adina walk back up towards the main road in the rear-view mirror. "Good."

"Yep."

Up ahead, light spilled onto the pavement. Warren stalked out of the doorway, his expression set into a heavy frown. A flame sparked within her when she remembered his voice rumbling in her ear as she touched herself. *Feed me your orgasm, kitten.*

His steps quickened when he saw the second security guard standing outside the car, and they shared a few terse words before he climbed into the driver's seat.

"I'll leave you." The security guard sitting next to her stepped out of the car.

Leaving her alone with Warren's emerald eyes glaring at her in the mirror.

The engine purred into life, a sharp contrast to the overloud sounds of the cars back home on the council estate. He didn't say a word on their drive back to Regent's Park. The light from every passing car seemed to strip her bare, pressing her further into the seat.

When they arrived back at the flat, Kate went to open the door.

"Stay," he told her. Like a dog.

She was tempted to hiss at him like a cat.

A moment later, Warren was beside her door, holding his jacket out for her. With a small smile, Kate slinked into it, sucking his dizzying scent into her lungs. Its warmth made her shiver.

What would it be like to have the real thing?

Kate gave herself a mental shake as her thoughts descended into filth. She followed Warren into the flat, watching as the frowning bodyguard that had stood watch whilst she was talking with Adina climbed into the driver's seat, steering the car off into the night.

"Where do they take the cars?" she asked, squinting at the bright lights in the apartment building.

Warren placed his thumb on the scanner next to the lift to Rhys's flat. The bruising on his knuckles had turned into a sickly yellow. She wondered what the corresponding bruises on her father looked like. The scanner flashed green a moment later, giving them access to the lift. "An underground carpark round the back."

When they walked into Rhys's flat, Warren's hand shot around her elbow. The lights flickered on as they traversed the corridor, all the way to the bedroom.

In a single fluid movement, Warren had her pinned up behind the bedroom door. He held both of her hands in one of his. "I'm told you flashed my entire security team."

"Accidentally," she panted, trying and failing to sound indignant. Her dress began to move down her body now she was no longer holding it up.

He ground his erection into her stomach, his anger turning into a smouldering grin at her breathy gasp. "Are you wearing the lingerie that Rhys mentioned?"

"Only if you tell me what you learnt from the brothel," Kate countered. "Or what you did."

"If we're bargaining, kitten," he rasped, "I'll want much more than a confirmation." He trailed his free hand down between her heaving breasts. "I'll want to touch."

"Touch me where?"

"Let's start here, shall we?" he smirked, cupping her breast.

Desperately trying to look as though her inner trollop wasn't squealing with glee, Kate nodded. "Over my bra."

"Fine." With one hand, Warren wrenched the remains of her dress away, leaving her far too exposed. Bending down, he growled at the lacy black bra encasing her breasts. Without padding, there was little more than transparent mesh shielding her nipples. He passed a lazy thumb over one, sparking a jolt that pooled between her legs.

Kate couldn't bite back the sound that escaped her, a gasp of shocked arousal. "Warren!"

"I learnt nothing in the brothel," he whispered, staring directly at her breasts. "I did nothing in the brothel."

"Wait, *what*?"

Warren's only answer was to suck her nipple *hard*, drawing an ecstatic moan from her lungs. The combination of the abrading mesh and his wet tongue was dizzying.

The first—the only—man she'd ever slept with had been Daniel, and his attentions comprised nothing more than getting her on her back and pumping into her. The only time he'd ever touched her breasts had been to twist her nipple almost painfully, pulling her away from arousal rather than drowning her in it.

Kate's head fell back against the door in rapture as Warren started on her other breast. She squeezed her thighs together, feeling her slickness. Her eyes rolled back when Warren used his free hand to play with the nipple he'd abandoned, working them together until she was immersed in nothing but desire.

A heavy knock on the door travelled directly to her brain, startling her out of her trance.

"Warren?" Rhys's voice came urgently. "We have a…" Rhys sighed "…a complication."

Warren stood up straight, once again towering over her. He shifted her just enough to crack the door open. Whatever he saw on Rhys's face had him stepping back a touch. "We'll be out in a moment. I'll bring clothes."

"We'll be downstairs."

He shut the door, ghosting a hand over her cheek. His eyes softened for a brief moment. "Put some clothes on." He moved to the chest of drawers in which she'd been storing her new clothes from Rhys.

Kate clutched his jacket together, stepping over the remains of her dress. The dress that probably cost more than her monthly income, judging by the designer label. With a pang, she thought of all the debts that were now past due, and the pile of letters she would come home to.

The panic threatened to overwhelm her with misery. She picked up the baggiest jumper there was and stared expectantly at Warren, about to tell him to turn away.

Only to find he was dangling a lacy thong from the tip of his finger with a smirk. "Have you worn this?"

"No." Kate snatched it away from him and threw it back in the drawer. "And I don't intend to."

"A pity. Find some of the less revealing clothes," he said softly. "There's a woman out there that needs dressing."

Saffron huddled in the corner, her right eye swollen and puffy. A tall young woman with a scraggly cloud of white blonde hair that fell to her waist. She'd drawn her legs up on the dark blue sofa, having been sufficiently clothed. Her nostrils flared as she tried to get a hold of her emotions.

"How did you end up with Graves?" Warren leant forward, his elbows resting on his knees, his hands clasped together.

Kate sat behind Rhys and Warren, feeling more nauseated with every word that left the poor girl's mouth.

"He offered refuge to my mother when my sister and I were younger. He seemed nice." Her voice broke on the final word. "Until he set her to work in his *operation*, and when I came of age I was set to work as well."

Rhys looked down at the floor, scrubbing a hand over his face. "Of age being?"

"My fourteenth birthday. My virginity was sold to the highest bidder."

"Fucking hell," Rhys got to his feet, strolling around to the back of his chair. He grabbed it, his shoulders hanging heavy, his knuckles white. "How old is your sister?"

"Thirteen." She looked at the three of them, pleading with her eyes. "I need to get her out. Please."

"But there was no one else at the warehouse," Rhys looked out across the window, to the darkened greenery and the glittering city lights. He gave Warren a side glance. "The Ruislip site Charlton gave us."

Saffron shook her head sadly. "The last time I saw her was a couple of weeks ago when she moved locations."

"Why was she moved?" asked Warren.

"There's a drug-growing operation just outside of London. The people who work there are..." Her face screwed up in disgust. "Slaves, for want of a better word. Like my sister and I. He lures them in, telling them that he can solve their problems. Graves says he just wants to give people a chance to work towards a better life. They're mostly illegal immigrants, like my mother. He shows them his police documentation, so they trust him, moving to where these so-called jobs are. Then they're isolated, and the intimidation begins. The abuse. The violence."

Rhys's face was strained. "He's hurt you?"

Saffron stared straight ahead, side-stepping the question altogether. "I just want to stop him hurting my sister."

Inhaling a shuddering breath, Kate's inner self-hatred came to the fore. She had facilitated this in helping her father with the Club. And how much money had he paid to Graves? How had that capital been spent?

To cause untold misery.

"Do you have a photo of my father on your phone?" Kate whispered to Warren.

"I have a photo of his driving licence, hang on."

She waited whilst he pulled it up, taking it out of his hand and presenting it to Saffron. "Have you ever seen this man? Has he… visited you?"

Saffron zoomed into the image before shaking her head. "I don't think so, but I wasn't always sober when I was working. Graves would inject us to prevent us from escaping. To get us addicted, keep us coming back for more."

"Inject you?" Kate asked.

"With heroin, mostly."

A harsh noise came from Rhys's throat. "Do you need us to get you any?"

Waves of icy blonde hair shook around Saffron's face. "I've been trying to escape for a while, to wean myself off it without him knowing. I…" Her lips pressed together. "No, I don't want anything. Perhaps some food, if you have any."

Rhys's smile was tight, but he offered Saffron a hand up. "We can get you some food. Come and look at some of the take-away menus I have. The Indian down the road is quite good. The chippy next door to them is *excellent*. We also have…" His voice trailed off as the two of them retreated down the corridor.

The hand that landed over Kate's own startled her.

"Stop it," Warren ordered her. A soft frown appeared on his brow.

"Stop what?" Her eyes flashed to his before darting away again. Thoughts of guilt were swirling around her head, dragging her down into an endless whirlpool.

"This was not your fault."

Perhaps not entirely, and certainly not directly, but the fault arrived at her door all the same. "Saffron can take my bed, if she wants it. I'll sleep in here on the sofa."

Rhys appeared in the doorway. "Er—no need. She can sleep in my room and I'll have the sofa. Or one of the others. We're getting an Indian in. Did the two of you want any food?"

"I'll have a gulab jamun," Warren said.

Kate shook her head. "No, thank you."

"One for each of us, Rhys."

Rhys disappeared as Kate stared at Warren. "I said I didn't want any." She didn't even know what gulab jamun was.

"And when we used to stop off and get sweet and sour chicken with salt and pepper chips from the Chinese shop after school, you'd always insist you didn't want any."

She bit her lip, knowing exactly where he was going with this.

"Then as soon as we sat down on the bench, your grubby little fingers would find their way into *my* food." Warren sat back in his chair, his legs spread wide. "Sound about right?"

Unable to stop a grin spreading across her face, Kate shrugged her shoulders. "Maybe?" she said, her voice higher than usual.

Warren's laugh was a deep rumble that warmed her chest. "That's the first time I've seen you properly smile since I found you."

Her eyebrow quirked up. "*Found*? Is that the word we're using now?"

Warren yanked her chair forward. Its ear-splitting skid across the wooden floor made her wince, but Kate yelped in fear of being dislodged, grabbing onto his arms to steady herself. "What would you call it, kitten?"

"Kidnapping?"

His arms gripped either side of her chair, imprisoning her where she sat. "So if I told you that you could go home right now, would you?"

The thought of endless final notices on debts she couldn't pay almost made her feel ill. "I don't know," she whispered, her voice wavering.

"You'd never see me again," he told her, eyes sparkling, jaw ticking.

Her answer was even fainter the second time round. "I don't know."

Warren's jaw clenched as he stood, backing away from her. He left without a second glance, his footsteps fading away into nothingness. She wrapped her arms around herself, thinking of the warm smile of the boy on the bench sharing his food with her.

She wondered whether she would ever see its like again.

Kate chewed slowly, her eyes fixed on Rhys's truly enormous TV. She had one hand in a pack of Maltesers, mindlessly feeding them into her mouth like a crab.

"What you watching?" Rhys flumped onto the sofa next to her. For the first time since she'd met him, he wasn't dressed in a suit. Instead, he wore a plain white t-shirt and, oddly, a pair of workman's trousers.

"*The Crown*," she frowned. "Have you robbed a painter and decorator?"

He snatched the bag of Maltesers with a wry grin before pointing at the telly, currently showing the Queen in Buckingham Palace. "She dies at the end."

Kate snorted out a laugh. "You're such an idiot."

"A lovable idiot, surely? Like a Golden Retriever."

She yanked the bag of Maltesers back. "A bloodhound at best."

Rhys opened his mouth in mock outrage. "No! I'm far too good looking to be a bloodhound."

"Um, Kate?"

The two of them looked over to see Saffron perched nervously at the edge of the room, her hands wringing together.

"Could you help me with something? In the bedroom." Saffron's lips pinched together so tightly they might have been sewn shut.

Kate got to her feet, letting out an *oops* of surprise when a half-melted Malteser rolled to the floor. Her lips twisted in a guilty grimace when she noticed the melted chocolate stain on her baggy shirt.

"You're an animal," Rhys observed casually, pausing the TV and picking up the Maltesers packet. "I'd better finish these."

After disposing of the singular Malteser and quickly changing into a clean shirt, Kate knocked on Rhys's temporarily reallocated bedroom door.

Barely a beat had passed before Saffron opened it, her eyebrows knotted together in worry. "Come in."

It was the first time Kate had entered Rhys's bedroom. It was luxurious without being ostentatious. As with the rest of the flat, the colours were themed. Probably by some ridiculously expensive interior designer. The furnishings were all tastefully shaded in green or gold, with two variegated *Monstera* plants on either side of the bed. The kind of bedroom she'd only seen in Instagram photos.

Kate glanced around her. "This is nice."

"Have you never been in here before?" Saffron's index finger rapidly tapped her thumb.

"No, I've only ever been in the other room." With Warren. That dulled the remainder of her good mood. He hadn't returned to the flat in the days since Saffron had arrived. She'd not mentioned him to Rhys either, stubbornly refusing to broach the subject.

Except now she was regretting her initial stance, wondering how he was and when he would be coming back.

Warren had grown up in foster care, having been given up by an underage mother. She knew that people leaving him had always been a sore spot. And she'd insinuated that she would do the same at the first opportunity.

"Oh." Saffron paused. "I thought you and Rhys were together."

Kate's face must have been a bewildered picture. "Not at all. I only met him a couple of weeks ago."

"Seriously?" Saffron's head tilted like a confused German Shepherd. "But you're living with him."

"He's a friend of a friend, and I had nowhere else to stay," Kate explained, keeping things as concise and detail-free as possible. "He's nice."

"He is nice," Saffron bit her lip before a quick exhale. "And I got my period unexpectedly and bled all over his bed."

Kate glanced at the unmade bedcovers. "Well that's all right," she said in what she hoped was a soft and encouraging voice.

Saffron shook her head. "It's not. It's gone through to the mattress too. The bloody thing even *smells* expensive and I've ruined it."

"You haven't put the sheets in the wash yet, have you?"

"No, but I've been trying to clean it with water and soap."

"Hot water?"

"Cold," Saffron replied. "Why?"

"Good," Kate breathed a sigh of relief. "Hot water will set bloodstains. I always seem to get my period in my sleep so you've no idea how many times I've had to get blood out of my mattress."

"I can remove it then?" A look of hope dawned on Saffron's face.

"We'll both do it, if you'd like."

"Oh my god," Saffron threw her arms around Kate's neck, bundling her into a hug. "I'm so glad you're here."

"Thank you," Kate patted Saffron's back awkwardly. "Me too," she replied, wondering whether she really meant it.

After quickly discovering that the flat had no hydrogen peroxide and that Saffron had no tampons, Kate made her way back to the living room, finding that Rhys had immersed himself in *The Crown's* pilot episode. Which was definitely not the episode she'd left it on.

"What?" he said, catching her looking at him. "I haven't got anything else to watch."

"I was more judging you for eating all the Maltesers but anyway, I need to go to the shops."

"No."

She began to argue back, but Rhys overruled her.

"No. Apart from the fact that I actually quite like you and don't want to see you strangled, Warren would imprison me in that torture chamber he calls a cellar for the rest of my life."

"But I really do need things, Rhys."

"Just stuff from a supermarket?"

She nodded.

He opened his phone, flicking across his screen until he found whatever app he was looking for. "Here. They'll deliver in less than an hour. Get whatever you want."

Kate took it. "Are you sure?" She scrolled down, only to be prompted to re-order the last delivery… A packet of condoms and a bottle of lube. Pretending she hadn't seen it, she quickly found the things she needed—and a few she didn't—and went to check out. "Delivery is £5!" she exclaimed, horrified.

"It's fine," Rhys waved an idle hand, his eyes glued to the TV.

A depressed prod in her brain reminded her that some weeks £5 had been all she'd had left for food. Ignoring it, she pressed the button to confirm the purchase, cleared the screen, and handed Rhys back his phone. "Thank you," she said quietly. Sincerely. "Do I need to go down to accept it when it arrives?"

"No, one of the security team will bring it up. I'll give you a shout."

Said shout came barely twenty minutes later.

"One of the benefits of being in London, apparently," Kate mused to Saffron, digging through the bag—which one of the security team downstairs had already pre-checked. She laid her order out on the bed. A bottle of hydrogen peroxide. Rubber gloves. Kitchen roll. Tampons. Pads. Two menstrual cups. A hot water bottle in a velvety soft cover. And the biggest box of chocolate seashells she'd ever seen.

"Oh my god, those look amazing," Saffron said, picking up the box of chocolates.

"They are amazing. My father got me a small box last Christmas and I've been obsessed with them ever since."

Saffron perused the period-related items.

"I didn't know what you used, so I just got everything."

Reading the packaging on one of the menstrual cups, Saffron looked at her questioningly. "Why two?"

"Well I actually need one," Kate opened the other box and gave it a squidge. The new cup was slightly smaller than what she had at home. "I didn't have a chance to pack before I came here."

Kate had decided that she wouldn't tell Saffron she was effectively imprisoned here, not when Saffron had so many issues of her own to deal with. The more time she spent here, though, the more it started to feel like an escape from the drudgery of her everyday life.

"I've never heard of a menstrual cup before. Are they good?"

"They're certainly cost efficient. I paid £8 for mine about four years ago and it's still as good as new." Kate picked up the bottle of hydrogen peroxide with a shake. "Right. Let's get to work. And put the gloves on. This stuff will sting and turn your fingers white if you get it on your skin."

The two of them spent the next hour carefully removing the bloodstains from the sheet, followed by the mattress. Saffron's eyes went wide when the hydrogen peroxide began to fizz when it hit the blood.

"Is it supposed to do that?"

Kate nodded, wiping the foam away to reapply another round of hydrogen peroxide. She repeated the process until both the sheet and the mattress were good as new. The final step was using a hairdryer to dry the damp patches on each.

Saffron visibly relaxed when the stains were gone. "Thank you so much."

"You're welcome," she smiled. "Do you want to choose a film to watch whilst I go and fill up the hot water bottle for you? Then when I come back, we can make a start on those chocolates."

The rest of the afternoon saw them tucked under the bedcovers, watching the entire first season of *Stranger Things*, which Saffron had never seen and Kate was pleased to revisit.

"Did you say there's five seasons of this?" Saffron asked, biting into a chocolate seahorse.

Kate nodded. "Four at the moment."

There was a sharp knock at the door.

"Come in," Kate called.

Rhys let the door swing open, resting his shoulders against the doorframe. "You two look very comfy." A frown. "Was the thing you urgently needed a large box of chocolates?"

"No, but would you like one?" she smiled sweetly, holding what remained of the tray up to him.

He took one. The hydrogen peroxide they'd left on the bedside table caught his eye. "You weren't dissolving bodies in here, were you?" he joked, rolling his eyes. "No wonder Warren likes you."

"Perhaps you should take another one," Kate said.

Rhys's smile echoed hers as he held the covers up, planting his arse on the mattress next to her. "Budge up, Kate. Ooh, *Stranger Things*. I only came in here to ask what you wanted to order for dinner."

"Order?" Kate asked.

"Of course. You don't expect me to cook for myself, do you?"

"Let me guess, you're too pretty for that?" Kate grinned, dodging his attempt to elbow her in the ribs. "Saffron, what do you fancy?"

By the time they began season two of *Stranger Things*, the three of them sat with trays of fish and chips balanced on their knees, huddled together in the bed. They chatted like old friends, with Kate finding herself in far too good a mood.

After leaving school, she had become so isolated that it became almost second nature. Her father often stayed at the club, meaning Kate was alone in the house for days on end, her only contact with the outside world being debt collectors.

But the companionship she felt, sandwiched between Rhys and Saffron, felt good. Her eyes grew heavy, and the sounds of their laughter lulled her to sleep.

For once, it had been a good day. She'd made a friend.

6

Warren

"Your leads were useless," Warren said quietly, rolling his sleeves up. His eyes were trained on Paul Charlton as the man fidgeted in his chair, having been given heroin for the first time since his imprisonment.

Paul's hands raised—as much as they were able to when they were strapped to the arms of the chair in which he sat. The fingertips on his right hand were blackened with frostbite, courtesy of the industrial walk-in freezer in which Paul had been stashed since the ramblers' attack. "I told you everything I know."

"You've worked with William Graves for a decade. Do you seriously expect me to believe you've only seen him on two occasions?"

In the corner, Brax lurked. A crocodile sitting beneath murky water, waiting for the opportunity to strike.

"He came to the club, Warren. I didn't go to him."

"And yet you were a regular visitor to the warehouse in Ruislip. A location only known to his closest associates."

"It was a drug transportation and distribution warehouse. The only people that Graves allowed on-site were people he held power over." Paul's greying hair was greyer—and thinner—than ever.

Warren smiled. "That must have been difficult for you. To know he held power over you like that."

"Not as difficult as you might think."

"Why?"

"Because I have just as much power over him as he has over me." Paul's victorious sneer made Warren's fist clench. "More so."

"The security footage of the accident?" Warren asked. Paul didn't deny it. "I'm impressed. You're smarter than you look."

"Damn right," he sniffed, the insult sailing straight over his balding head. "The only thing he's got on me is business records, condemning himself as much as me." His face scrunched up. "And a recording that would shame me."

Warren's smug smile faded. "Of you buying drugs from him?"

Paul's speech was slurred, his attention jumping. "Kate." His laugh shouted around the room. "You used to call her kitten. Do you remember?"

"What do you have on Graves?" Warren intoned dangerously. He *needed* the security footage from the night of Aaron's death. The crash had been right in front of a parade of shops. Their cameras would have a clear view of what happened.

Please, Paul. Don't do this! Please!

Paul's smile faded. "Something he shouldn't have been doing."

"Something illegal?"

He snorted. "Everything Graves does is illegal." His eyes traversed Warren's body. "You're a grown man now, aren't you? How was prison?"

"I made some friends."

Warren didn't miss the meaning behind Paul's raised eyebrow. "I'm sure you did. A good-looking boy like yourself would have been a breath of fresh air. I bet they bricked up when you strolled through the doors."

Strolled.

Warren shook his head. He'd been pushed through those doors in a fucking hospital bed. "Tell me what Graves is doing in the recording."

Paul narrowed his eyes, his skinny legs constantly moving. "Go fuck yourself." He looked down suddenly. "Did they re-attach your foot? I never thought to ask."

"Do you have a copy of the recording?" Warren's voice raised, his patience quickly being eroded. When Braxton had searched through Paul's phone, the only thing they'd managed to recover was an unholy amount of porn. Thankfully not homemade by the revolting man in front of him. But what Warren had *needed* was the recording of the night of the crash. They'd pulled his house apart to find it, but were still none the wiser as to its whereabouts.

Paul's blinks were becoming longer, his attention sliding away as quickly as Warren's patience. "I wish to negotiate my release. Then I'll tell you."

Warren caught Braxton's eye. "Not how it works, Paul. We want Graves and the tape. Then I'll free you." Warren wouldn't, of course. Paul Charlton would never see the light of day again, but he didn't know that.

"I don't know where Graves is."

Barely refraining from rolling his eyes, Warren had had enough. They'd been going in circles all day. He knocked on the freezer door, muttering an order to Brax whilst Talbot, who had been guarding Paul since they'd imprisoned him, opened the heavy door. "Lower the temperature again until he starts talking."

"Shall I untie him?" Brax asked.

Warren let a pitiless grimace spread across his face. "No. He can stand to lose a few more fingers." He looked down to Paul's feet. "And take off his shoes. He won't be needing those again."

Rhys's flat was dark when he entered it, the only light coming from the golden sky beyond, illuminating the world inch by inch. Warren strode over to one of the vast windows, staring out as the sun rose over London. Buildings glistened in the distance, but Warren made his way to his old bedroom.

He paused halfway down the corridor, realising that the door was open. Frowning, Warren dashed towards it, uncaring of how much noise he made. His heart stopped when he saw that the bed was empty. "Kate?" he called, running into the en-suite. That was empty too.

Terror held him hostage, taking him back to the day of the attack, of hands around her bloodied throat. "*Kate?!*" Warren raced through the rest of the flat, full of fears that her would-be murderers had returned, that he hadn't been there to keep her safe.

A low feminine murmur reached him a moment before his brain caught up. "Warren?"

The security team downstairs would have prevented anyone from either entering or leaving the flat. Rhys himself would have protected Kate, calling his security up here at the first sign of trouble.

He stopped outside of Rhys's bedroom door, breathing heavily.

What he couldn't figure out was why Rhys, Kate, and Saffron were all in one bed.

The fuck had happened whilst he'd been gone?

Kate tiptoed out of the room, gently closing the door behind her. "What's wrong?" she whispered, clasping her cardigan over her front, her mussed hair clustered over one shoulder.

He led her down the corridor, speaking in a low murmur. "I came home and saw your bedroom was empty. I panicked." Even now, his heart still raced, thumping a steady beat through his chest. "Why were you all in one bed?"

"We were watching TV," she shoved past him with a sense of urgency, heading straight for the en-suite in his old bedroom. "And my bladder is about to burst, excuse me."

Warren sat on the edge of the bed, giving his heart a much needed rest.

"Where were you?" Kate asked when she came out of the bathroom, her voice still raspy from sleep.

He saw no point in lying to her. "Tonight? Questioning your father. Before that I was sorting out the additional security work to the house." *And missing you.*

"Did my father tell you anything new?"

"No. He has a recording of Graves though. Did you know about that?"

Kate frowned. "No. A recording of what, exactly?"

"That's what he wouldn't tell us." Standing, Warren tucked a wayward brown hair behind her ear. "I don't suppose he's ever mentioned anything like that."

She shook her head. "Not at all. I'm sorry."

"Don't be sorry. It's not your fault." A wry smile curved his lips. "Sleeping in Rhys's bed, however…"

"Hmm," her eyes narrowed, though they held no bite. "Don't tell me you were jealous."

Warren let his eyes sink down to her lips. A promise. "What do you think, kitten?"

"I think you were right to order a second gulab jamun for me. I would have stolen the entire thing."

He chuckled. "Can I get that in writing?"

"No, but if you don't run away ag—"

A repetitive tone made Warren wince, and he took his phone out. His green eyes widened at the reminder. "Shit."

"What's wrong?"

He ached to stay here with Kate, but pulled away from her. "I need to leave again. I'm sorry, kitten." Rifling through the wardrobe, Warren found something more comfortable to wear than his usual three-piece suit; a loose cotton shirt and a pair of old jeans. They were Rhys's, but they'd have to do.

Kate watched him carefully. "How long will you be gone for?"

"I'll be back tonight," he called, hurrying into the en-suite to shower and change. It would be awkward without his 3D-printed shower prosthetic, but he'd manage. "You should get some sleep. It's still early." He was in and out in ten minutes, scrubbing the towel over his hair to dry it.

Kate wasn't in bed when he exited the bathroom. Instead, she was fully dressed and looking at him with a hopeful expression. The same hopeful expression he'd see when she wanted to steal his chips after school.

"Can I come with you?" she asked shyly, her hands twisting into the fabric of a knee-length gingham dress. "I won't be any trouble."

It wasn't her he was worried about. The first of June. Mattie's birthday. He should have remembered long before this, but the day had crept up on him. Paul fucking Charlton had crept up on him. Again. Mattie had heard enough about Kate, and Sarah too.

They'd love to meet Kate, Mattie especially.

"Fine," he smiled. "Let's go."

The long westward drive meant they entered into the seething arena that was morning traffic. Despite the fact that they were trying to get out of London instead of in, the roads were still rammed with cars and their bad-tempered drivers.

"Oh that smells so good," Kate sniffed as they sat in traffic outside a fast food drive-thru.

With a wry smile, Warren flicked on the indicator. "Get what you want, kitten. We don't have to be there till ten o'clock." He pulled out his phone and sent an order in through the app.

She fidgeted in her seat excitedly. "Are you sure?"

"I'm sure."

After they'd received their food, Warren pulled into the car park to eat. "Fucking savages," he muttered, eyeing a clapped-out Volkswagen Polo a few spaces down whose teenage occupants had regurgitated their rubbish onto the pavement.

"I know." Kate bit into her food with a moan that had his cock perking up like a dog hearing the rustle of a treat packet. "God, I forgot how good this is. I haven't had it in years. What did you get?"

He hid his bacon roll away, unable to stop a crooked grin raising one side of his mouth. "Why? Are your kleptomaniac tendencies returning to you?"

Kate chewed her lip. "Maybe." She held out a half-eaten pancake. "Would you like a bite of mine?"

Warren held her wrist steady. "Too right I would." He bit down, leaning across the gearstick.

Her cry was one of outrage. "That was half my bloody breakfast!"

He whipped out one of the two servings of pancakes he'd ordered. "I got another one, don't worry."

The bright smile that broke out across her face could have torn his heart in two.

An hour-and-a-half later, Warren turned off the motorway. In his rear-view mirror, the security car did the same.

"Andover?" Kate read the sign on the slip road. "We're going to Andover?"

"We are."

"Any particular reason why?"

Warren hesitated. "A couple of months ago, I hired a private investigator to find my parents."

Kate's lips parted as she sat up straight in the seat, leaving behind her slouched slump. "And they found them?"

"They found them. I wrote to my mother, and she replied. Her name is Sarah." Optimism practically dripped from Kate's expression. "My father's name is Andy, and I have a brother called Mattie. Today is his birthday."

"How old is he?"

Again, his answer wasn't immediate. "He's twenty-two. The same age as you. Mattie has Down's syndrome, but he isn't—" Warren let out a long sigh "—I don't want you to get the wrong impression. He's high-functioning, if that's even the right term. He's not a child, so please don't talk to him like one."

"Of course I wouldn't." Kate had twisted round to lay her cheek against the seat's pale leather. "I'm assuming this isn't your first visit."

"No, I've been here quite a few times now."

"Wait," she cried. "There's a big Tesco—can I pop in and get him a card?"

"Seriously?" he asked, the indicator ticking as they waited to change lanes.

"I can't show up to someone's house uninvited, on their birthday no less, and not have a card ready, Warren. I may not be a social butterfly but I'm not a hermit. Even I know that." She paused, her brows knotting together. "Or am I waiting in the car?"

"You're not waiting in the car, kitten. They'll be excited to finally meet you."

"You've told them about me?" Kate said, her hand lying on her chest.

It was either that or he told them about prison, but Warren just nodded. "I have. They know what you were to me." Even he had no idea what she was to him now. Someone that provoked longing and discomfort simultaneously, who seemed to see him at his most vulnerable.

"Can we get him a cake too?" she asked as they pulled into a space in the car park, unbuckling her seatbelt and opening the door. Her excitement was palpable.

"We can get him anything you want, kitten."

The shop was bustling with people. The two of them dodged trolley after trolley in their attempts to find the card section. A wall of gift cards gave him pause. "Do you want to get him a gift card too?" He chucked his thumb in its direction, grabbing her hand to pull her back.

Kate faltered. "I can't pay you back for that, Warren."

"I don't want you to. It's a gift from me to you." He halted. "To my brother."

She gave him a slight smile. "What does he like?"

"*World of Warcraft*. Books. *Warhammer*."

"*Warhammer*?"

"It's a game where you buy and paint your own little figurine armies and battle them against other people's little figurine armies." Not that he was an expert by any means. "I think." Warren picked up one of the multi-shop gift cards and examined it, searching for where it could be spent. "I think this one would be best," he said eventually. "He can buy *World of Warcraft* stuff with this and spent it in book shops."

"Thank you, Warren."

He waved it away. "Don't mention it. Let's go get a cake."

"And a birthday card," she nudged him with her shoulder playfully.

At five to ten, Warren stood with Kate outside Sarah and Andy's front door. His mum and dad, not that he'd ever thought of them as such.

It wasn't out of malice. Warren likened it to someone getting a new step-parent in their twenties; it would be odd to suddenly call a stranger 'mum' or 'dad.' His hesitation to refer to them as 'mum' or 'dad' was because they weren't. Not really. If he'd met them as a child, perhaps he would have been more comfortable doing so.

But he was an adult. So he didn't.

It wasn't a problem he'd ever had with Mattie.

"Hello, mate," he grinned at the sight of his brother opening the door. Sarah and Andy's little dog barked in the background. "Happy birthday."

Mattie squeezed him in a hug that almost had his eyeballs popping out of his skull. "Thank you, Warren."

"Mattie," he laid a hand on both his brother's shoulder and Kate's. "This is Kate."

"Kate," Mattie said, grinning. "I've heard so much about you."

"It's lovely to meet you, Mattie. Happy birthday."

Sarah hoved into view at the end of the entrance corridor. "Come in," she said happily, shooting Warren a fond smile, "before the dog gets out."

Ushered into the living room, Sarah was positively beaming when she met Kate. Leo the Jack Russell was similarly happy, jumping up to her knees with his short, surprisingly chunky legs.

Warren nodded to Andy, who waved at him from a recliner armchair in the corner, clasping a lit cigarette in his hand, his eyes on the TV. A decade or so older than his wife, the man's legs were propped up, but the corners of his eyes twitched as he surveyed the room. Sarah bustled about with a motherly smile, taking the cake into the kitchen to sort out the candles.

Kate and Warren joined Mattie in his gaming room—previously a small dining room, according to Mattie—where his miniature army was proudly displayed on a large table, including a handmade terrain. A computer sat in the corner, with both the keyboard and the case illuminated by matching lights.

"Did you paint all of these?" Kate said, bending down to inspect the miniatures strategically laid out on the terrain.

Mattie nodded. "This one," he picked up a colourful figure that seemed to be part tree, "is called Sylvaneth, and she's the daughter of Alarielle."

"Can I pick them up?" Kate asked.

"Only if you put them back in the right position."

"Of course. You're clearly in the middle of a battle here."

Kate's compliments and Mattie's passionate teachings rang through the air as Warren walked past the range of codexes stacked on a shelf, as well as the wide array of colours neatly displayed according to shade. Movement in the corner of his eye made him approach the computer monitor. Mattie's character was still in game. Others whizzed by, either on foot or on mounts.

"This is Stormwind, isn't it?" Warren asked, pointing at the screen. "In *World of Warcraft*."

"It is," Mattie smiled. "How do you know that?"

"I remember what you tell me." He'd also watched *World of Warcraft* videos on YouTube to ensure he didn't forget. "And you're playing as a druid? With *very* fancy armour."

His brother rushed round to the computer, sitting in his gaming chair to bring up a character screen that showed the armour to its fullest effect. "This is the Garb of the Astral Warden. I've transmogged it from other armour just because I like the look."

Standing behind the chair, Warren set his hands on Mattie's shoulders. "It looks great."

"Transmogged?" Kate asked, coming to stand next to Warren. "Ooh, that does look good."

"Thanks," Mattie grinned, turning to face her. "Transmogrification is an effect. So underneath this, I'm wearing other armour—better armour—but transmogging it gives it the appearance of the Garb of the Astral Warden."

"Oh I get it, so it's like an illusion."

Mattie held up his chubby hand for a high-five, grinning when Kate reciprocated. "Exactly."

Eventually, Sarah's head popped in from the entrance corridor. "Shall we sing *Happy Birthday*?"

"Come on then, mate," he said to Mattie. "Let's get some cake in you."

They settled back in the living room, and not a moment too soon. Sarah entered, holding the lit birthday cake aloft before placing it in front of Mattie.

"Don't forget to make a wish," Andy said gruffly from the corner. Leo jumped up at Andy's leg, his paws scratching at the sofa, and Andy shoved him away, muttering.

Mattie squinted for a moment before blowing out the candles and cutting the cake, passing slices around the room on a small set of plates. Mattie chatted happily to Kate, explaining his *Warhammer* army in more depth, whilst Andy's attention return to the TV. Leo, on the other hand, had made a home for himself on Kate's lap.

Jammy little bastard.

"Let me help you with that," Warren stood, taking the dirty plates from Sarah's arms and accompanying her into the kitchen.

"You should be out there with Mattie," she chided him. "He'll steal Kate away from you if you're not careful."

"Steal?"

Sarah's hand rested on her hips, a knowing smile playing about her lips. In such close quarters, he could see the bags under her eyes. "How have you been?"

"Fine," he said, perhaps a bit too quickly. "How's Mattie?"

"He's starting a new job next week."

"That's excellent," Warren said. "I bet he's pleased."

Sarah nodded, putting the kettle on. "He is. Andy isn't pleased about it, of course. Says it's too much work for the lad. But Andy spends most of the year working on cruise ships in the Mediterranean, he doesn't see Mattie day in, day out. It's all very well Mattie playing video games, but he needs to live his life, do you not think?"

That had often been a source of contention, Warren had gathered. Andy's insistence on treating Mattie like a child rather than an adult. "I do. I'm sure Mattie will be fine."

"That's what I said," Sarah agreed, getting a handful of mugs down from a cupboard, their bottoms scraping along the wood, before she fussed with the tea bag tin. "He's going to be working in one of those model gaming places anyway."

Warren snorted. "Hopefully he'll get a staff discount."

"I know. Prices are bloody extortionate." The kettle boiled behind her, and she turned, filling the mugs first with hot water and then milk. "So when did you see Kate again?"

Ah. He'd been hoping she wouldn't ask this question. "Recently," he said truthfully. "It was quite unexpected."

"Despite all the years that have passed, I still expected her to be a small girl in your shadow," Sarah said, sipping at her tea.

"So did I," he confessed. "She's quite… different," he eventually decided upon, choosing his words carefully.

Bewitching would have been more accurate. Mouth-watering. Irresistible.

"Sarah," a rough voice from the living room rasped. The voice of a heavy smoker. "Bring the biscuits in."

"Coming, Andy," she replied, quickly piling the cups of tea and the aforementioned biscuits on a tray and hurrying out the door to tend to her husband.

Warren followed slowly, frowning as he watched Sarah waiting on Andy hand and foot. Mattie and Kate had disappeared, and he found them back in Mattie's gaming room. He smirked, leaning against the doorway, as he watched Kate sitting in the gaming chair, controlling a character.

"So I can't turn into a cat yet?" Kate was saying. She looked down to see Leo at her feet, wagging his tail. "Sorry, Leo. No offence."

"Not yet," Mattie shook his head. "You have to be Level 20."

Kate caught his eye, grinning tentatively up at Warren.

"There is a good book about druids actually." Mattie stood, bustling out of the door. "Hang on," he called back to them, "I've got it upstairs."

"Are you having fun?" Warren asked, his voice low as he approached the desk. He leant on the back of her chair, enjoying the hitch in her breath as it tilted back beneath his touch.

She nodded up at him tentatively. "The game actually seems quite fun."

Warren bent down, taking Kate's hand in his own. "Thank you," he said softly, lifting it to his lips. "You're such a good girl."

The phrase rounded her eyes. Slowly, the tips of her lips edged up into a relaxed smile.

Ensuring they were alone, Warren let his hand snake up her neck, coming to rest just below her ear. "*My* good girl," he whispered possessively.

"Yes," she nodded, as though she couldn't get the word out quick enough. "Yours."

Warren closed the gap between them, taking her lips in a dominating kiss. He cradled her head with both hands, demanding more with every pass of his lips. She pulled back for air, but he seized control once more, tilting the chair back until it was in danger of toppling over.

"I can't control myself around you," he gasped between kisses. "You're this unquenchable madness in me." And *fuck* if he didn't want to punish her for it. He swept a hand down between her breasts, daring lower—

Footsteps thundering down the stairs wrenched him back from insanity, and he stepped back, leaving them both breathless.

"Here's the book," Mattie bustled into the room, none the wiser as to the tension their kiss had left. He plonked the book in front of her, letting it fall open.

Kate followed Mattie's instructions, but she spared Warren a brief glance. A bite of her swollen lip. A squeeze of her thighs.

And he smirked.

7

Kate

K ate deposited the suitcases full of new clothes back in Warren's vast bedroom with a sigh. They were home. The table she'd artfully decorated with tablets loomed in the corner, but she ignored it. The move back to Warren's house was vastly different from their departure. For one, she had two suitcases full of clothes. And two suitcases. By Porsche. Who made suitcases as well as cars, apparently.

She also didn't have a band of bruising around her neck from someone trying to strangle her.

"Holy shit, this bedroom is enormous," Saffron said from the doorway.

Kate turned to face her. "I know. I think this room alone is bigger than the house I grew up in."

"I thought the bedroom I'd been given was ridiculous. This takes the cake," Saf grinned. "Is Warren staying in here with you?"

"I honestly don't know."

Saf's eyebrow bounced up playfully. "An en-suite too?"

"Have you seen the gardens yet?" Kate pointed to the window.

All excitement left Saffron the moment she did. "Is that a koi pond?" she asked quietly.

"I think so."

With a sad smile, Saffron sat in the armchair next to the window. "My mum loved koi. She always said that when she finally paid off her debt to Graves, she'd get us a house. Just a small one, but it would be ours. Evie and I could decorate our own rooms however we wanted, and in the garden we'd have a little koi pond."

Kate sat in the armchair opposite. "It sounds lovely."

Saf shook her head sadly. "It was a fantasy. My mother must have known that she was never going to be able to work off her debt to Graves. It was nothing more than a story to help Evie and I sleep at night."

"How long ago did she die?"

Saffron looked out of the window once more. "Ten months, three weeks, and four days." Her eyes filled with tears. "I don't know how my mother did it. And Evie… She's 13. She's only a baby." She wiped her tears away with the heel of her palm. "She must be so frightened on her own."

"We'll get her out, Saf. Don't worry. Warren has an entire team of people working to find Graves—and Evie. I've told them every detail about my father's club." Brax had even had her go through the security footage, although it had been of little help. She knew the names of the employees and suppliers, but not their faces.

The only time she'd visited her father's club had been back when Aaron was alive.

Paul Charlton had been a shitty father, but at least he'd kept her somewhat separate from the business. She'd always wondered why, and now she knew.

It was because he was a shitty human being full stop.

Anger flared in her, as it so often did these days. The faces of the women—the *girls*—in the photographs were never far behind. Kate wondered how it started. At what point did her father choose to dip his toes into the ocean of human trafficking?

What had Saffron said? Graves turned the trafficked women into addicts. Was that what he'd done to her father too? Get him hooked on a drug he'd never be able to afford, and then offer him an out: funnel trafficked women into the club.

"I know," Saffron replied. "I've been questioned by them so many times I want to scream. I can't stop thinking that, without me there, he might have put her to work already."

There were no platitudes Kate could offer her there. "If he does, Graves will be punished accordingly."

Saffron rolled her eyes. "It won't take away what he might have done to her though, will it?"

No, it wouldn't.

A heavy knock at the door made Kate flinch. "Ms Charlton?"

"Brax?" Kate jumped to her feet, still slightly scared of the enormous man ducking into the room. "Is everything okay?"

"It is, but I'd like to run something by you. Follow me," he growled, setting off down the corridor, not bothering to see whether she'd obeyed him.

With a side glance at Saffron, Kate hurried after him, narrowly avoiding running into Linda, the plump housekeeper. Braxton's heavy footsteps led her into a section of the house that she had an inkling might be above the garage, judging from the views from the windows.

When Braxton opened the door at the end of the corridor, Kate's jaw dropped.

Inside was a wall of computer monitors showing every corner of the house, from Linda talking to Warren in the enormous living room to the koi swimming in the pond to Rhys leaning over the kitchen island, watching something on his phone. There were even cameras showing the grounds, right down to the meadow she'd been strangled in.

"Can you see everywhere on these?" she asked, simultaneously amazed and unnerved.

"Other than the bedrooms that are in use," Braxton answered, pointing to a chair in the corner. "Sit."

She sat, unable to tear her eyes away from the numerous screens, fiddling absentmindedly with her mother's locket as it sat on the new chain around her neck.

"As I'm sure you're aware, we've been questioning your father for some weeks about his involvement in an organised crime ring," Brax began, scowling down at her.

Kate looked away at the reminder that she shared blood with a man who had helped bring misery to so many people. Not just blood—his *name*. "I imagine you're helping him to repent."

Brax grinned maliciously at that. "I think it's fair to say he's quite uncomfortable, yes. But he's been, shall we say, reluctant to share any knowledge that he may have about Graves or his operation."

She snorted. "I would have thought the drug and alcohol withdrawals would have him singing like a canary."

"Not in the way we wanted."

"Is it possible that he doesn't have the information you need?"

Brax shook his bald head. "We've searched every inch of your family home, including his laptop and phone. He was conversing with Graves regularly—at least three times a week. The navigation history on his phone has demonstrated that he's been to sites that we know Graves has operated from. Other leads have all confirmed that your father and Graves were close partners, working together to feed trafficked girls and women into your father's club. Your father knows much more about Graves than he's let on, Miss Charlton."

Her face screwed up at the name like a bad smell had descended upon the room. "Do you know if I can change my name? My last name, I mean."

Taken aback by her question, Brax quickly recovered. "Off the top of my head, you're able to change it by deed poll for a fee. I'm not sure what it is though."

A fee. Everything always had a fee.

"I do think you're able to help with the investigation, however," he said.

"How?"

"Your father doesn't know you're here as a guest."

Was that what she was? A guest?

Brax carried on. "He thinks you're being held and questioned, as he is. Given his reluctance to provide the information we need…" He hesitated. "One of my team members suggested that your father may be more likely to answer our questions if he actually *saw* you suffering the consequences."

Her panicked eyes darted to the unlocked door, pondering her chance of successfully escaping. "You want to torture me in front of him?" Did Warren know about this?

"We would use special effects make-up to give the appearance of torture. You would not actually be harmed."

"So it would all just be pretend? Like acting?"

"Exactly," Brax's gruff voice was the deepest she'd ever heard. "Like acting."

Kate wasn't convinced. She was never very good at acting. "But what if he still doesn't talk? What if you go to all that trouble and then he sits there?"

Brax raised his enormous shoulders. "We'll take you away and apply heavier make-up."

Her nose creased as she scrunched up her face. "And if he sees through the make-up?"

Digging into his trouser pocket, Brax pulled out his phone. A few swipes later, he held it out to Kate.

An album of gruesome photographs was displayed. Some were clearly Halloween inspired, with black eyes or horns. Others were straight up gruesome, with peeled skin, acid burns, or exposed bone. "These are all fake, right? The injuries?"

She wouldn't put it past Brax to have a trophy album of his most grisly exploits.

"Right."

"Good," she said faintly. "That's good."

Thankfully, Braxton turned the phone away. "So you'll do it?"

Her lips parted when she saw movement on one of the screens. Saffron sat down on the bench in front of the koi pond, her shoulders visibly shaking as she sobbed.

"I'll do it," Kate decided, thinking of Saffron's mother, who had died imprisoned and prostituted. She thought of Saffron's sister too, a little girl in a terrible situation. "When do you need me?"

Kate had never realised how much she moved her fingers before.

Brit, the special effects make-up artist, had worked until Kate could barely look at her own hands without feeling unwell. "They're disgusting," she grimaced.

"Then they're doing their job well," Brit smirked crookedly, her tattooed hand working overtime tending to Kate's own.

Despite the fact that she knew well and good that all of her fingernails were attached, the sight of the wet, bloody mess that Brit had created still made her shudder. In the mirror, a black eye stared back at her, swollen and painful-looking. She'd had to change her clothes too. Gone were the clean, fashionable items that she'd been given, replaced by dirty rags that she'd been assured were cleaner than they looked.

"How long?" Brax leant in the doorway, his jaw locked.

Brit tilted her head sideways, her long, straight ponytail falling to the side. "Don't rush me, babe."

The growl Brax released would have had Kate shrinking in her seat, but Brit didn't appear to be affected by it.

Seeing Kate's worried look, Brit patted her arm. "Don't worry. He's a big teddy bear. Last night he had a tea party with our little girl."

"At a full sized table or a children's one?" Kate asked. Please let it be the latter.

"A bright pink children's one. He had to sit on the floor. It was adorable." Brit smiled, giving her husband a loving glance. "I don't know how the two of us managed to produce a girly girl. Did you know he used to work as a security guard for a metal band?"

Envy stirred beneath her. Not for Brax. God, if Kate was married to Brax she would shit herself every time he walked through the front door. But for the easy bond they seemed to have. The hidden smiles when they thought Kate wasn't looking. "Is that how you guys met?"

Brit's grin was nostalgic. "Yeah. Going on fifteen years ago now."

"I still had all my hair," Brax joined in. His phone briefly buzzed before he shut it off.

"It was down to his waist at one point," Brit revealed, her lip piercing twitching as she smirked.

Kate's mouth fell open. "Really?"

"It had to go," Brax said sadly. "I would have looked like Bill Bailey had it gone on much longer."

Brit's sigh was nostalgic. "It was fun to hold onto though."

Kate's eyes widened awkwardly, suddenly looking anywhere but at Brax or Brit. If only she had a free hand to fan herself with. She glanced down and her embarrassment was doused like a swimming pool falling onto a candle.

"I think Kate's horrified by that image," Brax chuckled.

She shook her head. "No, I just accidentally looked at my own fingers again."

Brit snorted out a laugh. "Don't worry. You won't have to look for much longer. You're all done."

"Now remember," Brax said, walking both his wife and Kate through what looked like an abandoned restaurant, "you say the word *Warren* twice in a row, and I'll pull you out of there immediately."

"And I'm okay with you grabbing or shaking me," Kate replied. They'd been through this a hundred times, and the covert words to use. *Stop* for 'keep going.' *Don't hurt me* for 'I'd like you to stop what you're doing, but I'm fine to keep going otherwise'. "Or grabbing my hair."

"But grab it at the base, Tommy. Otherwise it'll actually hurt her."

"I remember," he grumbled.

Kate turned to look at Brit. "His name is Tommy?" A grin grew over her. "That's unexpectedly sweet."

"Hence why I go by Brax." He stopped in front of a door with a long silver handle. Talbot, one of the men who had been at her father's house that night with Brax, stood in front of it, but there was no malice in his expression today. Instead, he simply nodded at her kindly. "Right," Brax announced. "He's in here."

"Good luck," Brit smiled.

"Thank you for your help," Kate replied, taking a deep breath. "And for helping me get out of the house without Warren noticing."

Brit waved a hand. "Don't mention it. It was a nice change from doing wedding and party make-up."

Brax's fancy watch flashed under the fluorescent lighting. "We'll need to get a move on if you're to get back before his meeting finishes."

"Okay," she replied, letting her shoulders fall in what she figured was a dejected manner.

"And I apologise for shouting at or grabbing you in advance."

"I forgive you," Kate smirked, sharply dropping it when Brax wrenched the lever to the side. The door squeaked open. Cold air, so at odds with the pleasant summer day, rushed over her as she walked in.

Her father sat in the middle of the room, his arms and legs zip-tied to the chair in which he sat. Kate wrinkled her nose at the smell of human excrement, whilst her eyes watered at the overwhelming scent of piss-tinged ammonia. Paul Charlton himself looked worse than Kate had ever seen him, even on the days after his benders. Brax had told her in advance of the frostbite sinking its teeth into her father's fingers and toes, but seeing it in person was another matter.

Had she really been laughing and joking in the other room whilst her father rotted away in here?

"Sit," Brax commanded. His loved-up expression was gone, replaced with the Brax that had first visited Kate that night she'd been taken from her family home with a bag over her head. "Paul."

Paul's sunken cheeks had aged him twenty years since Kate had last seen him—and he had never looked young for his age. Alcohol and hard drugs had robbed him of whatever good looks he'd once had. Finally, he met Kate's eyes, letting her see the exhaustion he felt.

"Dad," Kate whispered shakily, genuinely unsettled by his appearance.

"Hello, Katie."

She flinched. The last time he'd called her that had been just after he'd told her he'd lost everything they'd both been working for. *Let it fall*, she thought. "They've been hurting me, Dad." The tears that came to her eyes were genuine. Genuine upset at what he'd been doing all these years. The photographs that Warren had shown her came rushing back. The photographs of her father with a terrified girl who definitely didn't want to be beneath him.

"I can see that, Katie." Her father's throat bobbed.

"I don't know what they want."

Paul's cracked lips pressed together, but he said nothing.

"You know exactly what we want. The security footage from the accident." Kate cried out in shock as Brax's rough hand suddenly found purchase in her hair, tugging at her skull. "And Graves's home address. Multiple sources have placed you there on multiple occasions."

"Then perhaps you should ask one of your sources," Paul rasped sarcastically, pain lining his face.

"Dad, please!" she whimpered. "Just tell him, just tell him, just tell him."

"This is the last time I'll ask, Charlton," Brax snarled from behind her. "Your daughter could still get out alive. If not, I'll let my team have their fun with her and then start cutting her into pieces. Those fingers look like they hurt. I'm sure she'll be glad to get rid of them."

"Stop," Kate gasped. "Just please stop."

The expression on her father's face chilled her to the bone. "Then I guess you'll have to send me the pieces."

His words sent a visible shudder through her. "The day you brought me back from the hospital," Kate let the tears stream down her cheeks, "newly widowed, swaddling your motherless daughter… Is this where you thought my life would end?" She shivered, wishing she had warmer clothes on. "Is this what Mum would have wanted for me?"

"I'm sorry, Katie," Paul shook his head. If she looked hard enough, perhaps she could find a bit of sorrow hidden somewhere. "But they were never going to let you go."

"Did you ever love me?" she sobbed.

Paul shrugged, wincing like the movement caused him pain. "My ability to love died with your brother."

Braxton's enormous hand suddenly vanished from her hair. He crossed the room, whipping a backhand across Paul's face that would have laid out an ox. The force was such that Paul's chair teetered back, falling to the floor with a crash.

Brax grabbed her upper arm, lifting her from the chair.

Kate stood, looking at the blackened feet hanging uselessly in the air, the gruesome black nails. The man attached to them groaned on the floor, and a stream of bright red blood was already visible against the icy floor. "Goodbye, Paul," she said dully, before letting Brax escort her from the room.

The heavy white door had barely closed before Kate was sliding down it in a cascade of torment. No longer caring for the make-up on her nails, she wrapped them around her middle, trying to hold herself together. Sobs wracked her frame, but Brax knelt down next to her.

"He doesn't deserve to call himself a father," he said quietly.

Brit was there too, muttering something about body oil before she attempted to scuttle down the corridor towards her heavy case of supplies.

Only to run headfirst into a very solid, very furious Warren. "Jesus fucking Christ, kitten," he rushed towards her, sliding to his knees on the tiled floor and grabbing her hands.

"It's make-up," Brit's voice came quickly. "None of it's real."

"I knew he didn't love me like he loved Aaron," Kate managed as Warren held her through gasping sobs, "but he was perfectly happy for me to be gang-raped and tortured to death for crimes he committed, knowing full well I was innocent." She wiped her eyes, feeling some of the red wetness Brit had applied smear across her face.

All of that effort for a few minutes of devastation.

And yet she'd never felt more exhausted.

Kate had always known their relationship was different. Other men had proper bonds with their daughters, would protect them with their life. Men like Brax ,with his perfect pink tea parties. Kate had always looked enviously upon them, wondering what her father had been like in those early years preceding her memories. Would he have let himself be wound round her little finger?

With a rough, hyperventilative inhale, she met Warren's agonised gaze. "Take me home."

Kate peeled her eyes open. The raw feeling on her cheeks told her that she'd cried herself to sleep. Blinking, she realised she was no longer in the car, being held and comforted by Warren. She was in Warren's bedroom—in his lap, laid out on the midnight blue sofa.

"Kitten?"

A cream blanket fell from her shoulders as she sat upright, weighed down by the bleakness within.

Warren pushed away the little workstation holding his laptop aloft, its wheels squeaking. He gave her his full attention, twisting to face her.

Her lip wobbled.

"Oh, kitten."

Kate tried not to get lost in self-pity—again—but sank into Warren's embrace nonetheless. "What kind of daughter isn't loved by her own father?" she mumbled into his shoulder.

He retreated to cup her cheeks, staring deep into her soul. "The fault lies with him, not with you." A tentative smile lifted his lips. "You forget, kitten, that I met you as a little girl. A little firebrand. And you were *so* easy to love, with your wide smiles and endless energy. The little sister I never had. Even then I felt it, this consuming need to protect you."

She knew she shouldn't ask it, but she did. "And now?"

His gaze burned like an inferno raged within him, churning and spitting flames. "Nothing I feel for you is siste—"

A quiet, restrained knock silenced him.

"Come in," Warren answered.

Saffron entered, her brows knitted together. "Kate," she breathed, rushing to the sofa. "Are you all right? Brax mentioned you were upset."

"I'm okay," Kate wrapped herself in the cream blanket, the heat from Warren's eyes no longer keeping her warm.

"The food you ordered has just arrived," Saffron told Warren, "but Brax said you wouldn't be ready for it."

"Food?" Kate perked up.

Warren's lazy smile said it all. "Sweet and sour chicken. Salt and pepper chips."

"Several portions of it, I hope."

His hand rested on the small of her back. "What do you take me for?" The warmth of his touch disappeared as he stood. "I'll be back with your food, Your Highness."

Quicker than she'd expected, Warren returned with several bags, one of which had the heavenly scent of hot food. "There are quite a few different things down there, Saffron. Feel free to go and help yourself before Brax and the security team decimate it."

Saffron bounced up, closing the door behind her as she left, shooting Kate a knowing smile.

"Did you leave her food downstairs just to get rid of her?" Kate asked suspiciously.

"Yes," he said baldly, the corners of his eyes crinkling. "I want you all to myself. Is that a crime?"

As though the smell of the food alone had infused some life in her, she gave a quick retort. "Depends on how much food you've brought me."

They ate in comfortable silence, quickly emptying the little aluminium trays.

It was only when they finished that Warren opened the second bag he'd fetched up. He pulled out a sleek, A3-sized box decorated in a black-and-white colour scheme. Opalescent stickers flashed as it moved, drawing her attention.

"This is for you," he said delicately.

Her brow creased when she recognised the brand; the same as that of Warren's laptop. "Is this…?"

He nodded, carefully watching her. "I thought you might want one of your own."

"Thank you," she said sincerely, putting the laptop box on the table and throwing her arms around his neck. Her last gift had been a singular box of chocolates from her father on Christmas Day. A box of chocolates she knew for a fact he'd picked up from the petrol station at the last minute. To suddenly have new clothes, new suitcases, and a new laptop thrown at her was overwhelming.

Warren's hands came up to lock her against him. "Anything for my kitten," he whispered into her hair, sending a shiver through her.

She pulled back, just enough to look in his eyes. Only to discover that his attention had drifted south and had settled firmly on her lips. Immediately self-conscious, she darted her tongue out, pulling her lip underneath her front teeth.

The groan he gave was unexpected, as was the hand he slid along her jawline. "You drive me to madness."

Kate didn't know where her response came from, but it left her anyway. "Then go mad with me."

Warren seized her lips with his own, brushing once, twice, thrice, before she opened for him. His stubble was sharp against her skin, but the softness of his lips more than made up for it in silky, drugging apologies.

His delicious warmth drew her in closer, and before long her hands were exploring of their own accord, tracing the biceps of the arm he'd secured around her waist, exploring the contours of his neck, even sinking into the darkest depths of his hair. Kate treasured every inch she uncovered, and wondered how many more she would find.

When they finally broke apart, both of them were panting with exertion and desire.

The heavy-lidded eyes over his smirk suggested that Warren was more aroused than exhausted. "If I'd have known that was what it was going to take for you to kiss me, I would have bought you a laptop weeks ago."

Blushing, she couldn't help biting back. "If I awake tomorrow to find a new Range Rover parked on the drive for me, should I worry about your intentions?"

He kissed her again. "You should always worry about my intentions."

Recalling the events of earlier, Kate decided to ask him a serious question. "Can I ask what your intentions are regarding Brax and I?"

"What about the two of you?"

"I mean, we just left without telling you," she shrugged. "I know the rest of Brax's team were furious. Especially the one with resting bitch face." Her and Brax had effectively been glared out of the house.

"Resting bitch face?"

"Yeah, his face looks like a slapped arse."

"His name is Creer." Heat infused Warren's narrowed eyes. "And how would you know what a slapped arse looks like?"

She chose not to answer that. "I simply meant that me being the prisoner and all, I thought you'd be angry."

"You're not a prisoner, kitten." Warren blinked down at her, an odd look in his eyes. "But no, I'm not angry. Well, I was a bit miffed you left, admittedly, but it's not as if you ran away. You left with my Head of Security and three security guards—in addition to the two that are constantly there guarding your father anyway. You were safe." Warren twirled a lock of her hair around his finger. "And I'm told Brax broke your father's nose. Again." He shrugged. "That cheered me up *immensely*."

Kate's smile was a weak one. "Me too."

"Don't give him another thought, kitten. He's not worthy of you. He never was."

A message popped up in the lower right-hand corner of Warren's laptop. She squinted at the photo attached. A familiar young man holding a familiar Jack Russell.

"Is that Mattie?"

Warren turned, a dark lock flopping over his forehead as he yanked the workstation towards him. "He wants to know if I've given you your laptop yet." Another message came in whilst he was reading.

Mattie: Because I can help her set it up if she's unsure.

"Are they difficult to set up? I've never done it before," she asked worriedly, dragging her new laptop towards her. She hacked away at the security sticker with her blunted nails. Within seconds, she'd peeled it off and was opening the box.

"It shouldn't be," Warren said mildly.

"Ooh," she exclaimed. "I didn't expect it to be white." Kate held her new laptop as though it were as fragile as a newborn. An excited smile broke through. "Thank you. I love it."

The laptop was a breeze to get up and running, and in a few minutes Kate had logged onto social media and sent over a friend request to Mattie. He responded immediately.

Mattie: Do you want to play *World of Warcraft* with me?

"Can I get that on this laptop?" Kate asked.

"That was literally the most expensive laptop in the shop. If it can't run *World of Warcraft* then I'm sending the friggin' thing back." Warren paused. "Do you really want to play with him?"

Kate nibbled on her lip. "It did seem like fun."

Warren tucked her under his arm, sealing their embrace with a kiss. "Then let's get it downloaded."

8

Warren

"You want the underlying profit margins for each of the product lines?" Jensen asked, jotting down notes for the minutes of the board meeting.

Warren nodded. "If they can get them down to each individual product, that would be even better. Their current reports aren't even close to good enough. No wonder they needed a fucking buyout."

"Noted."

"I'd like to add that to the agenda for our next board meeting too. They have eight weeks to get the first report ready for us."

Jensen looked at Aldous and Rhys. "Any other business?"

Rhys shook his head.

"Not of that sort," Aldous replied unhappily.

Warren readied himself for a fight. "If this is another attempt to persuade me to hand everything to the police th—"

Aldous held up a hand. "It's not that. It's Mum's sixtieth next month."

"Oh for fuck's sake," Rhys whispered under his breath.

"Auntie Alison is sixty?" Jensen sat back in his chair. "Holy shit."

"Do you know, I would have thought she was closer to fifty?" Warren said, mildly impressed.

Rhys rolled his eyes. "No wonder she welcomed you into the family."

Warren's grin was smug. "It's not my fault her biological children were defective."

"Speaking of defective, how's your new prosthetic going?" Rhys bit back, running his tongue across his teeth, bared in a smug grin.

Mid-sip, Warren inhaled half of his Coke in an attempt not to laugh. He choked out a cough, tears running from his eyes from the fizzing in his nose. "Sounds like you're itching to do another shot from my prosthetic," he bounced a Cheshire cat smile right back at Rhys.

Rhys clapped a hand over his mouth as he retched involuntarily. "Don't!"

Even Jensen smirked as Rhys staggered to his feet, holding his hand securely over his mouth.

"It's one of my *favourite* memories," Warren called after him. "I really don't know how you got past the smell. And the taste," he mock shuddered. "I bet it's still there on the back of your tongue."

Rhys wiped his mouth, looking distinctly unwell. "I will never fucking forgive you for letting me do that."

"Mate," Warren said innocently, "you're the one that offered."

Sitting back down in his seat, Rhys took a sip of water. "You may not be defective. But you are a cunt."

"Cuntiness aside," Aldous pulled out his phone, looking mildly bored. "The venue that Mum booked for her sixtieth has had to pull out. A fire's gutted the ground floor apparently. Her party planners haven't been able to find a new one on such short notice."

"I did suggest the local community centre," Rhys piped up. "Apparently their colour scheme of brown-on-brown isn't quite what she had in mind."

"What *did* she have in mind?" Warren asked.

"Somewhere big enough to accommodate 200 people, sufficient parking, a champagne reception, an in-house casino, and a fireworks display," Aldous listed off his mother's requirements.

A long way from the council estate on which Rhys and Aldous had been raised, in other words. Alison had worked long hours as a midwife to raise her two boys, and occasionally caring for Jensen too. Warren knew first-hand how devastated she had been when Rhys and Jensen were sent to prison. They'd already been locked up for eighteen months when Warren arrived as Rhys's new cellmate.

At first, he'd been bewildered by how many letters Alison wrote to the two of them, particularly as they'd been sent down for murdering a pensioner. Then the jealousy began. In Warren's first twelve weeks in prison, he didn't receive a single letter. The fact didn't escape Rhys's notice.

And then one day Warren received a letter from Alison too.

"She can have her party here," Warren offered, remembering the woman who'd welcomed a motherless criminal into her heart. "There's plenty of room in the garden for a couple of marquees. We're in the middle of nowhere, so fireworks won't be a problem."

"What about parking?" Jensen queried.

"The fields abutting the house are all mine too. I'm not using them for anything."

Jensen ran his thumb over his stubble. "Alison did like the house when she first visited, if I remember rightly."

"I'll run it by her," Aldous said, tapping away at his phone. He stood, picking up his keys off the desk. "I do need to get going though. I'll let you know what she says."

"You're welcome to stay. All of you," he offered. "It's not like there aren't enough bedrooms."

"Or cells," Aldous muttered darkly. "But no. I want to get home."

Jensen was of a similar mind. "So do I. I'll see you soon, boys."

"You're staying, I assume?" Warren asked Rhys when the other two had disappeared into the night.

"If you don't mind."

"Linda's already made up your usual bedroom," he said, climbing the stairs. He left Rhys at the landing, heading for his walk-in wardrobe-turned-bedroom. Out of habit, he glanced in the two-way mirror, smiling when he saw Kate in the other room, intensely clicking away on her laptop. *Probably on that bloody game with Mattie.*

Shedding his clothes, Warren strapped the 3D-printed shower prosthetic to his leg and let the hot water wash his worries away. He was just leaving its embrace when a knuckle rapped at the door. "Yep?" he called, sitting on the large rectangular ottoman in the walk-in wardrobe, replacing the 3D prosthetic with his normal one.

The bedroom door opened.

That was when he realised his mistake.

Kate stood in the doorway, and Warren watched as her focus left him. It landed on the mirror that ran almost the entire length of the room—the mirror that gave him a front row seat to anything she was doing in her room.

"What the fuck is that?" she whispered, her face a stomach-turning combination of furious and humiliated.

"Kitten," he began.

She cut him off, shutting the door behind her and raising her voice. "You can see into my bedroom?" She pointed a finger at the camp bed underneath the mirror. "This is where you sleep?"

Warren nodded, standing to his full height, holding the towel around his waist. He should feel ashamed, but he wasn't.

"Why? Why is this even here? What lunatic puts a two-way mirror into their own fucking bedroom?!"

"Before I moved in, this—my walk-in wardrobe—was just a normal bedroom. I converted it and put a door in between the rooms," he gestured to the door next to the mirror he'd kept locked since she'd moved in. "Normally, I keep it transparent, but there's a button I can press to turn it into a mirror and back again."

Her eyes lingered on his, slowly making their way down to his tattooed chest. "Have you been watching me get changed?"

"No," Warren took a step closer to her, "because you get changed in the bathroom after you shower. It was awfully disappointing to discover."

"So you *have* been watching me?"

"Obviously I've been watching you," he admitted, backing her up against the mirror in question. The towel fell away. "You mumble in your sleep."

Worry flared in her eyes. "What have I said?"

"I don't know. It's a mirror, not a microphone. And I had the cameras in the bedroom turned off weeks ago."

Kate placed a hand against his chest. "There were cameras on me?"

He tilted her face up towards his. Thank fuck he had put cameras on her in those early days. If it hadn't been for the cameras, he and Rhys would have never seen her on the brink of suicide. "Before I trusted you."

She let out a little whimper at the feel of his cock pressing against her stomach. "Warren, you're naked."

He was aware. "Do you like the feeling of my cock against you, kitten?" He snaked his hand around the back of her neck and pulled until their bodies were flush, devouring her answer and her lips both.

"This is *not* the time!" she hissed, pushing away from him, her hand heavy on his chest. She huffed, apparently trying to regain her composure. It wouldn't matter. He'd tear it from her as easily as breathing.

Something else tore it away before he had the chance.

Her jaw slackened, as did her lips, reddened by their furious kiss.

"What is that?" she whispered, her voice barely audible.

Warren followed her line of sight, just to the left of where her palm was braced, landing squarely over his heart.

Fuck.

The little minimalist outline of a cat was the first tattoo he'd ever gotten. It perched between the extensive artwork on his chest, hiding in plain sight. From a distance, it was barely noticeable at all, but as close as she was...

"A cat," Kate said. It wasn't a question.

He swallowed, covering her small hand with his. "A kitten. So you would always be with me." A little piece of the home he'd lost upon entering the prison gates.

Kate's eyes were wide, sparkling with tears. Though her hand still rested on his chest, her arm was no longer braced against him. Instead, she came close, bringing her other hand up to join the first, until she was mere millimetres away from his favourite—and most treasured—tattoo.

He smiled when she kissed it, threading his fingers through her dark hair.

Then she wrapped her arms around his neck, pulling him downwards—although he went *more than* willingly.

"You're so fucking beautiful," he groaned into the kiss, seizing her floral blouse in his hands and rending it in two. Buttons flew in all directions, scattering across the room. A few tinkled across the tiled bathroom floor. "Why do you think I want eyes on you at all times?"

"Warren!" Kate gasped, attempting to cover herself.

He wrenched her arms away with a sly grin, holding them both in one hand. "Don't hide from me." With his other hand, he pulled the straps of her bra from her shoulders and freed her breasts with a satisfied snarl. It almost drowned out her self-conscious gasp.

But nothing could eclipse the noise she made when his lips closed over her breast, sucking its cherry-red bud. Her hands came up to grasp the back of his head, holding him in place.

In a cruel movement, Warren raked his teeth over her puckered nipple. Kate flinched beneath his grasp, crying out his name, but he'd already switched to her other breast, beginning the process all over again.

Once again, she cried out at his teeth, a mixture of agony and ecstasy. "Yes!"

Warren dragged her over to the large rectangular ottoman in the centre of the room, pushing her backwards onto it, her ample breasts bouncing. He crawled over her, trapping his weeping cock between their bodies. "You like being held down, don't you?"

"Yes," she said again, her eyes glazed with arousal.

"I saw it on the night you arrived, when I pressed you against the wall. You like it when I'm rough with you."

Kate nodded.

"You want to be at my mercy."

Another nod.

"Good," he growled. "Because I'm going to do whatever I fucking want to you." Without another word, he bunched her skirt around her hips, letting a groan loose from deep in his chest at the sight of her lacy black underwear. Savouring every moment, he hooked his thumbs underneath the lace and unveiled the prettiest, pinkest pussy he'd ever seen.

"Warren," Kate whimpered a few seconds later. "*Do* something. Don't just stare at me."

"You want me to do something?" he asked, his voice dangerously low.

"Please," she begged.

Nostrils flaring, he gathered her damp underwear in his hand and brought it up to her mouth. "Open."

"What?"

"Open your fucking mouth before I open it for you." He grinned when she finally obeyed. "Good girl. Can you taste yourself?"

Kate nodded, her eyes closing as he stroked her face.

Warren pushed her legs wider, exposing every inch of her. "You're to do *exactly* what I tell you and nothing more, do you understand?"

Her nod was immediate.

"That includes not coming." His smile was positively malevolent. "You're not to come. You *will* be punished if you disobey me." Warren cupped her face roughly, his erection painfully hard. *There's my perfect kitten.* "And trust me when I say that I'll enjoy hearing you beg for mercy."

Her eyes flashed in alarm, but he paid no attention. Instead, Warren delicately teased his hands up and down the insides of her thighs, absorbing every hitch in her breath, every judder of her chest. He pressed kiss after kiss around her pussy, never quite travelling where she wanted him, even as she tried to tempt him.

"Has anyone ever kissed you here before, kitten?"

Kate shook her head, her eyes wild with arousal.

"This is what you need, isn't it? You need my touch."

A desperate muffle escaped past the underwear gagging her. He could just make out the meaning of the garbled sound. *Please.*

Kate flinched as Warren buried his face between her legs, laving his tongue at her entrance. Arousal soaked his tongue, and he groaned at the taste of her honey, swallowing every drop he could find. Her knees drew together, blocked by the broad width of his shoulders, just as her desperate moans of pleasure were impeded by her lacy gag.

When he sucked her clit, Kate went wild. Her hands gripped his hair, holding him exactly where she needed him. Keen to have her on the edge for as long as he could, Warren inserted two fingers inside her. Her back arched, but he clamped her down with a heavy arm, holding her exactly where he needed her.

Come, he willed her silently, curling his fingers against her g-spot. He wouldn't voice it, wanting an excuse to punish her.

"Uh-uh," she mumbled, shaking her head desperately as she barrelled towards her orgasm.

Such a good kitten. Warren's eyes promised punishment, even as he pushed her towards the edge he wouldn't give permission for her to go over. *But your efforts are in vain.*

When Kate's eyes rolled to the back of her head, Warren knew it was over. Her scream as her orgasm hit her was biblical, even as her legs quivered unstoppably around his ears. On and on it went, her cunt squeezing his fingers with every wave that shuddered through her.

Warren prolonged it as much as possible, eagerly sucking her clit until she finally pushed him away.

Just like he had the first morning after she arrived, he tugged her into his arms—except this time he had to remove her lacy underwear from her mouth first. He turned the key to unlock the door next to the mirror, carrying her into her bedroom.

Settling the two of them in the large, luxurious bed, he kissed her forehead. "You were such a good girl," he whispered lovingly.

Kate looked up at him as though he was the only person in the world who mattered, her soft dark eyes searing him to his very soul. "But I disobeyed you."

"For much longer than I thought you would have. You tried so hard to resist, kitten. I'm proud of you."

She smiled out a sigh, not looking away for a moment. "Will you still punish me?"

"Yes," he replied, massaging her shoulder. "But I think you'll enjoy it."

"I like it when you care for me," Kate admitted, hiding underneath his chin shyly. Her nose rasped against his stubble, her fingers dancing over the kitten tattoo on his heart.

Warren inhaled the scent of her hair, moving his massage to her upper back. "I'll always take care of you, kitten." Over anyone. Over anything. "Now let me hold you as you sleep."

Warren blinked open bleary eyes at the distant buzzing. It stopped as he was rubbing the sleep away. Relieved, he let his head fall back on the pillow, smiling as his kitten squeezed him in her sleep.

Until the buzzing began again.

"For fuck's sake," he grumbled, shifting away from Kate's touch. The very last thing he wanted to do.

"Don't leave," Kate bleated. Her hand limped across the bed, searching for him.

He took it and brought it to his lips. "I'll be back, kitten."

Fumbling for the prosthetic he'd kicked off last night, Warren eventually made it to the walk-in wardrobe. He picked his phone up from the shelf on which he'd left it before his shower, panicking slightly at the five missed calls from Mattie displayed on the screen.

Before he had a chance to call him back, Mattie rang again.

"Mattie?" Warren answered frantically. "What's happened?"

"It's Mum," Mattie answered. "She collapsed, and I had to call an ambulance for her. She's in hospital and Dad's offshore for work. Can you come?"

Fuck. "Of course I'll come. Which hospital is it? The little one in Andover?"

"The big one in Basingstoke," Mattie sniffed.

Through the two-way mirror, Kate was getting out of bed, holding the duvet to conceal her nakedness.

"I'll be there in less than an hour, okay?" he ran a hand through his hair. The memory of last night, of Kate tugging on it, returned to him. "Do you need me to bring you anything? Or Sarah? Have you eaten breakfast?"

"No."

"I'll be there soon, all right? I'll send you my location so you know exactly where I am. Everything will be okay."

Kate was stood in the doorway when he put the phone down. "What's wrong?"

"Sarah's in hospital," he swallowed. "She collapsed. I need to leave."

"Do you want me to come?" she asked, slipping her soft hand into his.

He nodded in relief. "We need to be quick."

To her credit, Kate was ready to leave quicker than he was. They flew down the motorway, just avoiding the morning rush hour. Again, they stopped at a drive-thru for breakfast—for both them and Mattie—but there was no laughing or joking this time, no casual reminiscing.

Warren held Kate's hand in a firm grip as they rushed into the hospital, following Mattie's directions to the intensive care ward. They were buzzed in, and the receptionist quickly directed them to Sarah's bedside.

"Warren," Mattie stood, his cheeks stained with tears. His brother barrelled into his arms.

"Hey," he soothed. "I've got you. Everything will be fine. You're not alone anymore."

Sarah lay unconscious on the bed, dwarfed by the incessant humming of flashing machines. A ventilator blocked the lower half of her face. Her hair, which she usually styled in a tight, sensible bun, streamed against the crisp white hospital pillow. A hairbrush lay next to her head where they'd interrupted Mattie combing it out.

"They think she's had a seizure," Mattie revealed. "She's had a CT scan. They've only just brought her back." He gulped down a shuddering breath.

Warren did his best to comfort Mattie in a situation that lay far, far outside both of their comfort zones.

Mattie finally cracked a smile when Warren brought out the food they'd picked up on the way down. "Mum says I'm not supposed to have fast food unless it's a Friday. I put it on too easily, and my doctor says it's not good for me."

He nodded. "I think the doctor will give you a pass today."

Mattie was silent as he ate, his eyes never leaving his mother. "I wish I'd brought my PC," he said eventually, "just for something to do. I hate sitting here staring at her, wondering if she's ever going to wake up."

"Actually," Kate whispered, her hands disappearing into the bright yellow leather satchel at her feet, "I brought this with us. I thought you might need a distraction." She placed her new laptop on the portable table next to the bed.

"I'll turn on my mobile hotspot," Warren offered. The extra charges would probably run into the hundreds on his next bill, but it would be a small price to pay to take Mattie's focus off of their critically ill mother.

It came as no surprise to any of them when Mattie fired up *World of Warcraft.*

"Do you know when Andy will be back?" Warren asked. The last he'd heard, Andy was in the Mediterranean somewhere.

It took Mattie a minute to realise Warren had asked him a question. "No, but he should be flying home soon, I hope."

"Have you spoken to him?"

Mattie shook his head. "I left him a voicemail. I don't think he's allowed to use his phone whilst he's working."

With a comforting smile, Kate took Mattie's hand. "I'm sure he'll be here as soon as h—"

An older woman dressed in dark blue scrubs slid the privacy curtain back with a polite expression. Warren winced at the sudden metallic scraping of the eyelets against the pole. "Good morning, I'm Dr Tripathi, one of the doctors dealing with Mrs Harper's case." She paused, wearing the tight smile of someone about to deliver bad news. Her eyes ran down her chart. "Which one of you is Matthew Harper?"

Mattie raised his hand, his face suddenly pale. "We're her sons," he said, gesturing to Warren. "Is she going to be okay?"

Dr Tripathi's face was sincere. "We're going to do everything we can to help Mrs Harper. Now, we've sent her for some scans, as I'm sure you're aware. However, the good news is that her seizure doesn't appear to be a new condition. Rather, we're working under the hypothesis that it's an additional symptom of her glioblastoma. This is good news, as we've found that patients presenting with seizures do tend to have a more favourable—"

"Wait, what?" Warren blinked, his own panic reflected back at him in Mattie's expression. "Her glioblast..."

"Glioblastoma," Dr Tripathi supplied, when he failed to finish the word. She checked her notes. "We have it down here that Mrs Harper was diagnosed with glioblastoma approximately three weeks ago."

"And what is that, exactly?" Mattie asked.

There was a pause before the doctor answered, looking between them with a patient expression. "Glioblastoma is a type of malignant tumour found in the brain."

Malignant.

Something deflated inside his chest at the mere mention of the word.

Mattie squeezed Kate's hand. "Tumour... As in cancer?"

"I'm afraid so," Dr Tripathi answered, her tone not unkind. "But she's scheduled to start chemotherapy later this week. After her seizure this morning, we've already issued her a prescription for carbamazepine, which should help to control the issue in the future. We're hoping that carbamazepine should either reduce the incidence of future seizures or prevent them altogether."

"And the chemotherapy," Mattie sat up hopefully, "that will cure her cancer?"

Dr Tripathi's nostrils flared as she inhaled. "Glioblastoma isn't something that can be cured, per se, but it can be slowed with chemotherapy and other treatment options such as radiotherapy and surgery. She's already been scheduled in to start treatment soon."

"Good," Mattie said faintly, staring at the hospital bed—and its occupant. Warren lay an arm across his brother's back. "Good."

"Very well." Dr Tripathi began to list off potential symptoms that she might have been experiencing, attempting to ascertain whether any other signs may have been missed. Warren let Mattie answer the questions, given that his knowledge was superior to Warren's own. Eventually, the doctor reached the end of her list and hurried away, her heeled boots clacking against the linoleum floor.

A few minutes later, the nurses began to arrive. They were an ever-present feature in the intensive care unit, to the point where they were just as numerous as the patients themselves.

His mother, on the other hand, was eerily still, despite the rush and bustle of the nurses working around her.

Sarah had been a month shy of fifteen when she'd given birth to him. A baby herself. He hadn't even needed to ask why he'd been given up for adoption. Warren would never forget her look of joy when they met again as adults.

"I thought about you every day," she'd promised, wiping away her tears. "Every day."

He believed it too.

Kate's voice broke through the fog of the furious Googling he'd done since Dr Tripathi had departed. Every webpage had given him progressively shitter news. "*With optimal treatment, patients with glioblastoma have* a median survival of less than one year," one academic journal had told him.

He swallowed away the lump in his throat.

His mother was going to die soon.

"Warren?"

"Mm?" he lifted his face away from his phone to find Kate and Mattie on their feet.

"The nurses say we need to leave for the night, but we can come back to visit tomorrow." The two of them had packed up and were ready to leave.

"Right," he said, stretching his muscles after being stuck in the least comfortable chair in existence for hours. He took Kate's hand, suddenly desperate to be alone with the one person who held him together. "Do you want to come and stay with us, Mattie? Or would you prefer to go back home?"

"I'll come with you, if you don't mind. The lady next door—Charne—is looking after Leo. She was his breeder, so he can stay with Charne and his mum for a bit. Can we come back to the hospital tomorrow?"

"Of course. We can spend the whole day with her, just like today," Warren assured him. *We need to spend as much time as possible with her whilst we still can.*

Mattie engulfed him in a tight hug, his head only coming up to Warren's chest. "Thank you for being here."

"I'll always be here for you, Mattie. For you, and for Mum."

9

When Warren disappeared into the en-suite in his dressing room, Kate followed.

She pushed open the bathroom door, and there he stood.

Water flowed over his broad shoulders in rivulets, following the path etched into his body by his muscles. Kate bit her lip at the sight, remembering that *this* man had been on his knees before her.

She'd dreamt of it last night, and had awoken to the pulsing breathlessness of her release.

Wordlessly, she let her clothes fall to the floor. The metallic buttons on her jeans clinked against the tiles, but Warren didn't turn. The first tendrils of self-consciousness touched her, but she shook them off. He'd already seen her more intimately than she'd seen herself. There was no place for her fear between the two of them.

It was only when she opened the glass door to the shower that he turned, his eyes widening first at her face and then her body. "Kitten," he growled, dragging his gaze back up to her own. "Why are you in here?"

"Because I want to care for you," she answered simply, reaching up to stroke his cheek.

He hauled her up against him, skin to skin.

"Wait, I'm standing on your… uh, toes," Kate looked down, embarrassed when she realised it was his prosthetic.

But his teeth flashed in a smile. The first one she'd seen today. "I'm sure they'll recover." He stroked his knuckles across her cheek, leaving a wet smudge behind. "My good girl," he whispered softly.

The words warmed her to her core. "I am?"

Warren nodded. "My perfect kitten."

Kate leant against him, gazing up at him like he held the answers to the universe.

"Let me touch you." He grabbed the shampoo and applied it to her hair, working it into a lather.

Kate hummed with pleasure, lost in the sensation of his fingers massaging her scalp. "I came in here to care for you, Warren. Not the other way round."

"It pleases me to care for you."

Judging from the hard bar of his erection pressing against her skin, it pleased him very much indeed.

By the time he moved onto washing her body, Kate realised that she may have been out of her depth. He was teasing her, she was sure of it, working the shower gel into her skin, getting painfully close to her nipples but pulling away at the last minute.

"Touch me, please," she finally begged. Her voice was barely a whisper beneath the hot rush of the shower.

Warren groaned in satisfaction, digging his cock into her lower back. He bit her neck, hard enough to make her gasp. "You finally learnt some manners, then."

She cried out as his fingers brushed against her nipples, puckered so tightly every touch was agony. Eager to give as good as she got, she attempted to twist her arm backwards and seize his cock, but Warren grasped it tightly. "If you want to touch me, then you're going to do so begging on your knees."

The very thought sent a rush of arousal below her navel, and Kate clenched her thighs together.

"But first, kitten, I need to finish washing you." His fingers spread wide over her stomach before dipping deeper. Kate moaned when he cupped between her legs, but he whispered in her ear. "Hush. I don't want you to make a sound, understand?"

She nodded, leaning her head back against his shoulders. His touch turned intimate, exploring her with sensual, practiced movements until it took all of her willpower to hold back her moans, until she writhed in his arms and sent pleading looks at him.

Finally, Warren rinsed her off, taking a last opportunity to explore her intimately. "Good girl," he breathed, turning the water off. He dried both of them before leading her out past his walk-in wardrobe and into the bedroom proper. He took a seat on the midnight blue sofa, placing a cushion on the floor between his legs. "Kneel," he ordered.

With a pliability that was unlike her, Kate's knees bent. His cock jutted forward, as demanding as the man it belonged to. And she loved it.

"You know what I want."

"I do," she confirmed, licking her lips.

His heavy, strained breath was audible. "Then beg me for it."

"Please let me suck your cock," Kate said unabashedly, so turned on she couldn't stand it. "Please."

"Open," he snarled, fisting his cock in one hand and circling her neck with the other, pulling her closer.

The salty taste of sin and seed leaked onto her tongue, but Warren held her there by her throat.

"Stay," he hissed, his chest heaving as the reddish-purple head rested on her bottom lip. "Perfect," he said quietly, smiling down at her.

A heady calm relaxed her shoulders, even as it ignited her arousal.

"I'm going to fuck your mouth," he promised her. "If you want me to stop, tap my arm. Do you understand?"

"Mmhmm," she mumbled around his length.

And then he began to move. Slow strokes, at first, as though to test her boundaries, but soon his cock was hitting the back of her throat in increasingly fast motions that had her moaning around him. Her hands dug into his thighs until she remembered something from a porn video she'd once watched. Hoping she wasn't going to hurt him, Kate began to play with his heavy sac. Gently massaging him as he'd done to her in the shower.

Warren's answering moan had her thighs clenching together once more. "Oh *fuck*, kitten. I'm going to come. Tap my leg if you want me to pull out."

She didn't.

He came with a heavy, masculine groan, hot ropes of cum striking the back of her throat. Kate swallowed him down as his sac contracted in her hands, driven to madness by her arousal.

Exhausted, Warren's head fell down against the back of the sofa, his pants coming thick and fast. His touch changed from dominance to adornment, brushing gentle touches against her cheeks. "You're perfect, kitten. So perfect. Like you were made for me."

I was, she thought.

Kate rested her head against his thigh with a languid smile. She shouldn't enjoy this. She shouldn't enjoy kneeling at his feet like a dog, brushing her face against his leg and waiting for attention, but she did.

"Now, what do you say?"

"Thank you for fucking my mouth, Warren." The words sent a spasm between her legs.

Warren's nostrils flared, as though he knew exactly how wet sucking his cock had made her. "Get on the bed and spread your legs." He followed her like a wolf on the hunt, his long legs eating up the space behind her—real and artificial—and a snarl ripped out of his throat when she finally lay back to expose her wetness.

Pleasure forced her eyes shut when Warren pounced on her, his mouth closing over her clit. She cried out at the sudden heat, whilst he curled his fingers inside her until she had been reduced to a mindless, panting wreck.

Her fingers dove into his hair, holding him in place despite the fact that he clearly had no intention of leaving. As if they had a mind of their own, her hips rolled against his face. His short beard was sharp against her intimate skin, but Kate loved it. A reminder of exactly whose tongue worshipped her.

He drove her higher and higher, forcing her spine to bend and her thighs to close around his head, until her restraints finally snapped. Kate came with a hedonistic cry, digging her nails into his scalp. Her hips undulated as her sensitivity grew, but he moved with her, his tongue never leaving her clit.

"Stop," she choked eventually, and he rose up on his elbows with a masculine smirk that brimmed with possession, kissing a path up her body until he arrived at the sensitive skin under her ear.

"There is *nothing* better than you coming on my tongue, kitten."

Kate's lowered eyes narrowed. "I don't know," she smiled lazily. "That gulab jamun was pretty good."

A laugh rumbled out of his chest, warming her to her core. "My kitten," he whispered, playing with the wet strands of her hair. He kissed her, letting his forehead rest on hers. "I need you," he admitted, blatant vulnerability in his eyes. "I've always needed you. Thank you for coming with me today."

"I'm so sorry about Sarah, Warren."

Jaw clenched, he looked away. "She's going to die. Soon."

Kate didn't know what she could say to that. Her old neighbour had died of glioblastoma. Peter's father, with their unruly escape artist staffies. The doctors had said he had six months to live, and he was dead in six weeks.

"I've only just found her," he said, his expression desolate. "And now I'm going to lose her again. I wasted so much time. Prison wasted so much of my fucking life. It stole *so* much from me—and from Sarah."

And her father was responsible for it. Kate just listened. There were no words that could comfort Warren now. No apologies. On their way home, Mattie had been furiously reading the chemotherapy leaflets the doctors had given them, but Warren had already accepted the cold hard truth.

She wouldn't parrot pretty words at him. He was allowed to grieve for what he had lost. "I'll be here for you every step of the way," she promised him. "For you. For Mattie. And for Sarah."

Warren rasped his knuckles over his facial hair. "You're not a prisoner here anymore, Kate."

"I know." She hadn't felt like a prisoner in weeks. Not truly.

"No," he cradled her head with a tattooed arm. "I mean... I paid off your debt. I've transferred your father's house into your name to do what you will with it. And if you want to leave, you can. I'll give you the money you need to live a good life, and the security necessary to protect you."

Kate took her first proper breath in years, as though a hundred tonnes had just been lifted off her chest. Air flooded into her lungs. "*What?!*"

"I don't want you to feel trapped here. I don't want you to feel as though you have to do... *this* with me."

Whatever *this* was. She pushed him off her, barely hearing a word he was saying. "The debt's gone?"

"It is." Warren wiped his face into a guarded expression.

"Show me."

Warren strolled into his walk-in wardrobe, fully unashamed of his nakedness. His shower prosthetic was still attached to one leg, a strange mesh creation that he'd told her had been 3D printed. Even through her panicked, grief-stricken haze, the sight of his thick thighs and muscled arse held her attention. He emerged with his phone, flicking the screen with his thumb before passing it over to her. Her gaze momentarily rested on the little kitten tattooed onto his chest.

So you would always be with me.

Her jaw dropped when she finally dragged her focus to the phone. Not just because he had access to her bank account details—because *of course* he did—but because for once she wasn't deep in her overdraft. For once, she was very, very far away from her overdraft. "Half a million?" she asked faintly.

Kate barely saw Warren's gentle nod, instead bowled over by the possibilities opening up to her. She'd been living below the poverty line for so long that half a million could last her thirty years with careful budgeting.

"And the house I grew up in is mine too, you said?"

Warren took the phone from her, opening up a document. *Official copy of register of title*, she read. "That's the relevant information." He pointed to a paragraph at the bottom.

Her name was clear as day next to the achingly familiar address of home.

The first tear dropped without her realising, but soon a torrent joined it. The relief of endless pressure. She clutched the bedcovers to her front, smiling through her tears. When she felt his tentative hand on her spine, Kate clutched him too, weeping against his kitten tattoo as he crooned assurances into her hair.

"I'm sorry," he whispered, when her tears had been reduced to a small stream and her eyes were heavy with exhaustion.

"For what?" she croaked.

"For not telling you sooner."

Kate pulled back. "How long has it been gone for?"

"Since the night I took you out to dinner."

She coughed out a laugh. *Weeks.* All the worrying she'd done since then had been for nought. "Why didn't you just tell me?"

"Because I was selfish. Because I wanted you to stay." His lips touched the top of her head, and a cold spot formed as he sucked in a deep inhale. "I'm sorry," he said again.

"I'm sorry too. For you."

It was the last thing she said before sleep took her.

Kate didn't expect the first thing she saw when she awoke to be Warren bearing breakfast on a tray.

He paused when he realised she was awake, wearing a simple white shirt and dark trousers. "It's gone midday. I thought you might be hungry."

I could get used to this. Her stomach had started to rumble from the moment the scent reached her. She accepted the tray with thanks, making short work of the meal whilst Warren took his preferred seat on his couch, pulling his laptop towards him.

"Sarah's started her chemo," Warren broke the silence just as Kate was starting to wonder how she was going to move from the bed without any clothes on. "She's just messaged me."

Kate gasped. "I think I forgot to include the Pepto-Bismol in the little care package I made up yester—"

His soft eyes found hers over the laptop screen. "I packed it before I left, don't worry. She said thank you."

A little abashed, she shrugged slightly. "You paid for it all." Especially the *extortionately* expensive cashmere throw.

"And you spent hours researching chemotherapy to accumulate a list of anything she might need," he smiled at her, before frowning at his laptop. "I don't think Andy's handling it very well."

Kate could imagine. "When your wife of however many years is diagnosed with cancer, I imagine it would devastate anyone."

"He isn't coming home."

She blinked. "*Still*? It's been days since Sarah's seizure."

Warren read out from his screen. "*Andy says he's been scheduled onto back-to-back cruises for the next month.*"

Kate was appalled. "His partner of thirty years has got terminal cancer. I'm sure they'd give him leave to come home. What exactly does he do on the cruise ships?"

"Operational maintenance." His dark green eyes met hers. "I'd like to invite Sarah and Mattie to stay here with us."

Us? "It's your house, Warren."

He stood, coming over to sit on the bed. Their legs brushed against each other. "It is," he whispered. Kate's eyes flickered closed at the feel of his hands travelling up either side of her neck. "But I'd like it to be yours too."

For the second time in as many minutes, Kate was speechless.

There was no panicked backtracking from Warren, no shitty jokes. He seemed to be just as comfortable in his question as he was without clothes on.

"And if I want to leave?"

That was when he flinched. "Then I'll have Brax take you wherever you want to go. Unless that place is back to Rhys's bed. And my guards will be staying; that isn't negotiable. Graves targeted you once. He may do it again."

Despite the reminder of the attempt on her life, Kate couldn't help but smile. "I'll have you know, I got into bed with Saffron. Rhys just invaded our Netflix marathon."

"Will you stay?"

"I'll stay," she confirmed, goosebumps prickling their way up her spine as Warren's fingers danced over her skin.

"Naked in my bed, I hope."

"Considering *your* bed is the squeaky foldout behind your pervert mirror, I'm going to say no." She lay down, letting the covers unveil her breasts as she threw her arms wide. "I'll stay in the king-sized bed in here, thank you very much."

Warren let loose a tortured growl and tugged the covers down even further, leaning above her and momentarily taking a rosy nipple into his mouth. "Have I told you that you've got fantastic breasts?"

"No, but I think you should." Daniel, the ex-boyfriend who'd ghosted her, had called them droopy, but she wasn't about to ruin Warren's good opinion.

"You've got fantastic breasts."

Should she say 'thank you' after a compliment like that? The best she could come up with was to reciprocate. "You've got a fantastic arse."

"You only think that because we're not currently sharing a bathroom."

It took her a second, but she burst into laughter. "You're disgusting."

He nodded solemnly. "That's more like it, yeah." His strong arm wrapped around her shoulders, drawing them closer together. "Rhys and Aldous's mum, Linda, is having her sixtieth birthday here in a few days. I want you to come as my date."

Kate bit her lip playfully. "I probably shouldn't mention that I've had both you and Rhys in bed with me then?"

Warren's nostrils flared as he held her wrists above her head with a single hand. "Not if you don't want me to tie you to it, no."

The breath she released was one of anticipation. She'd spent enough time on the internet to know she wasn't completely vanilla, but she'd never been faced with her kinks *actually happening*. "He was against me all night," she baited him.

"*Don't* test me, kitten." His voice was heavy in her ear, his free hand teasing her breasts.

She writhed. "Or what?"

"Fucking hell, Kate."

Kate yipped as he bit hard into the flesh between her shoulder and neck.

"I'm going to send you a link to a questionnaire. Fill it out. Understand?"

"Yes," she panted. Warren placated her with a surprisingly tender kiss before getting to his feet. "Wait," she held out her arm, trying to entice him back into the bed. "Where are you going?"

"I have a meeting with the CEO of one of our subsidiaries in London. I'm sorry. It's urgent." Judging by the erection fighting at his fly, his apology was genuine.

Kate pursed her lips innocently. "But what am I supposed to do in here whilst you're gone?"

The corners of his eyes crinkled with understanding. "You're not to touch yourself." It was an order.

"And if I disobey?"

"Then you'll be punished, kitten." He shoved her laptop into her hands. "Now fill out the fucking questionnaire."

Warren: You're not to touch yourself today.

Kate nearly screeched with frustration when she saw the message. It had been the same every morning, coming at ten o'clock on the dot. The *only* thing coming. Her need, however, had grown exponentially. Filling in the questionnaire hadn't helped. It had sent her down a kink rabbit hole of terms like 'brat' and 'rope bunny' and 'subspace', and every image had her wanting more. Even things that she'd never heard of like predator/prey play had her thighs clenching together.

> **Kate**: I hope you're having to get up stupidly early to send me these.
> **Kate**: And if you're expecting a happy date at Alison's party tonight, you're going to be sorely fucking disappointed.

It wasn't Warren's fault he'd been away for so long. Whatever *situation* that needed to be handled at the subsidiary had nosedived off a cliff, and he'd flown to their New York office to sort it out. Jensen, the oldest of the four Stones, had gone with him, which Rhys said signalled bad news.

That was one of the benefits of Warren being gone. Rhys had been given strict instructions to keep her company, which helped Kate feel a little bit less… intimidated by living in a house full of security guards.

Saffron's continuing presence had helped as well, of course. Particularly in the getting-ready-for-the-party department.

They'd chosen their dresses together. With Kate's only real friends growing up being Warren and Aaron, her femininity was somewhat… underdeveloped. She'd had friends in secondary school, but they'd vanished after they'd graduated, confirming her suspicions that she'd effectively been a spare prick at a wedding.

It was nice to finally have a female friend, though. Saffron was full of suggestions about dresses and accessories, something that Kate had little knowledge of. Saffron had even suggested they book a make-up artist to get them both ready.

Kate had known just the woman.

Brit arrived several hours before the party started, once again dragging her suitcase of make-up. Her outfit, however, was a stark contrast to what she'd worn the day they'd questioned her father. Though her hair remained largely the same, tied in a long black ponytail that emphasised the shaved sides of her head, Brit wore a gothic evening dress complete with a high-low skirt and a corset.

"Oh my god," Kate gasped upon seeing her. "That looks like a goth version of the wedding dress from the *November Rain* music video."

Brit tilted her head, swinging her ponytail to the side. "That's a very specific image you have there."

Kate shrugged. "*Guns N' Roses* were my Dad's favourite band. But you seriously look amazing."

Unzipping her suitcase, Brit grinned. "Now let's do the same to you."

When late afternoon arrived, however, Kate looked up at her dress with apprehension.

"I'm not so sure about this," she whispered to Saffron, whose white-blonde hair had been twisted in an elegant up-do. Brit had disappeared once their make-up was finished, providing a somewhat worrying explanation of *I've always wanted to jump Brax's bones at work.*

"Come on," Saffron said encouragingly. "You'll be fine. And your boobs will look amazing."

"It's all right for you, you look like a fucking Targaryen!"

Saffron did an excellent job of not looking smug. "I'm sure we all have a little Khaleesi inside of us."

"Daenerys," Kate said automatically, trying not to think about Brax and Brit having sex in his office.

"What?"

"Khaleesi was just her title. Her name was Daenerys." Kate's lips hardened into a firm line, thinking about the last few seasons. "I shouldn't have brought it up, I'll just get mad thinking about the ending of *Game of Thrones* again."

Wrapping an arm around Kate's shoulders, Saffron leant into her. "But *House of the Dragon* seems to be good."

Feeling like a toddler being talked out of a tantrum, she nodded. "Fingers crossed it stays that way. I'm so excited to see Nettles and Sheepstealer."

"And the *Game of Thrones* showrunners lost their *Star Wars* job?"

"You know that did cheer me up," Kate admitted, nodding sincerely. She took a deep breath. "Right. Let's put on my fucking dress."

The needy, frustrated Kate who had decided to purchase the backless, sleeveless satin dress in a deep mauve was not the terrified, self-conscious Kate who crawled into it. Her hair had been lifted off her neck, artfully curled around her head in a dark brown corona. With every step, the slit in the long gown showed off more of her legs.

"What time did you say Warren was getting back?" Saffron asked, checking her reflection in the mirror at the end of the corridor. Even she looked nervous.

"He should have been back already."

"Kate!" a familiar voice called from the bottom of the stairs. Mattie wore a smart black suit, with a tired-looking Sarah holding his elbow, dressed in an emerald green gown that brushed her toes. Little Leo toddled around on his chunky legs behind them, sporting a new tuxedo collar Kate had bought for him.

"You're looking very handsome, Mattie," Kate bent down to kiss his cheeks on account of her heels. "You look gorgeous, Sarah." She looked down as Leo approached her. "And aren't you quite the gentleman, Leo?"

"You're looking very pretty. Both of you." Mattie blushed as he took in Saffron's Valyrianesque appearance. "You've just missed Warren, but people are starting to arrive for the party. Come on."

When the four of them moved to the garden, Leo followed, stopping to cock his leg on a small bush bordering the stone path. The marquee itself was enormous, a tall, white structure held up by three enormous inclines. Its interior was dotted with waiters sporting trays of champagne flutes like migrating spots on a ladybird.

At the other end of the vast marquee, a casino had been set up. Tables covered in green baize were carefully arranged. Kate felt an odd nostalgia at the sight of them. The last time she had visited her father's club had been as a girl, but she remembered the feel of the tables beneath her hands, the amplified chatter, the occasional roar at a big win.

Tonight, the real attraction was the river of pale blue roses flowing in the air, suspended by almost invisible wire and illuminated by fairy lights to ensure it sparkled in the night. The colour scheme was continued throughout the marquee, with pale blue sashes adorning each chair and cerulean curtains marking off private seating areas.

The more Kate looked, the more she saw. Fruit machines, cocktails with smoke bubbles, trays and trays of bite-sized canapés, a fully stocked bar, Instagram-worthy flower walls, champagne towers, a six-foot tall illuminated '60'.

Guests streamed around the marquee, clutching flutes of champagne and wearing clothes costing more than her monthly wage. Frowning, Kate saw Jensen and Aldous chatting in one of the seating areas.

"He was in New York with Warren," she told Saffron, looking round to see where Warren was hiding.

"I don't suppose you can introduce me."

"To which one?"

"I'll take either." Saffron's smile was filthy. "Or both."

Kate grabbed the nearest flute of champagne and took a healthy gulp. A prickling feeling ran down her spine, as though she was being watched. She ignored it. "You're corrupting Mattie."

Mattie's blush deepened beneath the silvery blue mood lighting. "You're four years too late for that one, Kate."

"Wait, *what*?!"

Mattie looked around—presumably to check Sarah wasn't listening. Thankfully, she was deep in conversation with Rhys. "You think just because I'm disabled I can't have an adult relationship?" he said tartly, cocking his eyebrow.

She hadn't really thought about it like that. "I suppose I just thought you were very into your models."

"I've been *very into* several things," Mattie muttered as Saffron began to cackle.

Kate resisted hiding her face in her hands on account of not wanting to ruin Brit's hard work. "Why is everyone getting laid but me?"

"Hello kitten."

She shut her eyes as soon as the dark, suave voice reached her ears. Pretending she hadn't heard it. Pretending she hadn't sent the man it belonged to a long list detailing each and every kink that tickled her fancy. Pretending that he didn't know her better than anyone else ever had.

Whilst Warren was distracted with Mattie and Sarah, Kate steadied herself with another flute of champagne.

"Saffron," Warren said, "I hear you've been keeping Kate company."

Saffron nodded, sending Kate a nervous glance. "I suggested we hire a make-up artist to get us ready. And her and Mattie have been showing me how to play *World of Warcraft.*"

A glass of liquor brushed Warren's lips, the dark liquid disappearing between them. "I'm sure Blizzard will be relieved to know Mattie's doing his best to increase subscriber numbers."

Mattie stood at his brother's elbow. "Saffron likes to watch more than play."

"Yes," he drawled. The verdant glint in Warren's eyes found Kate, ogling her body so blatantly she wanted to blush. "I hear that can be… entertaining."

"How was New York?" Kate blurted out, desperate to change the subject.

"Stressful. Come," he took her arm. "I'll introduce you to Alison."

Kate had no choice but to let herself be swept away, sending apologetic looks to Mattie and Saffron. The former was smirking, but the latter remained unconvinced. *I'll be fine*, Kate mouthed to her. Warren may have had the capacity to be an arse of the highest order, but he'd never hurt her.

The list of his kinks came to mind. Dominant. Primal.

Perhaps he would hurt her.

The thought had her navel swirling with warmth.

Warren had sent her his list of kinks after she'd sent him hers. She'd thought of little else in the days since. And in the nights.

Whilst they passed a throng of people at the centre of the dazzling marquee, Warren leant in close. "By midnight," he rumbled, "I want to see your lipstick marking my cock." His large hand slunk down her spine, stopping just above her rear. He cleared his throat before Kate could so much as widen her eyes. "Alison, I'd like you to meet Kate."

A deeply attractive middle aged woman stood in front of them, wearing a slate blue dress shimmering beneath the river of roses. Her striking amber eyes lit up as she saw them; eyes that Rhys had inherited, down to the last striation. "Darling," she grinned, kissing Warren on the cheek before moving down to Kate. "I've heard so much about you."

Kate shoved her thoughts of lipstick to the back of her mind as quickly as possible. "It's lovely to meet you."

"I was positively thrilled when Warren said he'd found you again. He used to write and tell me about you in his letters."

"Letters?"

Warren's hand tightened around her hip.

"It's how Warren and I met," Alison said politely. "Rhys would mention Warren in his letters—when they were in prison, you know. But we eventually started corresponding, didn't we, darling?"

"We did, yes," Warren answered.

"Did you know he didn't have a single correspondent before I started writing to him?" Alison clucked her tongue, her brow creasing with compassion.

Kate felt the gentle chiding beneath Alison's words. "I didn't," she said softly. In all probability, she could have guessed. A child bounced around the care system, with no family to call his own. After Warren was first arrested, Kate *had* wanted to visit him, but her father had overruled it, saying that he was a murderer who deserved his punishment. Her talk of sending letters to him had met the same fate. She addressed Warren. "I should have made more of an effort to write to you. I'm sorry."

His face flickered into a frown. "You were a girl, Kate. And from your perspective, I had just killed your brother."

"Still," she shrugged. "You were my friend." *And I missed you.*

"Well I'm glad you're friends again," Alison said gently. "And it's lovely to see your mum and brother here, Warren." She looked over to one of the seating areas, to the sky blue sofas and little cloud-shaped cushions, where Rhys, Sarah, and Mattie sat in deep conversation.

"I'm glad they're here as well," Warren agreed, taking another sip of his liquor.

"Your brother must be so worried," Alison frowned. "How is your mum getting on?"

Warren's throat shifted as he swallowed. "She's managing as best she can. And Kate has been keeping her company during her chemo, haven't you?"

"We've been going with her every day, Mattie and I," Kate smiled. Sarah had needed people to be with her, and with Warren in New York she had been pleased to fill that role, be it offering a shoulder to cry on or fetching refreshments—or anything in between. "I mean, technically it's chemoradiotherapy because she's having both chemotherapy and radiotherapy together," Kate chattered nervously, "but it's a bit of a mouthful." *Wrap it up. Stop blabbering like an idiot.* "So yes, um, we've been keeping her company."

"And Rhys has been staying here, I hear?" Alison's amber eyes flicked between them, like a cat waiting to pounce.

"And behaving himself," Warren's hand slowly made its way up to her neck; a proprietary touch that send goosebumps erupting over her skin.

"Of course," Kate nodded enthusiastically. "He's been very gentlemanly."

"I'm glad," Alison said wryly. "Don't be fooled though, Kate. He wasn't always like that. Between Rhys and Jensen, I was almost eaten out of house and home." She smiled at someone in the distance. "Aldous was always my little angel when they were younger."

"They were close growing up, then?"

Alison shrugged, her dress glittering in the movement. "Jensen would come down and stay for the summers, and he and Rhys were always thick as thieves. They're closer in age, you know. Aldous was a bit too timid for their roughhousing." Kate's face must have shown her amazement, given that Aldous had by far exhibited the most aggression in front of her. "Aldous learnt to protect himself after Jensen and Rhys were sent to prison," she explained. "I insisted on it."

Kate had known that Warren had met Rhys and Jensen in prison, but it suddenly occurred to her that she'd never wondered *why* they were there. "Whereabouts did they grow up?"

"On the Old Dean, it's—"

A familiar understanding dawned on her. "In Camberley?"

Alison fired a question back at her with a smile. "Are you local?"

"I grew up in Wildridings in Bracknell, so the other side of Swinley Forest."

"Oh, how funny. Jensen and Aldous used to go mountain biking in Swinley all the time."

"Loads of the boys on our estate used to do the same," Kate leant into Warren. "I remember badgering Warren and my brother to take me on my bike, complete with pink streamers and stabilisers."

Shaking her head, Alison smiled at Warren fondly. "I wish our lot had had stabilisers. Would have saved us endless grief. During the summer, half of the boys would end up down A&E with mountain biking injuries. The first time Aldous went with them—the only time—he broke his collarbone."

Kate winced compassionately, but Warren's hand pulled on her waist. "Alison," he said suddenly, smiling as Sarah approached them. "I don't believe you've met my mother, Sarah."

"No," Alison said warmly. "How wonderful to meet—"

"Come on," Warren whispered into her ear, pulling her away from the older women.

Kate glanced back, but the two were sharing a laugh. "Don't you want to say hello to your mum?"

"I already saw her before the party. But I've got plans for you, kitten."

Warren politely but firmly fended off other guests as he directed them out of the marquee. They were forced to pause to greet people, and Kate forgot their names as soon as they were spoken.

They soon left the carpeted paths laid out for partygoers, migrating to the stone path that would lead them inside. Just beyond the treeline, Kate spied security personnel lurking. The longer she looked, the more guards she saw. She would have sighed with relief, had her blood not been racing at the prospect of Warren isolating her from the rest of the party.

Once inside, Warren pulled her into a room she'd never been in before. A lounge, dashed with warm coral tones. He slammed the door behind them, catching her in his grasp to growl in her ear. "Your safe word is pepper."

"Pepper," she repeated, hiding the excitement that the mere prospect of a safe word brought with it. *Pepper. Pepper. Pepper.*

She had no warning before he unzipped her dress, the material sagging open around her. Warren shoved it to the ground as though its existence had personally offended him, leaving her standing only in her heels and lacy pants. "Warren!" she cried, outraged.

"If you didn't want me to act like an animal, you shouldn't have worn that fucking dress."

Kate bit her lip. She shivered as Warren circled her with a predatory gaze, though it had more to do with the idea of being prey than her state of undress.

He paused directly in front of her, reaching almost lazily into his pocket. Panic flared inside her when he drew out a penknife, but she remained still as he approached. The blade caught the light, throwing it into her eyes.

"Although I approve of your choice of bra," he murmured, trailing the blade across her nipple.

The sharp prick made her whimper. The questionnaires had discussed the use of blades—which she had consented to—but she wasn't expecting it to be the first thing he explored. Kate gasped when the tip found her other nipple, flicking back and forth. "I'm... I'm not wearing a bra."

"Exactly." Warren pinched her nipple *hard*, prompting her to cry out. "*Good* girl. I'm tempted to mark you here with the blade, just in case you forget who you belong to."

A strangled noise escaped her at his touch, followed by a quick gasp of relief when he let go.

Her reprieve was short-lived, however.

Warren hooked his fingers into the side of her underwear, slitting the fabric with the knife. He repeated the process on the other side, easily pulling the scrap of lace away from her body. Holding her gaze, he bunched it up in his hand and brought it to his nose, inhaling deep. "Damp already?" he taunted her.

She nodded—then yelped when she felt the cold bite of the knife's blunt edge between her legs. Warren moved it slowly along her folds, grinning at her whimper when it hit her clit. "Warren," she squeaked.

He only smirked, bringing the knife to his lips and licking her taste off its blunt edge. He quickly put it back in his pocket, letting his hand rest around her neck. "Kneel."

Kate's shoulders were the first to relax, as though that single word changed everything. She let out a cool, calm exhale before gracefully dropping to her knees. The carpeted floor hit her, hundreds of fibre strands caressing her all at once, but the only thing she was able to focus on was Warren.

His rough fingers lifted her chin with unexpected tenderness. "Spread your legs."

She obeyed, feeling so exposed it was maddening, but he rewarded her with a loving smile.

"You're perfect," he whispered, visually perusing her body at his leisure. Smirking, he stepped away and leant against the back of the room's Chesterfield sofa. "Take out my cock, kitten."

She went to stand up, but his voice made her pause.

"Ah-ah," he chided. "Crawl to me."

The order should have been humiliating. Infuriating, even. But even as that thought crossed her mind, a darker, more intriguing thread overruled it. Her body began to crawl before she'd had a chance to wonder *why* she found this so arousing.

And then he stood before her, casually leaning. There was no order this time, but his commanding gaze would have made it redundant anyway.

Kate's hands flew to his belt, tearing at the stiff leather. She yanked his trousers down and was rewarded by his long, thick length bouncing back up to meet her.

Except he hadn't said she could touch him.

"Did you do what I asked and not touch yourself?"

She nodded.

"Good girl," he crooned down at her. "Then take your reward."

She was on him in a flash, her tongue lapping at the salt-scented desire dripping from his length. Kate moaned, her legs spread, desperately wanting more, *needing* more.

Warren's head fell back, exposing the thick bump of his Adam's apple. He groaned when she began to suck in earnest, taking in more and more of him until he hit the back of her throat.

"*Fuck*, kitten." His laugh was interrupted by yet another groan when she began to massage his sac, just as she'd done the other night. "Stop," he hissed.

She did. Instantly.

"I don't want to empty myself down your throat tonight," Warren snarled. "Get up. Now go and lean over that table. Face down. I want your arse in the air."

The chill of the wood against her front made her jump. The table was slightly lower than her, especially wearing heels, meaning that Warren gained his wish.

"I don't want to hear a sound from you unless it's the safe word, understood?"

Kate almost said *yes*, but caught herself at the last moment, her cheek pressed against the wood. Instead, she nodded, wondering wha—

A hard smack on her arse forced out a shocked gasp. The sharp sound echoed through the room.

She was ready for the next one. It was significantly harder than the first; a punishment, she knew. His palm bit into her skin afterwards, massaging the flesh he'd sorely abused. No sooner had his touch disappeared before it returned with a vengeance.

Her arse began to burn. Warren varied his strikes, but his hand was large—and her rear only had so much available space before he overlapped. Kate shifted her hips between the strikes, her mouth falling open in bliss. They sent arousal shooting between her legs, and she almost moaned when Warren's harsh touch transformed into a teasing, rolling massage.

He found her clit, paying it a tantalisingly brief visit before dipping his fingers inside her. "You're dripping."

Kate went to nod, but something impish inside her commanded her to revolt. "Yes," she gasped, knowing that her punishment would be quick.

And wonderful.

He struck her arse; his hardest hit yet.

"Yes," she whispered, lost in the overwhelming *burning* of her skin. She must be red raw by now, but she didn't want to stop. His hands spread her buttocks roughly, his thumb caressing between them. The rough rumble of his laugh sent butterflies fluttering through her.

"Who would have thought my little kitten would crave punishment?" He flipped her over, not bothering to be gentle. Kate loved it; she wanted him rough and untamed. The bony ridges of her shoulders hit the wood first. His hand found her throat again, squeezing. "And who would have thought causing you pain would make me so fucking hard?"

Warren stood between her legs, the fiery intensity in his eyes hot enough to burn. "You've been taking the pill?"

"I started it today," she panted. "*Please.*"

He notched his thick cock at her entrance. "Good girl," he rasped, sheathing himself inside her in a single brutally powerful stroke.

Her eyes rolling back in her head, Kate's unabashed moan was one of ecstasy. She whimpered as he set a punishing rhythm, not waiting for her to adjust to his size—or the fact that his hand was still squeezing down on her throat. "*Yes!*" she choked. *Overpower me. Use me.*

"Take me." His voice was almost as commanding as his cock. Using his free hand to spread her knees wide, he absorbed every inch of exposed skin. "You're going to take all of me, and you're going to be thankful for it."

Kate could barely catch a breath, pinned down by both Warren's hands and his cock. A barrage of sensations hit her, each of them more pleasurable than the last. She drank in the sight of him like this; jaw clenched, throat exposed, eyes lowered, skin glistening with sweat.

Warren had never looked so utterly unhinged, fucking every ounce of his aggression into her, and she loved it with a potency that was almost alarming. She had offered her body up to this titan of a man, and *god* was she enjoying the results.

She began to pant as he pounded her into the desk, her breaths increasing in both speed and pitch, until she begged for her orgasm to take her, to finally throw her into bliss.

She didn't have to wait long.

"Come for me, kitten," Warren snarled hatefully, sweat dripping from his temple. He squeezed her throat again. "And have the fucking decency to look me in the eye when you come on my cock."

The climax that seized control of her body was unholy, to the point that Kate struggled to keep her eyes open at the onslaught. The noise that left her was inhuman, a cracked, imperfect scream that threatened to rip her throat apart. Her legs quivered uncontrollably, even as he pinned them against her.

But she followed her instructions. She gave him her eyes through it all.

"Fuck. *Fuck.*" Warren groaned, his stomach muscles going taut as her walls pulled him into bliss. His hot, rushing release hit her insides.

"Yes," Kate croaked, her voice as exhausted as her body. "Give it to me, Warren."

"Kitten," he bit out, riding out the rest of his orgasm. Breathing heavily, he let his head fall to her shoulder. Kate clutched him to her, smiling as he mumbled into her skin. "My kitten."

10

Warren

"Should I ask why you needed aloe vera cream delivered to a suspiciously remote part of the house during my mother's birthday party?" Rhys stood on his tip-toes, doing his best to look over Warren's shoulder through the sliver of open door.

"No." Warren snatched the cream out of Rhys's hand and shut the door without another word, locking it once more.

Rhys's muffled voice still managed to penetrate the room, tinged with notes of amusement. "Prick."

When Kate's form came into view beyond the high back of the Chesterfield sofa, Warren paused in his stride. All the stress and worry he'd endured in New York seemed to melt off him, sliding away into nothingness as he beheld her snoozing underneath his suit jacket.

Fuck, he'd missed her. Warren had never been one for offices, instead preferring the solitude of his own company, but even that was lacking in comparison to his kitten. How had he gone so long without her? He'd barely lasted a week, desperately wanting to tell the inept CEO to go and fuck himself before boarding the first flight back to Heathrow.

Her eyes flickered open as he approached. A smile lifted her lips.

He knelt beside her and gently kissed her temple. "I'm so proud of you, kitten. You did so well." He'd scooped her up off the table afterwards, cradling her within his arms until she'd fallen asleep, but the urge to care for her still reigned within him. "I want to massage this into your skin."

"Why?" She touched her face delicately. "Am I flaking?"

"It's for your arse, not your face," he swallowed, shame coming over him. He'd needed her too badly to be gentle. "You're bruised. I'm sorry, I should have been easier on you for the first time." He squirted a healthy dose into his hands and scrubbed them together to warm the lotion.

"I'm fine," Kate protested.

"Just let me care for you, Kate."

Sighing, she rolled onto her front, letting him massage the product into her skin. Warren took his time, expanding his attentions to incorporate everything from her shoulders to her feet, relishing in the moans he brought forth.

"Your calf muscles are tight," he informed her, watching her toes curl.

"Mmm." It was the only response he was getting at the moment, but Warren wasn't going to complain.

"I have a mind to do this every morning."

One eye flicked open. "Oh no," she replied dramatically. "How will I cope?"

Finishing with a kiss to her rear, Warren leant back on his haunches. "I hate to be a mood killer, but we should get back to the party."

"Is it still on?"

His eyebrow shot up. "We've only been gone for an hour."

Kate shrugged, dragging herself up into a seating position. "I lose track of time whenever I have a nap. It could literally be next year for all I know."

Over the next few minutes, the two of them dressed once more, with the notable exception of Kate's underwear. Warren had thought her hair would pose the most significant challenge, but Brit had sprayed and styled it to such a degree that it might as well have been fired in a kiln.

Warren felt like a conqueror walking back to the marquee. Pounding music heralded their arrival, with the restrained, polite conversation of earlier having transformed. Guests were letting their hair down on the dancefloor. Bite-sized canapés flowed from the kitchens and alcohol poured freely from the bars. He sighted Alison flirting with a silver-haired man out on the dancefloor and smiled.

Smirking, he leant into Kate. "Dance with me."

She shivered as his lips brushed her ear, but her *fuck me* eyes almost had him dragging her back out of the marquee. "I don't know how to dance."

Warren pulled her close, until their hips ground together. "Just move with me, kitten."

The stiffness of her limbs eased bit-by-bit, and by the next song she was grinning up at him. Her body swayed from side to side, but Warren couldn't keep his hands off her, never forgetting that he had her ruined underwear in his pocket, and that she was bare and bruised beneath the dress.

And that once the party was over, he was going to fuck her until dawn.

When the music reached its peak, Warren was pleasantly surprised when Kate threw her arms around his neck and drew him down into a passionate, possessive embrace. He gripped her back, lifting her off the floor, chuckling when her moan turned into a panicked squeal.

"Put me down!"

"Come over here," he smiled. "You look run off your feet."

"I am a bit hot," she admitted. "And I've got a slight headache."

"Rhys will have some paracetamol." He led her over to the quietest area of the party: the outdoor lounge next to the casino, with its fluffy cloud pillows and sky blue sofas.

Jensen and Rhys were already on one, engaged deep in conversation. Words like *New York* and *merger* were being thrown about, and Warren knew that Jensen wouldn't take long to get the others up to date on their business dealings over there.

By contrast, Sarah and Aldous seemed to be having far too much fun on the roulette table closest to them, sitting next to a young woman with chestnut brown hair, who—judging from her exaggerated *no* as she slid her stack of tokens back over to the croupier—appeared to have just lost a small fortune.

Warren flagged over a waiter carrying a tray of canapés and, instead of merely selecting one, lifted the tray out of his hands. "And can you bring over a jug of cold water, please? And a couple of large Cokes?"

"Thirsty?" Kate asked him.

He shook his head, placing the tray in front of her. "Eat. The water is for you. You need food. And sugar." He clicked his fingers to get Rhys's attention, not wanting to shout in Kate's ear.

"Ah, I see you two have re-joined the party." Rhys's flirtatious smile reached Kate. "Did the aloe vera help?"

There was a pregnant pause before Kate answered in a curiously high voice, her cheeks flushed red with exertion. "The what?"

"Kate has a headache," Warren interrupted Rhys before he could answer.

"I have some paracetamol you can take," Rhys offered, as Warren had known he would. Sharing a cell with him for years on end meant that Warren had had a front-row seat to Rhys's frequent migraines. He'd also known that his friend wouldn't go anywhere without adequate painkillers.

Kate thanked Rhys, waiting until his attention had returned to Jensen before speaking again. "I don't need all of this, Warren."

He frowned. "Did you read the links I sent you?" He dropped his voice. "Including the one on aftercare."

"Well, yes, but—"

"But nothing." He pressed a bite-sized Yorkshire pudding into her hand. "I've already told you I was too harsh with you, so let me care for you as you deserved to be cared for."

"I'm perfectly fine."

"Do you or do you not have bruises developing on your skin even now?"

Kate chewed. "I wouldn't know. I haven't seen them."

"Listen to me," he held her chin firmly. "I'm not just going to hurt you because I like it. I'm going to hurt you because you're *mine* to take care of afterwards. Do you understand? You don't get one half of the relationship without the other."

"Okay," she said quietly, her brattishness receding at whatever she saw in his face.

"Okay," he reaffirmed, kissing her forehead. He shoved another canapé into her hand. "Now be a good girl and eat."

He looked up with a grin to see Mattie and Saffron each carrying a small tray of drinks down the carpeted gangway.

"Where did you two disappear to?" Mattie exclaimed.

"I had a bit of a headache," Kate's eyes flicked to Warren's momentarily. "Sorry Mattie. I didn't mean to abandon you."

"Not to worry, Saffron has been keeping me company. Did you need me to go get you some painkillers?"

"Rhys has just given me some. Thank you though, Mattie." Kate swiped the drink nearest to her. "Whose is this?"

"That one's Warren's, Kate," Saffron said quickly. "I got you a Coke, I thought you didn't like alcohol." Saffron pushed a glass brimming with condensation towards her.

"You have it if you want it, kitten." Warren's hands worked her shoulders without pause as she swallowed the paracetamols and a gulp of whisky.

Instantly, she scrunched up her face. "God, that's *disgusting*." She looked outraged. "How can you drink that?"

"It gets better with every sip."

Her eyebrow illustrated her doubt as she put the whisky down, electing for a sip of Coke to swallow the second tablet.

Warren's chest puffed out with pride when Kate leant back against him, resting her head against his throat. *Mine.* He tapped the glass of Coke with a meaningful look. *Drink.* "Who's that dancing with Alison?" he asked Rhys, just as the waiter arrived with yet more drinks.

Rhys tore his eyes away from Kate. "Hmm?"

"The silver fox grinding against your mother."

Rhys spun around frantically, like a meerkat sighting a predator. "Don't ask," he grumbled. "Some oily property developer."

Warren caught Rhys's eye with a grin. "Aren't they all? Smug pricks who've paid thousands for unlicensed *courses*."

"All on a property *journey*," Rhys volleyed back, "to lose their money before they've even started, that is."

Jensen interrupted them with a cough. "I hate to break it to you, but Euan was a nurse back before he was a property developer. Plus he's perfectly nice. They've actually got a lot in common, with Auntie Alison being an ex-midwife."

"How the fuck did he afford to start investing in property then?" Rhys wondered.

"His wife died. He used her life insurance policy to create a nest egg for their daughters."

Rhys sighed. "Well now I feel like an arsehole."

"You are one," Warren clapped him on the shoulder with a smile.

It wasn't long before Euan and Alison joined them, having exhausted themselves on the dancefloor. Alison looked positively delighted at the attention, and even Warren had to admit that Euan looked smitten.

She deserved it. Rhys had filled him in on his upbringing whilst they shared a cell, and the woman was a saint. Alison had worked full-time to raise Aldous and Rhys alone after their worthless father scarpered with a barely legal secretary. Not to mention that Jensen's visits frequently increased her number of dependents to three. Then Jensen and Rhys had been sent to prison for murder, leaving a traumatised Aldous behind for Alison to care for alone.

Even so, Alison was always wreathed in smiles when visiting the prison, having taken Warren into her heart as well.

It was Warren's good luck that afforded Alison the lifestyle she enjoyed now, coupled with Aldous's determination and Jensen and Rhys's hard work.

For so many reasons, Warren thanked his lucky stars that he'd invested in Bitcoin when he had. Aaron had heard of it first, convinced they would become millionaires overnight if they sunk their lifesavings into the currency. The lifesavings of two adolescent boys hadn't been much, but with the astronomical rise in the price of Bitcoin, it hadn't needed to be.

He clenched his jaw, holding Kate close. Would she still want him if she knew the truth? That he'd effectively stolen Aaron's share of the Bitcoin purely to spite Paul Charlton?

All the hardships she'd endured these past few years could have been avoided if Warren had returned Aaron's share to them.

Before Braxton had taken Kate from her house, he'd have called it collateral damage.

But now his conscience prickled unhelpfully.

Perhaps sensing that he was the least protective of Alison's four boys—both adopted and biological—Warren soon found himself talking to Euan, whilst Kate had been persuaded by Sarah to join her at the roulette table.

"When did you buy the house?" Euan was saying, ducking down to see the property beneath the cover of the marquee.

"Not long after I left prison."

Euan raised his eyebrows. "Hell of a change—from a cell to a mansion."

He shrugged. "When I was locked up, all I ever wanted was to be alone. I endured years of being surrounded by people when all I really wanted was peace." Warren couldn't help squeezing Kate slightly tighter. "This is my peace. A house in the middle of nowhere."

Sipping his beer, Euan nodded. "I can understand that. After my wife passed, I was inundated with well-wishers, all trying to make me forget that my soulmate was gone. The only time I was able to grieve was when I shut the bedroom door at night."

"How long ago did she pass?"

A sigh lifted Euan's shoulders, followed by a long, slow exhale. "Fifteen years next month."

"I'm sorry," Warren said genuinely. "But Jensen said you have daughters?"

"Two. Nattie and Darcy. The apples of my eye," Euan grinned. "Darcy is over by the casino, losing her inheritance, and Nat is in America at Columbia University."

"Ah," Warren smiled, "I only just got back from New York this afternoon."

"I was speaking to Jensen about your trip earlier this evening," he gave a wry smile. "I only wish he'd introduced me to his aunt a little sooner." His eyes drifted over to where Alison stood, sitting next to Sarah at the roulette table with Kate. "My daughter—" Euan pointed to the chestnut-haired young woman next to Kate "—Darcy, looking as though she's racking up her last loss. Is that the young lady you were, ah, dancing with earlier?"

Warren nodded, feeling his shoulders relax as he gazed upon Kate. His little tigress had taken every ounce of animalistic need he'd had in him earlier. He'd taken her hard and fast, her arse bright red.

And yet here she was, smiling and laughing.

"Kate," he confirmed. "And I'm going to see how she's doing at the tables. Excuse me."

"I'll come with you," Euan offered, finishing his beer as he stood. "I want to see how much of my money Darcy has lost."

At the table, Warren was surprised to realise that Kate was merely watching rather than playing. He crept behind her, kissing the delicate skin under her ear. "Are you not in the mood to play?"

Kate leant back against him, humming with pleasure when his arm wrapped over her shoulders, coming to rest just under her throat. She dropped her voice. "I don't have any money."

He caught the croupier's attention. "Give her what she wants. Add it to my bill."

"Warren," Kate tried to hush him. "I don't even know how to play."

"Call it aftercare," he whispered into her ear. "Besides, all family members play on the house." On the house being on his bank account.

"Family? Is that what I am?"

"It's what you've always been, kitten. Now go and do your best to bankrupt me. You deserve it."

"No!" Darcy cried out from across the poker table, letting her head rest in her hands. She halted the words about to leave Euan's mouth. "I know. I *know*. I just want to win back what I had originally and then I'll stop."

Euan's smile was one of loving amusement as he wrapped her in a hug. "I don't think that money's ever coming back, baby girl."

Kate stiffened in Warren's grasp.

"Are you all right?" he asked.

She nodded, conjuring up a smirk and gesturing towards her little stack. "I think I'm getting the hang of it."

On his other side, Sarah sat, Leo on her lap, attempting to look magnanimous behind her much larger pile of chips. "You're doing brilliantly."

"I wasn't expecting you to be such a skilled player," Warren admitted to his biological mother. Her hair was thinning already, he noticed.

Sarah looked round, as though to check the coast was clear. "I go to a book club once a week—or what started out as a book club. Don't tell Andy, but over the years it's transformed into a poker club. Or poker and crocheting, at any rate."

"Why crochet?" Kate frowned.

"When someone wants to watch instead of play, they can crochet. And we don't play with real money; we play with little crocheted coins instead. I find it's quite nice without having money involved. Like tonight," Sarah gestured to her stack of chips, "it's all very well and good but it's a lot of money to lose."

"As Darcy has discovered," Kate added. "I'm not used to betting. My father... He ran a casino."

"Oh! You must be a dab hand at all this then."

Kate's back pressed against his front, as though seeking support. "The last time I entered his casino was before Warren was sent to prison. I've never even placed a bet before tonight. He's not a good person," she admitted delicately. "Not a good father."

Warren held her a little tighter.

"I suppose I didn't want to gamble and find that I had a taste for it, like he does. It's more important to him than even his own daughter."

Sarah took Kate's hand with a touch only a mother could provide. "I'm sorry, sweetheart. But you don't have a taste for it, do you?"

Kate shook her head. "I don't know whether that makes it better or worse."

"In what way?"

"Because if it was some irresistible magnetic pull towards the gambling, it would be better."

Sarah's face was blank, but Warren understood. "But now you know he's made a choice to put you last," he said. "He didn't abandon you because of the gambling. He abandoned you because he didn't care enough to stay."

The wobble in Kate's lip told him he'd been right on the money.

"Kitten…" he murmured.

"Any parent who chooses vice over their child's happiness is not worthy of the title," Sarah reassured her fiercely, with an uncertain look at Warren. He could see the pleading there, plain as day. The pleading of a mother who'd given her son up for adoption in the hope he'd have a better life.

He gave her a small smile before tucking Kate under his arm. "Come on," he told her. "You've had an emotional night, and it's late. Let's get you to bed."

Saying goodbye to Sarah—and little Leo—he led Kate past the table at which Mattie played, Rhys and Saffron by his side, just as a victorious roar went up. Judging by the wide smile on Mattie's face, he'd just won big, but Warren could congratulate him in the morning.

Or afternoon, judging by the empty glasses surrounding the players.

Kate, bless her, made it to his bedroom before breaking down. "I'm sorry," she gasped, drawing in choking breaths even as she apologised, allowing Warren to engulf her in his arms. "It's just the gambling and *Darcy* and—"

"What did Darcy do?"

The silence lasted so long it was as though he hadn't said anything at all. Eventually, she gave him an answer. "Darcy has a father that loves her unconditionally, because she *deserves* unconditional love," Kate said bleakly, her eyes thick with tears. "I'm sorry for the pity party," she tried to push away from him, but he held her firm. "I've had too much to drink."

He began to unzip her dress, letting it fall to the floor for the second time that evening. She was naked beneath it, but he quashed any arousal beneath his skin. "You're allowed to feel your feelings," he told her, bending down to undo the clasps on her heels.

Once she'd stepped out of them, he guided her to the bed. "Lay down, kitten." He gave her an encouraging smile when she obeyed. He sat level with her feet, taking them into his lap, kneading the reddened skin highlighting the path the straps had taken.

She began to relax then, letting out sighs laden with pleasure. Her sighs progressed to moans the longer he worked, until he left her feet to lavish attention on her ankles and calves. "You shouldn't be doing this."

"Why?" he said mildly, hiding the annoyance prickling his veins.

"Because I don't deserve it."

He moved to massage her thighs, not missing the way they fell open, attempting to lure him between them. "You're wet."

Watching him through hooded eyes, she nodded, spreading them further. "Touch me. Please. I need you."

Warren deliberately avoided the sensitive skin of her inner thighs. "Do you remember the questionnaire you sent me?"

Another nod.

"Tell me what was on it."

"I... I want to be dominated. I want to be cared for. I want punishment."

He finally acquiesced to the signal sent by her spread legs and trailed his hands upwards, coming to rest on her labia. "You want to be taught a lesson?"

"Yes," she all but whimpered.

Spreading her wider, he asked her, "Are you sore from earlier? I was rough with you."

"I feel no pain whatsoever, Warren. And I like it rough."

"Good. Do you remember the safe word?"

"Pepper," she replied breathlessly.

"Stay." He left her on the bed, strolling into his walk-in wardrobe. "I bought something for you," he called to her, smirking when he found what he was looking for.

"Oh?"

"Oh," he confirmed, plugging it in next to the bed. Not bothering to be gentle, he manoeuvred Kate where he wanted her, pinning her legs open with his body. She jumped when he pressed the magic wand to her clit.

"What's that?"

"Never you mind what it is." Ensuring it was on the lowest setting, he switched it on.

Kate yelped. "*Oh!*"

He pulled it away, before gently brushing it back over her clit. The stimulation was gone as quickly as it appeared, with him letting her feel nothing but the barest of sensation. He repeated his movements intermittently, wanting her to remain uneasy and expectant.

It didn't take long before she was squirming under his grip. To keep her still, he straddled one of her legs and held down the other, enjoying the feeling of her fighting against him. "You seem to be in difficulty," he observed smugly. This time, he let her feel the vibrations for a full two seconds before they vanished.

"This is cruel," Kate hissed as her pussy wept, jolting whenever the vibrations returned.

"I enjoy hurting you. What did you expect?"

"Warren, please!"

The pause between vibrations was longer this time. "I bought you something else as well," he mentioned casually, picking up the metal chain and dragging it across her nipples to sensitise them. "Something you said you definitely wanted in the questionnaire."

Her lips parted. "Oh?"

He let the clamp bite down on her nipple.

Kate's shriek was immediate, but he gave her no mercy, quickly fastening the second clamp on. "They hurt," she whimpered.

Giving the chain the gentlest of tugs, he savoured her pain, picking up the magic wand once more. "Do you remember the safe word?"

"Yes," she gritted out.

"Does this hurt?"

"*Yes!*"

"Good. Seeing you in pain makes me so fucking hard, kitten." Turning the magic wand on again, he held it against the chain, enjoying her strangled gasp. "And knowing that *I'm* the one inflicting it makes me even harder."

When she eventually relaxed again, he gave the chain a gentle tug, moving the wand down to her clit. She moaned in relief, throwing her head back on the pillow.

"I love seeing you like this," he told her as she writhed, her hips rolling in endless movements. Kate's gasps became fully-fledged moans, her voice breaking at the imminent arrival of her climax. "Vulnerable and desperate and *mine*."

"I'm going to come!"

He pulled the magic wand away instantly.

"*No!*" she cried. "More! Please. Please, Warren, I was so close."

Anger hardened his jaw. "Tell me you deserve unconditional love."

The twitch at the edge of her lip betrayed her emotion. "No."

Furious, he pressed the magic wand back against her clit, leaving it until the last second until he pulled away.

"Warren!" she sobbed.

"Tell me you deserve unconditional love and I'll let you come."

"I can't," she sniffed, blowing out a shaky breath.

"Why not?"

"Because I don't! Even my own father doesn't want me, Warren. You should have heard him that day with Brax. I worked for *years* to help him but I never earned his love. I was never... never good enough for him, no matter what I did."

Tears tracked their way down to her hairline, but he held her focus. "Eyes on me, kitten. From the moment we met, *I* have loved you unconditionally. Back then, you were the little sister I always wanted, and then the day Brax brought you here," his eyelids fell as he rested their foreheads together. "When I first saw you, I rebelled against it, this *power* that you have over me. This maddening, bewildering, utterly incomprehensive pull that your body has over mine. But in the weeks since then, kitten, I've fallen in love with you. I don't just love you anymore, I'm *in love* with you. Have you ever known me to be a liar?"

Kate's eyes were as round as dinner plates. "No," she whispered.

"Then tell me that you're loved unconditionally. Tell me that you deserve to be loved unconditionally."

There was a brief flicker of doubt before she answered. "I'm loved unconditionally."

"And the rest?"

"I deserve to be loved unconditionally," she croaked.

"Good girl," he smiled, rewarding her by removing the nipple clamps. "Again."

Her cry of pain was music to his ears, but it wasn't the response he was looking for. "I deserve to be loved unconditionally."

He pressed the wand back against her clit. "And who loves you unconditionally?"

"You do—*oh!*" Kate's brows knotted together as the orgasm he'd denied her returned with a vengeance.

Warren grinned as her climax seized her in its clutches, her legs shaking uncontrollably through her cries, but the gush of liquid squirting onto the bed was a surprise. "That's it, kitten, you're so fucking beautiful when you come. I will give you the sun and the moon and the stars because *they are what you deserve.*"

Her eyes opened just enough for him to hold her gaze, his chest heaving with pride and love.

With her energy exhausted and her orgasm ebbing away, Warren pounced, freeing his erection and sliding it home in a single thrust. He slanted his lips over hers, groaning as her limbs wrapped around him. "You're perfect, do you understand?"

"I understand," she replied.

"I'm never going to let you go," he snarled, frantically chasing his own pinnacle, devouring her moans and replacing them with his own. "You're mine now, kitten, whether you like it or not."

"I like it. I love it."

His hips worked furiously, audibly pounding into her, following some primal rhythm older than mankind itself, until finally he exploded, groaning his pleasure into her neck. "And I love you," he choked as her pussy drained him. "I always have, and I always will."

11

Kate awoke with a noise halfway between a grumble and a retch, yanked from sleep by something poking her in the shoulder. She swiped it away with a lazy hand, but it returned, as incessant as ever.

"Kate?" Saffron whispered, sounding terrified.

Only then did she open her eyes. "Mmph?"

Saf crouched there beside her bed, white-faced. "Oh thank god," she took a deep breath. "I thought you were dead."

Her throat was as dry as sandpaper, but she was alive. "Why would I be dead?"

"It's quarter to seven. In the *evening*. You've slept the entire day."

With her faculties returning, Kate held the covers to her breast as she sat upright, fully aware that she must look like she'd been shoved through a hedge backwards. If she was honest, she probably looked better than she felt. "Where's Warren?" she rasped, glancing down at the unmade bed beside her.

Apparently satisfied, Saf stepped backwards. "He's cooking dinner for everyone downstairs."

"Everyone?" Realisation came a moment later. "Oh god, they all stayed for the party, didn't they?"

"Yeaaaah," Saf said slowly, grimacing slightly. "You might want to shower. You're covered in—"

"Don't finish that sentence."

"I mean I was going to say sweat but judging by the vibrator sticking out from under the bed, there's probably other fluids there too."

"Oh god." Kate wanted the ground to swallow her up.

Saf bit down on her bottom lip. "But you *are* okay?"

Well, her arse was sore. As were… other places. "My head hurts," Kate conceded, feeling the soreness between her legs more with every movement. "I think I'll have a shower before I come downstairs."

After her shower, the intoxicating smell of food tugged her towards the kitchen, her stomach rumbling. She found a crowd of people around the breakfast bar, perched on tall black stools. Warren saw her first, just as he placed a ceramic baking tray loaded with food onto the bar. The others dived in like animals crowding around a watering hole, but Warren gazed only at her, the corners of his eyes crinkling.

Hi, she mouthed, his declaration of love still hovering in her mind.

Brushing past Rhys, Warren approached her whilst the others were occupied. "I was going to bring your dinner up to you," he murmured.

Quirking her eyebrow, she smiled. "If I'd have known that, I would have stayed in bed."

He dipped his head, taking her lips in full view of the rest of the room. It only lasted a moment before he pulled back, slipping his arm around her waist. "Come and get some food. You must be starving."

She wasn't—until she neared the food. Her stomach began to growl in earnest at the breakfast bar, piled high with steaming chicken, roast potatoes, Yorkshire puddings, and pigs-in-blankets.

Kate winced as she sat down, the tenderness in her lower half making itself known once more. She dragged her attention away from her body to listen to Saffron's idle chatter, focused on the broadness of Warren's back as he moved about, fetching jugs of gravy and glasses of wine—and inconspicuously placing two tablets of paracetamol in her hand.

It was a strange sensation—to observe a man after she'd slept with him. Daniel had effectively disappeared into the ether after she'd given him her virginity, discarding her as quickly as he'd picked her up.

But Warren was still here.

She felt as though she'd been permitted membership to some exclusive club. To have known this man when he was lost in pleasure. To know what he was like at his most vulnerable; untamed, unhinged, and aggressive.

And then there was the soft side of him. Those wonderful moments afterwards when he'd collapsed in her arms, utterly spent. Or when he'd spoken tender, intimate words that had lulled her to sleep. Or when he confessed that he loved her.

That had been a surprise.

The conversation was a subdued purr around the table, with Saffron and Darcy producing most of the noise. Euan sat next to Alison. So close that Kate had a suspicion she and Warren weren't the only couple that spent the night together.

When Warren finally took a seat, it was at her side.

"I'm surprised at all this," she admitted quietly, as Mattie told Euan about his models.

"All what?"

"You. Cooking. You order take-away so frequently that I would have bet money on you not knowing how to turn on your own oven."

Under the table, his hand came to rest on her leg. "I'm a man of many surprises."

"Like needing aloe vera deliveries in the middle of birthday parties," Rhys grumbled on her other side.

"Fuck off, Rhys," Warren responded immediately, not looking away from Kate. "I have another gift for you, by the way. Don't let me forget to give it to you."

"What kind of gift?" she asked, shooting an alarmed look at the dinner table. Considering his last gift had made her squirt—something she wasn't aware she could actually do—she wasn't sure this was conversation they should have in company.

"A *normal* gift."

An excitable shout from Mattie tugged Kate's head to the left.

"It's Dad," he exclaimed, holding his phone out for Sarah to take. "He says he'll be home in a fortnight."

Sarah took it, frowning as she read the message. Reservation was clear on her face, but she attempted a smile back at Mattie. "That's good news."

"He's been away, hasn't he?" Alison asked.

Sarah nodded. "He works on cruise ships in the Mediterranean. I haven't seen him since before I started chemo."

"You must be looking forward to it."

Sarah's smile was tight. "I am."

"How long have you been married now?" Euan asked, sipping his wine.

"We married not long after I turned eighteen. It'll be twenty-three years this year."

"And I came along eighteen months later," Mattie grinned happily, crunching down on his Yorkshire pudding.

Kate didn't miss Alison's eyes flicking towards Warren. "I didn't realise quite how young you were when you gave birth to Warren."

"I was a month shy of fifteen," Sarah smiled, her eyes softening as she gazed upon Warren.

"Oh my god," Darcy's jaw hung open. "I'm three years older than that and I couldn't imagine having a kid *now*."

"That's why we gave him up," Sarah replied, her chest falling slightly. "To give him a better life."

Alison took Sarah's hand. "That must have been so difficult for you."

"It was."

"I'm thankful you did it," Warren reassured his mother. "For both of us. You needed to be a child for a while longer." Beneath the table, his hand squeezed Kate's. "And I found more family than I ever imagined."

"Oh my god, is that Bloodraven?" Kate could barely draw in breath as she perused through the hardback books Warren had ordered for her. Illustrated collector's editions of *A Song of Ice and Fire* by George R. R. Martin.

Or what GRRM had written so far, anyway.

"They arrived days ago, but I wanted to be here when you opened them. Forgive my selfishness."

"I would literally forgive you for murder if you buy me more collector's editions," Kate laughed, before gasping as she flicked to the next page. "Is that Shireen with Wun Wun?" She let loose a girlish squeal. "These are amazing, thank you so much."

A large hand scooped its way around her chest, whilst another settled across her hips. Warren pressed a kiss to the soft skin between her neck and her shoulder. And then another. "You're sore," he said. It wasn't a question.

She let the statement linger for a beat before responding. "A little bit."

Gently, he took the book from her hand, placing it back on the table in front of them. "I should have been more considerate," he said, pulling her into his embrace. "I couldn't stop. I'm sorry. I lost myself in you."

"It didn't hurt at the time."

His eyebrow lifted with amusement. "I should hope not." The words were a whisper against her lips—a moment before he took them for himself. His kiss was softer than she'd expected, his intent not to plunder but to coax.

To savour.

Kate couldn't stop herself from asking the question that played on her mind. "Why are you being so nice to me?"

His fingers intertwined with hers. "I've stopped fighting this. I've stopped punishing myself for the way I want you."

"Why would you punish yourself?"

"When we were children…" He swallowed, hesitating. "It was my job to protect you. I *wanted* to do it. You were so… alone."

The happiness brought about by the last twenty-four hours died a quick death.

"But then so was I. I never desired you. The thought never even crossed my mind—you were a child. You were my *kitten*, and that was all."

"And now?"

"Now the day is a waste if it doesn't end with me between your thighs, little kitten," he snarled, sinking his teeth into her neck before licking away the hurt.

"I think you might need to keep away tonight." Kate tried on an apologetic look, holding him by the shoulders. "I am sore, but that's not why you need to keep away. I've been having some period pains. It'll probably be, um, starting soon."

Warren didn't even blink an eye. "I've heard sex can help period pains." He paused. "Although it's only ever men I hear saying that so I'm not sure their opinions are unbiased. How about I pamper you instead? I'm sure Linda's stocked the en-suite with extortionately priced bath products. You can take your pick. I think there's some lavender—" Warren couldn't have come to a standstill more quickly if he'd run into a brick wall. "Or do you still despise the smell of lavender, you little heathen?"

"I still despise lavender and I refuse to apologise for it," she said baldly. "You're all the weirdos here, not me. It's disgusting."

A grin cracked his stony façade. "You know, I couldn't adore you more if I tried."

The snarkiness drained from her face, quickly replaced by undisguised shock.

Warren took advantage of her silence, kissing her until her cheeks were stained pink with need.

"And as soon as you're not sore, kitten, I'll be wanting you again. If you think I care that you're on your period, you're very sadly mistaken. What's the point of a sword if you never get it bloody?"

"Kate," Braxton began, staring intensely at his phone, "you know that prostitute you met?"

"Give me a second," Kate called, furiously clicking away during a dungeon in *World of Warcraft*. "I'm getting killed here." *Because the stupid tank isn't taking aggro off their fucking healer. Mattie, why did you move back home just as I decided to start healing?*

"Just pause it."

"There isn't a pause button. Jesus, have you never played an online game before?" Kate sagged as the last glimmer of green on her health bar vanished. "Bugger." Without her healing, the other dungeon players began to fall like flies. "Never mind. We're all dead anyway. What do you want?"

"The prostitute you met. The night you went out to dinner with Warren. Do you remember?"

Kate scrambled through her memories for the woman's name, shooting an unhelpful glance at Saffron and Rhys on the opposite sofa, now watching the fourth season of *Stranger Things*. "Adina, I think."

Brax nodded, shaking the phone in his hand. "She's sent a message to my colleague's number."

Feeling like a dick, Kate messaged a quick *sorry* to the other players and abandoned them to their fate.

"I'm sorry," Rhys's voice piped up from the other sofa, a grin unfurling across his face like a flirtatious banner. "You visited a prostitute with Warren?" He leant forward, his elbows on his knees. "Do tell me more. Not the Warren part, but you and the other girl."

Saffron narrowed her eyes. "You're disgusting."

Rhys's arm slid across the back of the sofa, precariously close to Saffron's neck. "I'm just an admirer of the female form, Saf."

Saffron's expression indicated that she couldn't have been more disgusted if a pile of shit had been flung at her face. "Do you not have your own home to fester in? It's been a fortnight since the party and you're still hanging around like a wet fart."

"It'll be lonely there without you."

"And yet strangely enough, I prefer it here."

"What did she say?" Kate asked Brax eagerly, cutting over Rhys and Saf's snipes. "Is she okay?"

"She doesn't say. Her text was simply an address followed by her name. And it's not the same address as the brothel in which she was working that night. What did you say to her?"

"Oh," Kate stalled, thinking back to their conversation in Warren's car. "I can't remember exactly." All she *could* remember was her dress hanging off her, baring her arse to the arse end of London. "I presume I asked her if she'd seen Graves. Or if she knew of anyone who had."

"So the address could conceivably be Graves's location?" Saffron joined in.

Brax honed in on her. "You were imprisoned in his properties for years. Would you recognise the address?"

Saffron shook her head. "I never knew the addresses of where we were. We travelled in the back of a windowless van. I'd probably know it from the outside, but Graves never used a location for long, and they all started to look the same after a while."

"So if he's there…"

"He won't be there for long." Saf looked round at Kate for support. "But my sister worked belowdecks, Graves called it. In the laundry room or kitchen. It's where I worked until I aged out." She chewed her lip. "My sister could be there, Kate."

Kate nodded eagerly. "Then it's worth checking out, Brax. Right?"

"You met this woman for all of five minutes, Kate. And she's a prostitute."

"So was I!" Saf stated, her voice thick with outrage. "Half of Graves's girls are working off debts and half are hooked on the drugs he supplies. None are there by fucking choice, Braxton! And just because a woman is a prostitute doesn't mean she's suddenly worthless. We're still people."

Brax's hands rested on his hips, he took a deep breath, but—

"They're right, Brax," Rhys laid his hand across Saffron's arm, sending a comforting smile her way. "Send a drone in first. There's no need to go in guns blazing. Speak to Warren. He'll agree with me, I'm sure. You're a father, Brax. Imagine if it was your little girl in the hands of Graves. What would you be doing right now?"

Brax's glare shrivelled Kate's insides. "You know exactly what I'd be fucking doing." He checked the phone again. "When's Warren supposed to be back from Andover?"

"I'm not sure," Kate said. "Not for a few hours at least."

"How far away is this location?" Rhys queried.

"An hour."

He nodded. "Then go and watch them for a while. Send out a drone or two first."

"Aren't they usually quite loud?" Kate asked. "One of the kids on the estate had a drone and everyone always knew when it went up." Followed by several OAPs fear-mongering on social media about how it was *spying on them*.

"Not the ones we have," Brax replied, huffing a defeated breath down at his phone. "I've sent a message to Warren to get his approval."

"Is mine not enough?" Rhys asked, his hands spread wide.

"No."

Rhys touched his hand to his heart. "I thought we were friends. I'm truly offended, Brax."

"I truly don't give a shit."

"Has he messaged you?" Saffron asked, her words muffled behind her hands.

On her laptop, Kate hadn't closed the tab since the last time Saf had asked, but her answer remained the same. "Not yet. I'm sorry." She shared a worried glance with Rhys when Saf lowered her head to her bent knees.

Warren had barely walked through the front door before he'd been squirreled away by Brax, but Kate didn't begrudge his changing focus. Saffron's presence in the house was a constant reminder that there were real people behind Graves's trafficking operation.

"I can't remember her name," Kate realised. "Your sister, I mean."

"Evie." Saffron's anxiety cracked for just a moment, long enough for a gentle smile to appear, like a ray of sunshine appearing behind the clouds. Kate blinked, and it was gone. "They're not even going inside the property. They're just checking it out. I *know* that. But… I can't help…"

"Hoping," Kate finished for her. All her life, she had been the younger sibling—up until Aaron's death had made her an only child. What would it have been like to have had a little sister to look after whilst working to put food on the table?

A nightmare. Kate had barely managed to keep herself alive some weeks.

And to have to do that in the centre of a human trafficking organisation…

A shiver went through her.

"Exactly," Saf said sadly.

"Tell me about her," Kate asked, watching Rhys jog to the front door to collect the food they'd ordered.

Saf's grin was a little crooked. "You know I told you about my mum always wanting a koi pond?"

She nodded.

"Well Evie decided when she was about five that we'd have to call all the fish Bob, regardless of gender." Kate's bewildered expression made

Saffron laugh. "Because it's the only word they can say. Five-year-old logic for you."

Rhys came back in with the food—Japanese food, which Kate had never tried before. "Aldous had some of the best one-liners when we were kids."

"Oh?" Kate accepted her bowl of ramen.

"Once he saw Mum without her make-up on and cried out 'Bleurgh! What's wrong with your face?'"

Saffron covered her mouth with an expression of horror. "Oh god, what did your mum say?"

"She burst straight into tears. It was, like, the week after my dad walked out on us as well."

"Your poor mother."

"It's okay though," Rhys grinned, "because Aldous offered to call her an ambulance to get her face fixed."

After her first clumsy attempts at using chopsticks, Kate settled for a fork. "How much younger is he than you?"

"Six years," Rhys answered, using his chopsticks like a pro. "Which meant I was old enough to corral him away from Mum and make him promise never to say anything bad about her face ever again."

Saffron followed Kate's lead and picked up a fork. "And did he?"

"Well not long after that he walked in on her getting changed and said that her boobs were much longer than he thought they were."

Kate choked on her noodles. "Jesus Christ."

"How did your mother not murder him?"

Rhys shook his head. "I genuinely don't know. What do you think?"

Kate's brain came to a standstill. "Of your mother not murdering your little brother? I mean, I'd like to give her a *well done* but—"

"Of the food, you eejit."

"Oh! It's great. What about you, Saf?"

Saf nodded, chewing furiously, giving them a thumbs-up.

It was past midnight by the time Warren and Brax returned. Kate, Rhys, and Saf were still sitting like sentinels in the living room, attempting to pass the time by binge watching TV shows. In the past hour, Saffron had finally begun to doze, curling up like a cat on the sofa.

Neither Kate nor Rhys had been able to sleep. The two of them had exchanged worried looks when Saffron wasn't looking, particularly as the hour grew late.

But she finally broke out in a smile when Warren walked through the door, hitting him like a freight train. "You're back," she mumbled into his chest, into his kitten tattoo, wrapping her arms around him in a vice-like grip.

He looked down at her with a quirked brow. "You were worried?"

"Of course I was bloody worried. Did you see Saffron's little sister? Or Graves?"

Saffron's head popped up at the noise, and she gasped at the sight of Warren. "Did you see her?"

Warren paused, his lips pressing together. "No, I'm sorry." He nodded a greeting to Rhys. "We *did* see a couple of young girls coming out to put things in the wheelie bin, but none of them were blonde."

Attempting to pull Saffron out of the slump she'd settled into, Kate spoke up. "But that doesn't mean she's not there, Saf. The fact that there are young girls there means there's still a decent chance she's inside."

"Exactly. But Graves was there."

Kate's eyes shot up. "He was?"

"Only briefly. He couldn't have been there for more than fifteen minutes, but we saw him, kitten."

"Then call the police," Saf begged, her voice high. "Please. You know there's girls in there Warren. You know the location. Let the police deal with it—Graves was one of their own. They'll come down on him like a brick shithouse."

But Kate knew by the hard glint in Warren's eye that Saf's pleas would go unheard. "It's not enough, Saffron. Think of what was done to you—to your mother. Graves worked her into the fucking ground. If he's put away, he'll be safe and cared for. And chances are he'll be out within a decade."

Hugging her arms around her waist, Saffron turned away.

"But," Warren carried on, "if we wait until we're able to trap him, you can be damn well sure that I'll give him the kind of justice he deserves."

Saffron's shoulders shook, but Rhys grasped them. "We'll get your sister out, Saffron." She tried to turn away, but Rhys held her chin. "Hey, listen to me. I promise."

She sniffed. "Okay." Saf turned back to Warren. "I'm sorry," she sniffed, her voice breaking.

"You don't have to apologise, Saffron." He gave her a small pat on the shoulder. "But Rhys is right. We know where Graves is now. We have a possible location on your sister. Once I have Graves, we'll call the police."

Kate nodded. "We're a step closer. We should celebrate—anyone fancy a drink?"

"I'll get it," Saf offered, wiping underneath her eyes and heading out to the kitchen. She returned a few moments later with a bottle of some fancy cream liqueur that Kate had never heard of. It certainly wouldn't be seen in the shabby corner shop on the estate.

Warren accepted the glass Saf offered with a smirk. "My favourite shot glass."

"The cat paw one?" Rhys's eyes narrowed, holding out his own shot glass—styled in the form of a woman, complete with heavy breasts and obvious nipples—for Saf to fill. "I prefer this one."

"Mmm," Saffron grumbled, catching Kate's eye. "I thought you might. Low hanging fruit and all that."

Kate's own shot glass was plain, thank god. She didn't much fancy her shot having its own nipples.

Half the bottle later, Warren ended the night with a, "Right." He held his palm out to Kate. "Bed."

Obediently, she followed, waving goodbye to Saf and a smug-looking Rhys before attempting to keep up with Warren's rapid steps. He barely looked at her, almost dragging her up the stairs.

But when he closed the bedroom door behind them, Warren let loose, slamming her up against it so hard her breath gushed out. "Warren!"

His hands found her throat in a strangely tender grip. "Shut the fuck up."

And then he descended, his body crushing her against the luxurious wood. His kiss was punishing, an all-consuming embrace that was as aggressive as it was loving.

When she tried to wrap her arms around his neck, he pinned them above her head, letting his other hand roam over her body at a leisurely pace.

Kate let out a little moan as his hands skated across her breasts, never staying in one spot long enough to enjoy. "Please."

He ground his hips into her, his erection *just* managing to graze her clit. Kate opened her legs, needing more, but his smirk was cruel as he dragged her roughly towards the bed.

She loved it. The roughness. The aggression. The primitive need to be overpowered.

And *fuck*, did Warren do it well.

He threw her on the bed with a snarl, but Kate barely had a second before he was on her again. He wrenched open her blouse, sending buttons scattering across the room.

"Stop ruining my bloody clothes," she panted, lifting her hips so he could yank down her jeans—and her underwear with them.

Warren grabbed her chin. "You're lucky I give you any fucking clothes to wear at all, kitten. You're lucky I don't spread your legs and tie you to the bed so you're ready for me to take any time I want."

The image had her moaning, but then he hooked his hands behind her knees and bent them back. Spreading her wide, just as he'd promised. "Like this?" she whispered.

"*Just* like this," Warren nodded, his eyes poring over her exposed flesh. "You're glistening for me already. My pretty pink kitten." He looked back to the bedroom door. "I could use you however I wanted. And there would be nothing you could do to stop it."

Kate's head fell back against the pillows, whimpering. Fucking hell. *Why does that turn me on so much? Why is that so fucking hot?*

"Would you like that?"

Slowly, she nodded.

"Good girl," his voice slipped over her skin like warm honey. "Now stay like this. Spread wide for me."

She nodded again, desperate to surface from the lake of desire in which she was drowning. She felt like a cat in heat as she watched Warren's clothes fall to the floor, piece by piece. Was it possible to be driven mad by bliss? She felt *empty*, needing to feel him inside her. "I need you. I need you. I *need* you."

When he stood bare before her, she admired him from between her thighs. As beautiful as she remembered. As savage as she needed. Beneath the trail of jet black hair leading down his navel, her attention caught on the soft inclines carved into his hips. A bottleneck for her gaze. And below, his cock proudly jutted forward, hard and wanting.

"Take me," she begged. "I'm yours."

"Fuck, kitten. You are so very, very beautiful." He smirked. "Especially when you beg." He ran his hands over her thighs as though he were a pilgrim tracing his hands over some sacred monument, savouring every inch of her skin.

Then he descended, falling over her to press her back into the bed. She delighted at the feel of his naked body against hers, his cock propped against her opening. Wrapping her arms around his neck, she pressed a gentle kiss against his lips.

"I need to taste you again, to see every inch of you," he murmured desperately. "It's all I can think about."

Warren carried the kiss down her neck and in between her breasts. His lips continued their downward path, claiming between her legs with the enthusiasm of a lover returning home from months at sea. Her cheeks burned as he inhaled her scent greedily, his nose pressing into her curls. Growling his approval, Warren parted her legs with his hands and her folds with his tongue. He lapped at her clit eagerly, filling the room with her moans. His arms wrapped around her legs, running his hand along her skin reverently. She cried out as Warren alternated the speed and intensity of his caresses, his tongue swirling around every inch of every corner as she begged for more.

When she was almost overwhelmed with pleasure, he allowed his fingers to glide inside her again, fluttering as she arched her back. Warren moved faster and faster; holding her firmer as she fought to move with the utter bliss he was giving her.

Kate found a strange duality there; her hips fought furiously to move with her pleasure, but the tighter he held her the hotter her arousal burned. She wanted to fight, but she also wanted to be overpowered.

Because she was free. Free to want. Free to explore. Free to need.

Panting, she fisted his hair, holding him in place even as her hips attempted to move with his rhythm. Kate chanced a look down and moaned; the sight of his dark hair dancing between her thighs was overwhelmingly alluring.

His emerald eyes hooked her. Intensely. Adoringly. A wantonness rose within her, slyly meeting his gaze. In response, she raised an emboldened eyebrow and tightened her hand in his hair. A wordless challenge. *Don't you have something to be concentrating on?*

Warren snarled in satisfaction, a grin dancing behind his arousal. Every rough sound of enjoyment that tore through his throat sent vibrations to her clit as she climbed higher and higher. The edge was right there, she could almost feel it. Warren was taking her there; his tongue against her, his fingers inside her.

She was lost.

Kate cried out as she came, the waves of pleasure crashing against her at such a relentless pace she fought to catch her breath. Warren didn't seem to have the same problem. He fuelled her pleasure, until she was so sensitive she couldn't bear it any longer.

"Stop," she gasped, her chest heaving as it fought to drag air into her lungs. "Jesus Christ," she smiled faintly, her eyes half closed as Warren straightened above her with a smug look of masculine satisfaction.

His kiss tasted of her, a metallic twang that she couldn't get enough of. Because it meant he was *hers*.

And when he swiped his cock through her folds, bathing the head in her slickness before sliding inside her, she was his.

They moaned together at the bliss of their joining. A simple act that brought endless pleasure.

Warren teased her at first, rolling his hips to stir his cock inside her, hitting her somewhere that even she'd never been able to find. He played her body like it had been made for him. And maybe it had—because how else could it feel so good?

It didn't take long for his rhythm to quicken. Sweat beaded on his forehead, but still he worked on, and Kate was happy to reap the rewards of his efforts, crying out at the impact of each thrust. Her fists tangled in the bedcovers until her fingers screamed for release—almost as much as the rest of her body.

Kate came with full-throated carnality, but even then Warren didn't let up, groaning out his own pleasure as she contracted around him. Their gazes locked, and Kate tried to commit every second to memory. The rasping groan when he came. His clenched jaw. His rough hands on her skin. The intent look in his eyes—and the softness hiding within.

When the storm of her orgasm began to recede, she pulled him on top of her, desperate for the intoxicating weight of his body.

Was he too heavy? Yes.

Did she give a shit? Absolutely not.

He was hers. And she was his.

She always had been.

12

Kate

The sound of retching swept her into consciousness, as though the Goddess of Sleep had shooed her out with a broom. Kate peeled her eyes open, grumbling at the bright morning sunlight. She tugged the covers over her head to shield them. Why had she drunk so much?

And by the sounds of the noises coming from the loo, she wasn't the only one regretting her choice.

"Kate," Warren's voice came from the bathroom. Even that small sound made her wince.

"Mm?"

"I think I need to call my doctor. I'm throwing up blood. Can you bring my phone?"

That woke her up. Kate scrambled to her feet, blinking away light-headedness as she hurried over to the bathroom in time to catch Warren binning a toothbrush and spitting mouthwash into the sink. He was wearing his 3D-printed prosthetic instead of his regular one, presumably because it was quicker to attach and remove.

"Oh Christ, that's so much more than I was expecting." The bright red toilet bowl distracted her from the nose-wrinkling stench.

"Take a photo of it on my phone to show the doctor so I can flush it. Fucking smell is making me want to keel over."

"Right." Her tender head becoming a priority of the past, she followed Warren's instructions as he collapsed on the ottoman cradling his stomach. His face had become alarmingly pale. "The NHS website says," she started, "gastritis, ulcer—"

"Call my doctor."

Kate flicked through Warren's contacts. "Name?"

"Roger Burley."

The doctor answered on the second ring. Kate left Warren to talk to the man, taking the time to fetch him his regular prosthetic and a fresh liner from the drawer. To stop herself from hovering, she washed and dressed, albeit in the bedroom ensuite, purely to avoid the stench of sick.

Warren was holding a small bin under his chin when she came out of the shower, whilst his phone had been put on loudspeaker, haphazardly lying on the ottoman. The bin's contents—paper and an old deodorant can—had been turfed out onto the floor. "Are you sure that's necessary?"

"Yes," the disembodied voice replied forcefully. "You called me for my opinion. My opinion is you need to get to a hospital as soon as you can. You're bleeding internally. The cause could be benign... Or it could very much not be. The last thing you want is to have ignored a problem until it's too large to solve."

Kate inserted a £2 coin into the hospital vending machine, going back for her sixth fizzy drink of the day. Letting out a yawn, she ambled back to the ward.

She seemed to have spent half her life in a hospital recently, what with Sarah's chemo and now Warren's gastritis. It had been a relief to have Warren's diagnosis be something simple, however. A quick blood test had been all the doctors had needed before starting him on a course of antibiotics. He'd thrown up several times today, but the doctors were optimistic that the nausea and stomach pain would calm down soon. Indeed, it seemed to be calming down already.

Warren levelled a frown at her when she opened the door to his room, sitting upright on the raised hospital bed. "It's gone ten. You should go home."

Ignoring him entirely, she planted her arse on the bed and cracked open the can. "A lady will go where she pleases."

He curled his hand around her throat, pulling her closer. "A lady will be punished if she doesn't follow orders."

"Don't threaten me with a good time."

"You enjoy force, don't you?"

Kate bit her lip. "Maybe."

Warren lowered his voice to a whisper. "And what about fighting me?"

Kate frowned. "Fighting you?"

"It's known as CNC. Consent non-consent. Did you not read the links I sent you?" Warren looked away, freeing a long breath. "Role playing, essentially. You act as though you don't want it, you fight me. You act as though I'm forcing you, but in reality you *do* want it."

"Right," Kate said breathlessly. She had read about that, now that he mentioned it.

"I wouldn't want to *actually* force you. I want you to know that." His hand found her cheek, and he smiled. "If you don't want to do it, it's not a—"

With an impish smirk, Kate crept her hand under his hospital gown. Heat flared in her when she found exactly what she was looking for: his thick cock, hard and wanting.

"Kitten…" Warren shot a glance at the door before his eyes closed, losing his struggle against her wandering touch.

"You want me to struggle as you pin me down?" she breathed, keeping her voice low, stroking his length.

He nodded, leaning back on the raised hospital bed. "Fuck, yes."

"Would I scream?"

"*Yes,*" he snarled. "But then I'd gag you."

Kate squeezed his cock, quickening her strokes. She clenched her thighs together, her arousal skyrocketing. "I'd be so helpless. Tied down. Gagged. You could do whatever you wanted to me."

He seized her face with his hands. "You're damn fucking right I would." His kiss was cruel. A conquering, biting embrace that had her moaning in pleasure. "I'd spank you until you screamed for mercy."

Fuck. She bit her lip, sucking in a breath when his hand meandered underneath her skirt. "You'd hurt me?"

"I'd *punish* you." He swore, and she widened her legs for him. "You're fucking soaked. You want this?"

Kate nodded. "I want to scream for you until my throat is raw. And then I want you to force me to drink your cum."

A ragged rasp escaped from his throat and he grabbed her hair with a rough hand, forcing her face down to his cock.

"Then drink, kitten."

Kate fastened her mouth over the head of his cock, sucking, desperate to taste him. He groaned above her, and the hot lashes of his seed hit the back of her throat. Her mewl was victorious. She swallowed every drop, teasing the tip with her tongue—

The door handle depressed; a sound that pierced the room like a knife.

Warren yanked the bottom of Kate's skirt back down to her knees, but Kate had barely thrown the hospital gown over his cock before a nurse rushed into the room.

"Oh!" the nurse said, coming to a standstill, her gaze flickering between the two of them; Warren breathing heavily, Kate's face still inches from his groin. "Um," she pointed at one of the machines Warren was hooked up to, smacking her lips. "Your heart rate was elevated. I thought you were in need of assistance but now I can see…"

He's already received it, yes.

The red-faced nurse trailed off, letting them bask in their shame.

Kate would have stayed silent forever—avoiding eye contact, twiddling her thumbs, and swallowing the rest of the cum in her mouth—but Warren took a different approach.

"My apologies," he said suavely, as though he hadn't just been forcing his cock down Kate's throat. "I wasn't aware that it would send out an alert. It won't happen again."

"That would be much appreciated," the nurse nodded, backing out of the room.

A long, silent second passed between the two of them. Then Kate's resolve broke, and she burst into laughter, pressing her face into Warren's shoulder.

He pulled her close, a reluctant smile curling his lip. "You're a bad influence on me, kitten."

Still giggling, she shrugged. "You love it."

"Mmm," he nodded, his shoulders dropping in a sigh. "I think I just might."

"You're quiet today," Kate said to Saffron. Her friend sat on the opposite couch, staring at the floor. Her attention was quite clearly miles away—it certainly wasn't on the TV show playing.

Saffron faked a smile. "I'm worried about my sister." She shook her head, the moisture in her eye catching the sun's rays. "I'm sorry."

"You're entitled to be worried."

Saf looked away. "Are you not going to the hospital today?"

Kate shook her head, her heart threatening to burst with excitement. She couldn't keep the loopy grin off her face. "I'll see him when he's discharged later."

"You love him?"

The question was unexpected, but not unwanted. *Did* she love Warren?

Excluding the calamities, the last few weeks had been… wonderful. Particularly the fortnight since the party, after consummating their relationship. She couldn't help thinking of the contrast between Warren and Daniel.

Daniel had pleased himself. There had been no consideration for Kate's feelings.

Whereas the pull between her and Warren…

It was inevitable.

"I love him," she admitted, pulling up her knees and sliding her arms around them. "I've loved him for a while now, I think."

"I'm pleased for you," Saf said quietly.

A throat cleared behind them. Kate swung round to see Rhys's tall figure striding across the room. "Saf, we need your help."

Kate perked up instantly. "What kind of help?"

"The kind of help that would involve staking out what we think is a cannabis farm and identifying the people going in and out of it."

"Why would Saf know about that?" Kate asked, turning to her friend. "You worked in the brothel side of things, didn't you?"

"When women were on their periods, Graves sometimes sent them to watch over the farms at night." Saf chewed her lip. "That's what I was doing when you found me."

"Will you come?" Rhys asked.

Saffron nodded. "Not that this house isn't gorgeous, but I could use a change of scenery."

Kate said her goodbyes to Saf and Rhys, choosing to dive into levelling up her new Warlock character on *World of Warcraft.* Her and Mattie had been levelling up her druid as a team, so it didn't feel right to work on it without him.

She was enjoying the Warlock, however. Especially the little pet she got along with it.

Minion, she could hear Mattie saying.

It was called a Felhunter, apparently, and she was enjoying it a good deal more than her previous pet-slash-minion—which was a scantily-clad woman that made her roll her eyes every time she summoned it.

Kate was three bars away from level forty when Mattie finally logged on.

> **Kate**: Lol, what time do you call this? How's your mum getting on being back at home?
>
> **Mattie**: Promise you won't call my phone.
>
> **Kate**: ...I promise? Why?
>
> **Mattie**: I need your help.
>
> **Kate**: Has your mum had another seizure?!
>
> **Mattie**: My dad's just got back from his latest cruise, but he's trying to kick me and Mum out of the house.

Kate: I'm sorry, *what*?

Mattie: He clearly didn't expect my mum to be home, but
he's going ballistic, Kate. He says because he owns the house
that she's got no right to live here. He's already on the phone
to the council saying he's making her homeless. And he says
I've got to go with her.

Kate stared at the screen, her jaw hanging open, but before she could
reply, another message came in from Mattie.

Mattie: He's smashing my models up, Kate.

Kate: I'll be there as soon as I can, Mattie. I swear.

Slamming her laptop screen down harder than she'd intended, Kate
leapt up. Her socks skidded across the tiled floor. She took the stairs two
at a time, rushing towards Brax's office—

Only to quite literally run into the giant man himself on the landing. She
stumbled back, precariously close to falling backwards down the stairs,
but Brax grabbed her arm and tugged her back to earth.

"We need to get down to Andover. Mattie's dad's throwing Mattie and
his mum out of the house."

Brax scrubbed a hand over his head. "I was just coming to get you.
Warren's started seizing, Kate. It's not gastritis. We need to get to the
hospital *now*."

When they arrived at the hospital, the wheels hadn't even stopped turning before Kate vaulted out of the SUV, ignoring Brax's voice. "Wait! For Christ's sake, Kate."

Kate ignored him, turning to open Sarah's car door. "Here," she smiled, taking Leo from her lap and offering her an arm. Six weeks out from her diagnosis, Sarah was steadier than Kate had expected—particularly when it came to leaving little Leo behind.

Andover had been unpleasant; an ugly, in-depth look into the breakdown of a marriage.

Half of Mattie and Sarah's possessions had been strewn across their front garden when Brax and Kate had screeched to a halt outside their house, but Sarah was fighting tooth and nail to keep Leo.

"You don't even want him!" Sarah was hissing at Andy when they walked in. "You just don't want me to have him."

Whatever retort Andy had been about to make had died at the prospect of an audience. Kate had an idea that his silence was more due to Brax's presence than it was hers, but she wasn't going to complain. The second SUV had pulled up a minute later, and Brax had wasted no time in ordering the two guards about in packing up the bulk of Mattie and Sarah's possessions.

Then there was nothing else to do but tell Sarah and Mattie about Warren's seizures.

Kate hoped she'd done the right thing in choosing to go help Warren's mother and brother first. Brax's phone had remained piercingly quiet throughout the journey to Andover and back, but that was a good thing.

She hoped.

If he was dead, they would have called. There would have been nothing else for the medical team to do. Brax had said Alison had already made her way there, and she would have contacted them had the worst happened.

So there must be no news yet. Surely.

Silent bargaining had lasted her this long, however. Her nerves were sky-high when they entered the hospital, with one of Brax's guards staying in the car to look after Leo. It was only twenty degrees Celsius, but even Kate—who had never had a dog—wasn't ignorant enough to suggest leaving Leo alone in the car. She'd seen enough videos on the internet of people smashing open car windows to rescue overheated dogs.

Complete with the owner returning half an hour later protesting that they had only been 'gone for a minute.'

The characteristic smell of hospitals was becoming almost homely at this point. The constant rush of people walking down the main thoroughfare was seemingly never-ending, but all the three of them had to do was keep close behind Brax and the other enormous security guard carving a path through the crush.

After shutting the door on Andy, none of them had made another mention of the man. Kate was fine to let Sarah bring it up as and when she chose. Mattie, on the other hand, had managed to rescue most of his models, which had been loaded in little purpose built cases full of black foam. Several had been lost in Andy's tantrum, but Mattie had assured her that they'd mostly been old models that he didn't play with anymore.

Although with the wobbling of his lip, Kate wasn't quite sure she believed him.

And then they entered Warren's room, and the air whooshed from her lungs in a single, bleak moment.

Warren was as still as a corpse on the bed, his face white and his lips worryingly blue. A cannula was embedded in his arm, attached to a clear bag of fluid hanging next to the bed. The band of worry and nausea around her torso loosened somewhat at the sight of his steady heart rate.

Something inside her died when she realised it had been less than eighteen hours ago that she'd been *assisting* him, causing the nurse to rush in on a wave of embarrassment.

It felt like a thousand years ago.

A gentle touch at her arm made her jump. How long had she been standing there staring at him for?

Alison, Rhys and Aldous's mother, stood there with a kindly expression. "Come and sit down, sweetheart. We've saved you a chair."

Kate allowed herself to be steered past the entire Stone family and plonked in the chair beside Warren's head. Sarah sat opposite her, focused on nothing but her son. "Will he live?" Kate croaked, her voice wavering as it met the open air.

The Stone matriarch bit her lip. Her eyes were stained pink with tears. "Maybe."

"He was… he was fine last night."

Rhys spoke up then, but Kate didn't bother looking at him. "It's not gastritis, Kate."

"But he tested positive for that bacteria. Didn't he?"

"He did, but in light of his seizures they've reassessed his diagnosis. The bacteria test was a false alarm. Apparently it's present in more than 50% of the popula—"

Sarah spoke over him. "Then what's wrong with him?" she asked, taking Warren's large, limp hand.

It was Aldous who answered. "The doctors think he's consumed some kind of toxin."

"A toxin? Like a drug?" Kate asked, taking Warren's other hand, mindful of his cannula. His skin had a faint yellow tinge.

Aldous shook his head. "We don't know. Whatever it is, it's affecting his liver—significantly so. That's having a knock-on effect on the fluid in his brain."

"Neither of which are good things," Rhys finished, his arms crossed.

"So what are they going to do about it?" Kate glanced around the room, hoping someone would have a simple answer.

"We wait," Alison said patiently. "They've given him a charcoal mixture to prevent his body from absorbing the toxin. The mistaken diagnosis has meant the toxin has been allowed to work for longer than it should have done. They're doing what they can to save his liver, and in the process stop the fluid from accumulating in his brain."

Kate needed more. "And… and if they can't do that?"

The question hung in the air, but no one dared to answer.

13

Kate

Warren's liver failed three weeks after his hospital admission.

He spent eight-and-a-half hours in surgery for a liver transplant. Which meant that Kate, Sarah, and Alison spent eight-and-a-half hours waiting in his hospital room, making stuttered, dead-end conversation and staring at the clock.

Second by second.

Minute by minute.

Hour by hour.

Nothing could have prepared Kate for the sight of Warren's bed being wheeled back into the room. A posse of medical staff accompanied him, but it was the tubes that drew her eye. Tubes coming from his nose. Tubes coming from his mouth. Tubes coming from the foot-long gash travelling from his diaphragm to his navel.

With the kitten tattoo perched on his heart, as always.

She broke into sobs, not even trying to stop herself from hyperventilating. Her efforts would have been wasted. Usually, she cared for Warren during the day, saving up all her tears for the shower.

Because going back to the house was somehow worse than being in the hospital. Despite there being Saffron and an in-house security team, the property was empty without Warren. Last night, even the sight of his shower prosthetic had her bursting into tears.

Another reminder that he wasn't there.

"He should wake up soon," Farida said kindly. She was one of the nurses that had cared for Warren most often during the three-week nightmare they'd all endured. "But we'll be watching him from the nurse's station," she pointed to the little desk that had a direct view into Warren's room. "All right?"

Alison and Sarah both nodded and thanked the nursing team, but Kate just sniffed, taking her permanent position next to Warren's head. And avoiding the monitor that she cracked her skull on at least once a day.

True enough, after a terse twenty-minute wait, Warren's bleary eyes opened, peering around the bright hospital room.

Kate's first words were more of a grief-stricken noise than actual speech, but she took a second attempt. "You're awake."

He blinked slowly, but the hard-edged grin was all Warren. "I'm awake. I'm sore, but I'm awake."

Alison and Sarah dived in then, the former asking all sorts of medical questions. It was a relief to know that, prior to becoming a midwife, Alison had worked as a nurse for a brief period. As a result, she'd be able to recognise if anything was 'off.'

Or that was Kate's reasoning, anyway.

Kate simply sat on Warren's other side, holding his hand and pressing the occasional kiss to his knuckles—albeit through her facemask. Unable to think of anything other than *we nearly lost you*.

Abrin.

That, apparently, was the cause of all the turmoil. A toxin she'd never heard of before, but it had almost taken the person she loved most in the world.

It had been a week since Warren's liver transplant, and Kate had read everything she could about abrin. The nurses had told them that there was no definitive test for the poison, but after reviewing Warren's symptoms and his blood results, that was the hypothesis they were going with.

The nurses had also told them that Warren's exposure was unlikely to be accidental.

Even now, the night before Warren would be discharged from hospital, Kate could see the broad shoulders of a security guard lurking outside the room. Each day was the same. A security guard would be here twenty-four hours a day, and when visiting hours were over, another would arrive to escort Kate, Alison, and Mattie home—and sometimes Sarah too, when she was feeling up to it.

Today was no different. At eight o'clock in the evening, the three of them readied themselves to leave the hospital. Their facemasks prevented them from kissing Warren goodbye, but given that Warren was now on immunosuppressants, all of them understood the need for physical distance.

Kate waited until the others had cleared the room before saying her goodbyes. "Promise me you'll be here in the morning, bright eyed and bushy tailed, ready to go home."

He snorted weakly. "I promise I will be in the building in the morning."

She knew exactly what he was implying. "The morgue doesn't count."

"You're no fun." His thumb slid across the back of her hand.

"I need you." Tears came to her unbidden; they seemed to have become a permanent fixture recently. "In the space of—what—three months, you've tunnelled your way into my heart." She gasped out a watery laugh. "And I'm keeping you there, I hope you know."

"Kitten..." he said tenderly.

She squeezed his hand. "You don't have to say anything, Warren. I just want you to know; I need you. I have done since you stormed into your room that first night."

A quirked eyebrow signalled his doubt. "Even when I pinned you against the wall?"

Though he couldn't see it, the sly smile beneath her face mask was filthy. "*Especially* when you pinned me against the wall."

"My dirty, dirty kitten."

Kate nodded. "Your kitten needs you home, Warren."

He leant back against the bed, lowering his eyes and squeezing her hand. "Tomorrow."

The orange wash of the streetlights sailed over her face as Brax drove the three of them home. Kate rested her head against the cool window, letting the car's movement jostle her about. The way onwards was recovery, surely. The past few weeks had been fraught with worry and terror, but that hurdle had been crossed now. The barrier had been overcome. They were on the home stretch.

They had to be.

An incoming call on the car's Bluetooth had her eyes flying open. Brax answered it with a curt, "You're on speakerphone."

The answering voice was just as polite. "Take me off speakerphone."

Well then.

Kate shared a look with Alison as Brax tapped a button on the interface to direct the call to his earphones. "You're off." There was a few seconds of silence before he interrupted the caller. "Wait, *now*?"

She let her imagination loose with the other side of the conversation. "*Yes, the projectile diarrhoea has struck now. It's even on the ceiling.*"

"You're sure?"

"*Yes, we'll never get it out,*" Kate's imaginary voice said.

Brax agreed that this was bad news. "Fucking hell, just do what you can. I'll be there ASAP." He tapped his ear to hang up.

"Is everything okay?" Sarah, who had been well enough to join them today, asked from the front seat.

With his jaw firmly set, Brax managed to nod. "It's nothing to worry about, but I'll need to drop you all off at the house instead of coming in with you."

At home, the three of them were ushered into the house by the security guard with resting bitch face. The most attractive of the security guards, Saf had said. Kate was doubtful. The front door had barely closed before Brax high-tailed it out of the driveway, the reverse light painting the brickwork white.

Mattie's familiar voice rang through the ground floor. Kate caught enough words to know he was talking through his headset with someone in-game, and she had a mind to join him.

"Kate?" Alison asked quietly. "Do you mind if I have a word?"

"Of course," she replied, surprised.

"Come."

Kate obeyed, saying goodbye to Sarah—who headed in the direction of Mattie's voice. Alison, meanwhile, directed Kate up the stairs and into Warren's bedroom with a somewhat apologetic expression.

"I don't want to be overheard," she explained. "And there's security cameras downstairs."

"Yes, I imagine they're currently getting a front-row seat to *Hellfire Citadel*." Seeing Alison's blank look, Kate waved her hand. "It's a thing in the game we play. What did you want to talk about?"

Alison's cheek hollowed inwards on one side as she bit it. "You know I was a midwife."

"I do."

"For thirty years."

"Quite a long time." Longer than Kate had been alive.

A nod. "It was, but it's afforded me quite a lot of experience in midwifery in general."

"Right."

Alison patted her face, just along her cheekbones. "You have darkened skin pigmentation around your cheeks, Kate."

She shrugged nonchalantly, not seeing the issue. Was this what Alison had wanted to discuss? Kate's new tan? "I must've caught the sun."

"You've lived in that hospital for weeks. You've barely seen the sun. But it is a common pigmentation pattern for women… during pregnancy." Alison held out her hand when Kate started to speak. "I'm not saying you *are* pregnant, I'm saying," she rustled about in her expensive leather handbag, "it's better to know sooner rather than later. And I didn't want you to be blind-sided after it's too late to do anything about it."

She held out a pregnancy test box, but Kate just stared at it.

"I'm taking the pill. *Religiously*. And Warren's been in the hospital for weeks."

Alison's lips tightened. "Have you been having your period?"

"Well no, but the doctor said it was common for women not to get their period when taking it."

"And it is," Alison's brows furrowed. "But if I were you, I'd want to be sure."

Kate took the box, hearing the tests shuffling about inside. She brushed her thumb over the little smiley face on the packaging. "I'll take it," she decided. The thought of a child bubbled up inside her, but she ignored it. There was no point even considering being pregnant until she'd actually taken the test.

"And if it's positive," Alison came closer, until her familiar perfume cradled Kate in a motherly embrace. "I'll help you with whatever you want to do. Don't think that just because I was a midwife you can't talk to me if you'd like to abort. All right?"

"All right." She'd had a pregnancy scare after Daniel, and it had been her first instinct back then. "You wouldn't judge me for it?"

The corner of Alison's mouth twitched. "I wouldn't judge you, because it's a choice I made myself."

Kate couldn't quite blink away her surprise. "You did?"

Alison nodded. "After the boys' father disappeared, I found out I was pregnant. Though I worked full-time, I still received benefits. I could barely keep the children I had clothed and fed. Adding another one to the mix would have sunk me. And it was the right decision to make. So no, there's no judgement here, Kate."

"Thank you," Kate replied sincerely.

"I'd recommend you take the first this evening and the second with your first wee in the morning, when your hypothetical HCG levels would be at their highest. Have you used one of these before?"

"I have. I, um, I had a wee before I left the hospital though," Kate explained sheepishly. "I'll need to wait."

Alison moved to leave. "Will you let me know if you want help with… with *things*?"

"I will." A thread of excitement stirred within her, but she quashed it. *Not yet.* "I'll speak to you in the morning."

Opening the door, Alison smiled gently. "I look forward to it."

"Fuck's sake," Kate muttered, having accidentally pissed on her own hand. Clipping the lid back on the test, she wiped it as best she could with toilet paper before placing it beside the sink and scrubbing her hands clean.

Her reflection stared back at her in Warren's enormous bathroom mirror. She squinted, inspecting her cheekbones. It *did* look like she'd caught the sun slightly, but it was summer. Surely a bit of a tan didn't mean she was pregnant? And she was on the pill. The doctor had been very clear about taking it at the same time every day.

22:00.

She took it at ten o'clock every day. She even had the alarm on her phone to prove it.

To kill time, Kate stepped into the shower, letting the warmth of the water wash her worries away. By the end of it, she had herself firmly convinced. She wasn't pregnant. She couldn't be.

The little digital indicator said otherwise.

Kate's stomach dropped like a stone as she darted forwards to pick up the test, letting out a cry of shock. She poked the little indicator, as though that would make any difference, but the message remained.

Pregnant 3+

Unbidden, her hand came to her navel, and she sniffed. Warren's baby was in there. With the next sniff, there was a smile. There was no stopping the waterworks then.

Kate made a beeline for the bed. Was this where their child had been conceived? *Or,* her brain interrupted, *was it in the room downstairs during the party?* She crept into bed, freeing her hair from the messy bun she'd placed it in before her shower.

When would she tell Warren? Was he well enough to handle the news? Would he be happy?

Kate hoped he'd be happy. Curling up into a ball and putting a soothing hand below her bellybutton, she pondered his reaction.

She was keeping it.

There was no chance that she'd get rid of it. Kate hadn't forgotten that Warren had placed half a million into her bank account, not to mention she now owned her house outright. Financially, she was set. She had choices now, rather than simply having choices thrust upon her.

Kate grinned like a lunatic when she thought of telling Warren of her pregnancy. Even the thought had her happy tears returning. *He's going to be as excited as I am*, she knew.

With that conclusion reached, Kate settled into sleep, dreaming of nurseries, the smell of babies, and happy families.

She woke drenched in sweat.

The dull, indistinct light pervading through the room told her that morning approached. Fanning herself, Kate stumbled across to the window, half tempted to press herself against the cool surface. Instead, she threw the window open, poking her head out as far as she could, relishing the feel of the crisp morning air against her skin.

Letting her weight rest on the windowsill, Kate grew drowsy, drifting in and out of consciousness where she stood.

The sound of a pained grunt had her eyes flying open.

She searched the dim gardens, past the koi pond and down the steps beyond. Was that movement in the woodland or her eyes playing tricks on her? Flashes of white drew her attention—*too* white. Nothing natural could be that white. Not for long anyway.

A huddle emerged from the woodland. Four or five men, perhaps.

Fuck.

A start of icy cold fear propelled her into action like a horse spurred into movement by the flick of a whip. She bolted to the door, taking a right down the corridor, following the path to Brax's office.

Adrenaline made her movements jerky and panic made her shake. Memories of the attacker's hands round her throat brought terrified little squeaks from her lungs, and Kate was glad that the house was deserted at this hour.

Even as she ran, she remembered that Brax was called away this evening. Panic threatened to overwhelm her then. How many of the guards were away? What would those men do when they broke in?

She burst through the door to Brax's office.

The only guard there was the one with resting bitch face.

She had never been so glad to see anyone in her entire life.

"Jesus, you scared the life out of me, woman," he scolded her, but she spoke over him.

"There are men," she panted, bursting through the door, "men in the woods at the back of the house. They're coming."

He looked at her like she was daft. "You mean those men?" he asked her, casually pointing towards one of the screens.

With the camera's night vision, Kate could see them more clearly. Her eyes drifted from man to man and, with a gulping sigh of relief, she recognised Brax and three of the security guards, Talbot among them. The former was moving stiffly, cradling one of his massive arms with a wince. "Oh thank god," she blurted in a single breath, resting her arms over one of the empty chairs in the room.

Her attention was then drawn to the fifth man—the one being dragged up the path with a bag over his head. "Who is that?"

Resting bitch face gave her a long look, his brows pulled down. "William Graves."

"You found him?" Kate rasped excitedly. "What about the girls that were with him? Do you know if they found Saffron's sister? Evie, her name is, she—"

He held up a hand. "You should get back to bed. I haven't received word about anything other than Graves. We'll know more soon."

Kate nodded, a hopeful smile splitting across her face. It was over. Her walk back to the bedroom was far removed from her earlier panicked dash; a thousand thoughts rushed through her mind, resulting in a leisurely stroll through the corridors.

God, she hoped they'd found Evie. And she hoped that this would bring Warren's crusade to an end.

The timing couldn't be better either. In her panic, she'd almost entirely forgotten about her pregnancy. Placing a hand against her lower stomach, she grinned. Warren would be safe. The baby would be safe.

That was all that mattered.

Her smile fizzled out when she passed the lift.

The cellar lay at the bottom of the elevator shaft, and right now Brax and his men were likely imprisoning Graves, ready to face Warren's justice. The same justice that her father had been facing since that fateful night he'd gambled away his club.

Had Kate not seen photographic evidence of her father's crimes, she would have been truly disturbed at what Warren was doing to him. She had never loved her father, but even she would have protested.

But now whenever she thought of him, she saw those girls underneath him. All she saw was their pain, their terror.

Graves was guilty of so much more. She forced herself to walk on, leaving the lift behind, reminding herself that whatever torture Graves would face, it was earnt. He'd *enslaved* people, trafficking them into sex work. When he worked as a police officer, he'd accepted bribes. He'd raped the women he trafficked, and facilitated the rapes of others, selling things that weren't his to sell.

When she re-entered Warren's bedroom, her thoughts were so consumed with the endless list of Graves's crimes that it took her a moment to realise she wasn't alone.

Movement was coming from the dressing room, and the fear that had so recently dissipated returned with a vengeance.

Please be Linda. Please be Linda. Please be Linda.

Though why the housekeeper would be rifling through Warren's possessions at dawn was a mystery.

Kate edged towards the doorway connecting Warren's bedroom to his walk-in wardrobe, hoping against hope that whoever was in there couldn't see her through the mirror.

At her first glimpse of the intruder—and her long, white-blonde hair, Kate's knees almost buckled with relief. "Saffron," she breathed, laughing away the tension.

Saffron yelped, jumping out of her skin. "Kate," she stammered, resting her hand on the open watch drawer in front of her.

"Is everything okay?" Kate stepped closer, frowning out her confusion. Her eyes drifted to the drawer. It was usually full to the brim, with Warren's watches neatly organised in plush fabric. But now it was nearly empty...

And at Saffron's feet lay a dark satchel, bulging with watches. A small black cylinder hung from its side, reminding Kate of a deodorant can.

"Saffron," Kate said again, her voice heavy with uncertainty. Saffron was... *stealing* them. "What are you doing?"

Despite the low lighting, she recognised the faint twinkle of a tear in Saf's eye. "I'm sorry," she whispered.

"What are you sorry for?"

The tear fell, but Saf zipped up the satchel and swung it over her shoulder. "For everything."

"You're leaving? But they have Graves, Saffron. They've just brought him in. Your sister—"

"I know. A friend has managed to get Evie out in the uproar of Graves's capture. I had a message. She's safe."

Despite everything, Kate's relieved smile was genuine. "Oh thank god. Is she all right?"

"He doesn't say," Saf shrugged, edging closer to the door that led out into the corridor. "But I need to get to her, Kate."

"You don't have to sneak away like a *literal* thief in the night, Saf. Graves has been captured. Warren's coming home in the morning. We'll give you whatever you need. You don't have to steal. Warren gave me money. I'll give you anything." Kate bit her lip, almost ashamed at the admission. "You're my friend."

"I almost killed you." The admission was so faint that Kate nearly missed it.

Even so, it trickled down her spine like icy water, leaving a shiver in its wake. "I'm sorry?"

Saffron gestured to the window. To the gardens beyond it. "The party. I… Graves made me do it. He was going to do to my sister what he did to me, Kate. He wanted Warren out of the way, so I agreed to be planted in the Ruislip warehouse."

"Where Rhys found you," she remembered.

"Exactly. I was to put the fentanyl—"

"*Fentanyl?*"

"It's a drug. An opioid. It's used for pain relief." Saffron bit her lip, looking away. "I put it in Warren's whisky the night of the party, but then he gave it to you." Her breath shook, her voice getting higher and higher. "And then the next day you wouldn't wake up."

Kate remembered Saffron shaking her awake, white-faced with terror—and suddenly her terror made sense. "You drugged me?"

Then Kate's heart skipped a beat.

She was an idiot.

She was a fucking idiot.

The night before Warren fell ill, they'd had shots of some fancy liqueur. With the ridiculous shot glasses.

And Saffron had fetched them both. Meaning she'd had plenty of time to slip the abrin into Warren's glass. And what had he said at the time?

His favourite shot glass. A cat… Or a kitten.

Saffron had known it too.

"The abrin," Kate hissed, her face scrunching into hatred.

"He had my sister," Saffron replied softly, fingering the little cylinder attached to the satchel. "It's not like I had a *choice*, Kate."

"You nearly fucking killed him." Rage roared through her like wildfire. Kate advanced, intending to claw Saffron's eyes out, but Saffron aimed the black cylinder in her direction and pressed the top down with her thumb. A thin stream of liquid shot out—

Directly into Kate's eyes.

An overwhelming, inescapable agony forced her eyes shut. Kate cried out at the wet flames licking at her eyeballs. Her hands scrambled about in the carpet, but she had no idea when she'd hit the floor. Her entire body locked up, her eyelids sealed shut by the pain, until it was as solid and palpable as those black moods she experienced, dragging her down to an inescapable pit of torment, and somewhere within it, a door slammed.

14

Warren

Warren sprawled lazily in the chair. He'd had fantastic ideas before—particularly when it came to his business dealings—but this really was his finest hour. Graves's agonised groans were music to his ears.

Given that he was still recovering from his liver transplant and Brax's arm was broken in two places, he hadn't been able to deal with Graves with brute strength. Admittedly, he could have asked one of his remaining security guards to mete out Graves's punishment. Most of them had grievances with Graves—it had been how he'd recruited them in the first place.

Ultimately, though, Warren was of the opinion that if he wanted to do a job properly, he needed to do it himself.

Sulphuric acid was doing the rest.

Graves was strung up by his wrists from either side of the room, his muscles stretched too far to allow him any purchase, but low enough that his feet dangled in a bath of acid.

Or what was left of them.

Every so often—or whenever Warren felt boredom creeping over him—he'd add a teensy bit more hydrogen peroxide. The result was, if he was being honest, a little unnerving. Whatever chemical reaction was at play would heat the combined liquids until they were boiling, eating away at Graves's feet until there was nothing left. The acid even dissolved Graves's bones.

The only thing that remained was the watery brown soup in the bathtub.

So Graves didn't bleed out, he'd then cauterise the wounds. That was good fun too, although the bastard eventually fainted each time.

As he had done so often over the past few hours, Warren topped up Graves's bath. "You know," he said, raising his voice to be heard over the furiously bubbling liquid, "I'm surprised you can feel anything at all at this point."

He screwed the cap back on, conscious of the fact that if he wanted to draw this out—which he absolutely did—then he couldn't add too much at a time.

Graves didn't even fight it. Perhaps his strength had been depleted after being strung up for so long, or perhaps he'd merely accepted his fate. Or was he delirious?

Warren knew how to fix that.

His laptop sat on the table on the other side of the room. The same table at which he'd once tried to interrogate Kate, before mistakenly presuming her to be innocent of her father's crimes. The first mistake of many.

He swivelled the laptop round. "Shall we have another look at this? It might cheer you up."

Graves's pain-filled gaze was low, his eyes barely opening.

Warren pressed play. He didn't even need to watch it. He'd replayed the video so many times since his men had discovered it on Graves's phone that he knew it by heart. A hundred times since he'd ordered his men to lock Kate in his bedroom once more.

"Will it hurt?" Kate's voice came. Despite himself, Warren turned his head. He was greeted with the sight of Kate, her hair shorter than she wore it now. The rest of her, though…

Her breasts were just as perfect, her skin just as soft. There was a brief glimpse of her pussy before Graves slotted between her spread legs, palming his hateful cock. "It'll be fine."

Kate gasped as Graves penetrated her, twisting her nipple as he did so. She turned her head to the side, screwing up her face, but Graves took no notice. He set a quick but steady rhythm, slapping his hand across her breast.

Warren tilted his head at Graves, suspended in the air. "Your technique is piss poor, by the way."

For the first time since his last cauterisation, Graves seemed to perk up. "Does she ever give *you* that look when you're fucking her?" he asked, his voice painfully raspy after the prolonged screaming.

"I've never touched her."

"My sources say otherwise. They say she sucked you off in the hospital." Graves let his head rest on his arm, lacking the strength to hold it up. "Do you see her face there?" Graves nodded to the video. "With the first slide of my cock, her head falls back and her eyes close. And that moan…" Graves's gravelly laugh was a mockery. "Like all was right in Kate's world, and it was all thanks to my cock."

"All thanks to your cock?" Warren said, his voice dangerously soft.

"I took her virginity. Does that annoy you? That she gave me something you'll never have?"

Warren said nothing. He merely picked up one of the empty jugs of sulphuric acid and dipped it into the murky brown acid solution, waiting until it was reasonably full.

And then he poured it over Graves's groin.

"It doesn't annoy me in the slightest," Warren replied, holding the jug steady as Graves began to scream and writhe, desperately fighting against the restraints preventing him from moving each of his limbs. Warren leant back slightly to avoid the fumes. "Because you won't have a cock left by the time I'm done with you."

The ravenous acid tore at Graves's shaft, peeling back layer upon layer of skin until it was a raw, bloody mess. Graves's screaming became constant; a shrill, undulating wailing that never ceased. Even then, Warren just refilled his jug and went again.

He only stopped when he heard the affirmative beep of the door's fingerprint scanner.

With his arm in a heavy cast, Brax stopped short at the sight of Graves's exposed skin. "Fuck me."

Warren narrowed his eyes, raising his voice to speak over Graves's agonised moans and pants. "I'm really not in the mood. What do you want?"

"I've noticed something… *off* about the recording. The one with Kate."

He knew exactly where Brax was going with this. And, if he was honest, Warren wanted to follow him there. But Kate had fucked Graves. What else was there to say? "You're only doubting because you like her."

"You like her too," Brax shot back. "More than like her."

"My feelings for Kate are irrelevant. Whether she was working with Graves or not, she certainly *fucked him*." He winced at his anger, putting a hand over his healing surgery scar. "Someone poisoned me, Braxton—on *his* orders. Someone close to me. She had ample chances."

Brax spread his uninjured arm. "*I've* had ample chances to poison you. And yet you're not suspecting me."

"Because you didn't welcome *him* into your fucking bed!" Warren roared, pointing at the pitiful figure strung up between them, his skin still fizzling even now.

"Go and see her," Brax pleaded with him. "She's locked in your room. She knows Graves has been captured. She thinks she's been locked in the bedroom for her own safety. Hear her side of the story whilst she's still in the dark."

Warren's gaze drifted down to the recording playing on the laptop. "I can see her side of the story, Brax. Plain as day."

"Your family is asking questions, Stone," Brax said simply, shrugging his massive shoulders. "They want to know where you are. Why Kate is in the bedroom."

"What have you told them?"

"You're in a business meeting, and Kate is feeling unwell."

He snorted. "Pepper sprayed, wasn't she?"

Brax nodded.

"Any sign of Saffron?" Creer had delivered the news upon Warren's return from hospital. God knows what had gone wrong between the two of them. He had been apoplectic with rage at first...

And then he had been shown the recording of Graves and Kate in bed.

"Saffron left through the woods, according to the security cameras. There are signs of a car being parked in the lay-by to the east of the house, so presumably she was picked up by someone." With a long sigh, Brax held the door open for him. "I can't hold your family off forever. Go and see them. Let them see that you're okay. And then go and see Kate."

Silenced reigned for a long moment, until Warren made up his mind. "Let the rest of the guards have their fun with Graves. Creer especially." Creer's daughter had been violated by Graves, the poor thing. "Give them free reign, but tell them to keep him alive as long as possible. He's not allowed a quick death."

He slunk from the room without a second glance, opting to take the lift directly up to the bedroom corridor. Even that stole his breath from his lungs, his hand never leaving the painful incision screaming at him every step of the way.

It was with trepidation, therefore, that he unlocked his bedroom door.

"Oh thank god!" Kate's gasp came. She had been perched on the armchair overlooking the garden window, but scrambled across the room. Twenty-four hours ago, her bloodshot eyes would have had him pulling her into his arms.

Now he just stood there, with the image of Graves fucking her burnt into his brain.

Kate clasped his cheeks, an odd softness to her gaze. His skin inwardly recoiled at her touch—at the fact that she had given a monster like Graves her virginity. "Brax said you'd left the hospital. Are you feeling okay? Come and sit down. You're as white as a sheet."

Watching her every move, he allowed himself to be led over to the couch.

"I should scold you for leaving the hospital without me." A smile played about her lips as she fussed over him. "I'm glad you're here. *Finally.*"

Are you?

"I've been busy," he replied.

The smile died a little. "I can imagine."

"What have you been imagining?"

"I don't know. Something abstract and awful and bloody. After seeing what you've done to my father, I prefer not to think about it too much. After everything Saf…" Kate's voice suddenly dwindled down to nothing. When she picked up again, her tone was despondent. "I caught Saffron stealing your things this morning."

"Brax told me." The watches were no matter. They could be replaced.

"She's the one who poisoned you," she said tearfully, her hand seeking out his in search of comfort. He let her take it, wanting to hear her speak, wanting to find any discrepancies he could. Instead, she simply shuffled closer to him, sighing into his neck. "She nearly killed you."

Kate smelled awful. Despite the hours that had passed since the pepper spray, there remained an acrid tinge to her scent.

Even so, the idiotic part of his brain wanted to give in and hold her.

The other half wanted to wrap his hand around her throat and never let go.

"Why did she pepper spray you?" he asked, trying to occupy his thoughts with something slightly less murderous.

"I may have been about to throttle her."

He snorted sarcastically. "Our minds work in much the same way, I see."

"Actually..." Her touch left him. Kate padded over to his bedside table, picking something up and concealing it in her hands. "There is something I need to tell you."

Warren sat up straight. Now that she was utterly cornered, was she going to confess to having a relationship with Graves? He'd expected her to flatly deny it. "What is it?"

She held out a thin white device with that crooked, excitable grin he had loved so much. "I'm pregnant."

All thought vanished. His entire world shrunk to him and Kate, both of them glued to what he now recognised as a pregnancy test.

A *positive* pregnancy test.

Warren choked in a breath; a storm rose within him, annihilating his plans for Kate after today's *revelations*. His eyes could do nothing but rest on Kate's stomach. "You're having a *baby*?" he asked incredulously.

Her crooked grin lessened slightly. "*We're* having a baby. We *made* a baby."

His brain whirred into action. *Now.* She was only telling him this *now*, after Graves had been caught. After that option had been extinguished. Was that why she hadn't escaped with Saffron? To try and pass the baby off as his, to gain a cushty position as mother to his child?

In her situation, he would probably do the same—except she didn't know that Warren knew about her relationship with Graves.

But there was still a chance that the baby was his. Unlocking his phone, he pulled up his doctor's number.

The man answered on the third ring.

"I need a pregnancy scan," Warren announced without preamble. "Tonight."

Warren sat like a sentinel, quietly observing Dr Baranovska fussing over Kate. An older woman with an Eastern European accent, she had been rather brusque with him, but appeared to view Kate as nothing more than a sweet lamb to be cherished.

If only she knew.

"This will be a bit cold," the obstetrician said, squeezing a thick gel onto Kate's stomach. There was no visible bump as of yet.

Kate jumped. "That is a bit chilly." She glanced at him, an excited glint hiding in her eye.

Warren was saved from having to reply by the obstetrician's question. "Are you wanting to find out the gender?"

"Yes!" Kate gasped immediately. "Are you able to tell now?"

Dr Baranovska shook her head. "We'll take a blood test after the ultrasound. That'll give you the results in about forty-eight hours. We need to check if there's a baby in there first." She glided what Warren presumed was the ultrasound scanner over Kate's stomach.

After a few moments of silence, the obstetrician turned the screen towards the two of them. "Say hello to your baby," she smiled.

The screen flickered, brimming with movement. But there in the centre sat a black-and-white blob that had Warren's chest expanding painfully, just as his stomach dropped. "That's it?"

"That's it." The obstetrician smiled. "Around nine-and-a-half weeks, I would estimate."

Kate's teary-eyed expression wrapped itself around his chest like a boa constrictor. "Is that the heartbeat?" she asked. "That little flicker at the centre."

"It is," she pressed a button on her machine, and suddenly a rapid beating seemed to pulse through the room.

"Oh my god," Kate whispered. "It's so strong!"

"And fast," Warren added.

"All perfectly normal," Dr Baranovska confirmed gently. "You can see all the different chambers of the heart have formed, and here—" She moved the mouse to hover over the baby "—are the arms and legs."

Warren swallowed. Nine-and-a-half weeks. What did that mean for the date of conception? He chewed on his thoughts whilst the obstetrician printed off copies of the ultrasound scan and took Kate's blood sample.

To test the baby's gender and, more importantly, its paternity. Not that Kate knew about the latter.

It would be another two days before the results came in. Two days of furious, endless waiting.

"Isn't this amazing?" Kate asked him after the obstetrician had left, wheeling the portable ultrasound equipment out with her—in addition to the cheek swab Warren had surreptitiously handed over. Kate cradled the ultrasound with a singular reverence, smiling and dragging her finger over the image. "This is our *child*."

Your child, he thought, closing the calendar app on his phone. *And Graves's.* The last brief tendril of hope had been firmly quashed, and he grieved its loss.

Nine-and-a-half weeks.

The first time they'd slept together had been at Alison's 60th birthday party—eight-and-a-half weeks ago.

The week before Alison's 60th, however, he'd been in New York, whilst Kate had been free to roam his home. He remembered sending a text to her every day. *You're not to touch yourself today.*

He was an idiot. A cuckolded idiot.

She'd been pregnant before he'd ever fucked her.

His mind made up, Warren escorted her upstairs, once again using the lift to avoid running into his family.

"Can we get the scan framed?" Kate asked, walking into his bedroom.

A non-committal noise left him. "A frame?"

"So I can put it on the bedside table," she said shyly. His beat of silence had a frown creasing her brow. "Is everything okay? You're very quiet. You're not in pain, are you?"

He closed in on her, pushing her up against the wall. Just as he had when he'd first brought her here. The feel of her body had his cock hardening, but he ignored it. A hate-fuck was *not* what he wanted right now. "Was it him you thought of when I touched you?" he snarled.

Panic grew on her like a weed. "Excuse me?"

"Did you ever tell him of how you begged for my cock?" His hand came up to her throat. He applied no pressure, merely holding her as a reminder of at whose mercy she now remained. "Or how you swallowed my cum like a prized whore?"

"Warren…" Injured eyes flickered between his, but her voice trailed off. She looked away, ashamed. *Good. You fucking should be.*

He laid his cards on the table. "When we seized Graves, we searched through his possessions. Including his phone. Imagine our surprise when we found a video of *you*."

"I've never met Grav—"

Warren grasped her jaw, digging his fingers in painfully. "Shut the *fuck* up." He shook his head, hate coursing through his blood like venom. "I've watched the video." A hundred times. "I've watched his cock entering you, Kate. Eight-and-a-half weeks ago. That's when we first slept together. Eight-and-a-half weeks. The baby isn't mine."

Her lips opened. "There must be some mis—"

"*Stop* lying to my face," he raged. "I may not be going to torture you, Kate. But I have evidence of Graves's crimes. And—wouldn't you know—now there's someone to pin it on." He seized the scan photo with a derisive snort and threw it to the floor. "If you think you're raising your child, think again. As you'll be in prison, it'll be taken from you and adopted. And let's hope it has a better childhood than I had."

He pushed away from her and headed to the door, taking care to tread on the scan photo as he did so. Hating Graves. Hating Kate. Hating himself most of all. Kate followed him, her pleas bleating in his ear, her arms holding onto him for dear life. Warren extracted himself from her grasp just long enough to slam the door, locking it with a hollow *click*.

The angry façade slipped away almost instantaneously. Like water slipping through his fingers.

Warren made it to the next door along the corridor—his walk-in wardrobe—before the sobs made it out of his throat, but when he closed the door there was no holding them back. Everything in here remained the same. The temporary bed he'd set up. The two-way mirror. The expensive ottoman. The empty watch drawer.

And yet in the space of a few days he'd lost his entire world.

The cold, hard truth stared back at him as he looked through the mirror. It was not his own reflection he saw, but Kate. She had slid down the back of the door he'd slammed in her face, tears streaming down her cheeks, hugging her knees as though that would comfort her.

She looked as heartbroken as he did.

Warren rested his forehead against the mirror. The moment he'd seen the scan, the moment he'd seen the *child*, it felt like everything had fallen into place. Children had never fallen onto his radar before, but he'd lost himself at the merest hint of one.

He wanted Kate. He wanted their child. He wanted to believe everything was a mistake.

Except that Kate had lied to him. And his child wasn't his. Kate not only knew Graves, she had fucked him—whilst she'd been with Warren, no less. She'd been *impregnated* by him. He gasped for breath amidst his sobs, lost in grief and misery.

Through it all, she had made him love her.

And that was a crime he couldn't forgive.

15

Kate

K ate glared into the mirror. It wasn't her puffy-eyed reflection she saw, nor the havoc she'd wreaked upon the room in which she'd been imprisoned—for the second fucking time. No, it was Warren.

She remembered his panic upon rushing into the bedroom on the day she'd contemplated suicide. Or the day he'd found her with the attacker's hands squeezing her throat.

It would have been better if he'd let her die.

There it was. That little voice that whispered black thoughts into her ear when she was at her lowest, always eager to kick her when she was down. It was the one thing she could count on. There was nothing else, only her and her suicidal thoughts.

Except now there was a new voice; the one that reminded her she had a child counting on her. A child that would be taken from her. Tears slid from her eyes, irritating the sensitive skin beneath them. Kate didn't even bother to wipe them away anymore.

She clutched the scan photo that Warren had crumpled beneath his feet, holding it against her heart. He'd turned on her—on *them*—without warning. More tears escaped when she closed her eyes. What kind of man did that to his own child?

But she knew the answer.

A man like her father.

It had never been a conscious thought, not really. But at the back of her mind, Kate had always known that she'd choose a better father for her children than her mother had chosen for her.

Failure, the malignant voice hissed.

And it was right. She'd failed her child before it was even born.

The black thoughts surrounded her then, swirling around her in a teeming whirlpool of misery, luring her towards the relief that death promised. Kate clutched the scan photo closer, as though it was a talisman of goodness, of *life*, but the black thoughts feasted on her anyway.

The bedroom door opened—and Kate's eyes opened with it.

Brax addressed her from the doorway, a crease between his eyebrows and a cast on his arm. His jaw twitched as he glared down at her, no doubt recalling the day before yesterday when she'd asked him if she could write 'CUNT' on it. In her defence, people should be warned. "Come with me."

"Go fuck yourself," she answered tonelessly.

He sighed. As though *he* was the one being inconvenienced. "Kate, I'm trying to help you here."

"Really? Because it looks like you're literally acting as Warren's guard dog. Does he tell you you're a good boy and give you belly rubs?"

"For god's sake," Brax muttered under his breath. His heavy footsteps stomped over to where she sat, but Kate went limp as he tried to lift her to her feet, doing her best impression of a child mid-tantrum.

Unfortunately, however, Brax was well versed in her strategy. He bent, hooking an enormous arm behind her knees and hefting her over his shoulders. Kate yelped as he stood to his full height, not used to the view from the top of the beanstalk.

"Put me down!"

Brax snapped out an answer as he bent to walk through the doorway. "I refer to your earlier response of *go fuck yourself.*"

"I hate you," she hissed, her hair swaying around her head as Brax strolled down the corridor. As much as she wanted to try and kick him in the balls, she also recognised that he was holding her one-handed, and a fall from this height could be fatal if she landed on her neck. And she didn't want to hurt her baby.

When he entered the lift and pressed the fingerprint scanner that would take them down to the cellar, however, Kate flailed like a trapped animal. There was only one reason he would take her down there. "No, no, no, no, no," she squealed. "He said he wouldn't torture me!"

"Calm down," Brax urged her, tightening his grip. "You're not going to be tortured."

Kate didn't believe him, but it made no difference.

The cellar was much as she remembered it. Dark, cold, and intimidating. The room in which Brax deposited her was different to the one Warren had questioned her in before. Steadying herself, she looked around to gain her bearings, her breath fogging in front of her face. A security camera perched high up on the wall, and Kate's eyes narrowed immediately.

But it wasn't the camera that held her attention; it was the long metal table in the centre of the room, a strange lip running around its edge. Although a shiver ran up the back of her neck, it had nothing to do with the freezing temperature.

A body on the table had her backing up against the wall. A sheet covered the corpse, but there was no hiding the congealed blood underneath.

"Is that my father?" she whispered, attempting to swallow her horror.

Brax didn't answer. He merely walked over to the corpse and pulled back the sheet.

Her gasp was a garbled, "*Daniel!*" She rushed over to the table, clapping her hands to her mouth. "Oh my god, oh my god, oh my god." Words of disbelief tumbled out of her, coupled with a barrage of guilt that nearly sent her to her knees. "What did you do to him?"

An immobile Brax watched her like a hawk.

"He didn't…" She gulped, seeing the crispy, blackened skin at his shoulders. Her shaking hands passed over Daniel's corpse, not quite daring to touch him. Had they set him on *fire*? "Daniel didn't have anything to do with this. He didn't deserve to die, Brax! He was a teacher." Kate sniffed, her voice shrinking until it was almost inaudible. "He had a *son*…"

At Brax's continued silence, the helplessness overflowed. Daniel may not have been the perfect boyfriend. Could she even call him that, when he'd ghosted her after he'd taken her virginity? Her gaze fell to the floor. "Is this what Warren plans? To torture and kill anyone who ever—"

Warren burst into the room, the door slamming against the wall. Paint flaked off, crumbling to the floor. The very sight of him sent Kate scrambling away, but his long legs tore across the room. Shaking with fear, Kate flinched away from him when he opened his mouth to speak.

A ringtone interrupted him.

The tension in Warren's face drained away. His hand disappeared into his suit pocket, retrieving his phone. Kate caught a glimpse of the caller's name.

Dr Baranovska

Instead of putting it to his ear, Kate frowned as he answered it on speakerphone. "Stone."

The accented voice of the obstetrician was a soft, out-of-place echo around the room. "Good afternoon, Mr Stone. The gender and paternity results have just come back from our laboratory. Is now a good time to talk?"

Paternity results?

But that was the least of Kate's worries. Daniel's corpse loomed large behind Warren. Moisture brimmed her eyes once more. No, this was not a good time to talk. The father of her child had apparently tortured her ex-boyfriend to death, and he lay in a pool of thick, congealed blood.

She thought of gender reveals, of happy couples learning the gender of their babies in clouds of pink or blue smoke, or popping balloons full of confetti, or even biting into cupcakes, surrounded by excited crowds of well-wishers.

Kate had the burnt corpse of her ex-boyfriend.

It wasn't what she wanted for her child.

Warren didn't share Kate's reluctance. "Yes. The gender. Are they a boy or a girl?"

"A girl," Dr Baranovska replied.

Incredibly, Warren smiled, his face suddenly lit from within as though they had indeed been transported to some fantastical gender reveal party. Kate blinked up at him, downright anxious at his mercurial mood changes. She had no space in which to rejoice at the news she was having a daughter, but Warren chuckled, rasping a hand over his face. "A baby girl."

Dr Baranovska continued. "Now, as for the paternity resul—"

Warren cut her off. "Delete them. I already know she's mine." He ended the call abruptly, looking down at her with the excitement she'd wanted to see when she'd first told him she was pregnant. His laugh was sweet. "We're going to have a little girl, kitten."

Kate couldn't laugh. Not when Daniel's corpse stared her in the face. "You tortured and murdered an innocent man," she whispered, huddling her arms around her middle.

Was that triumph in his expression? "This—" Warren pointed to Daniel's frozen corpse "—isn't Daniel. His name was never Daniel. He was never a teacher. This is William Graves."

Now she was utterly lost. "Excuse me?"

Warren walked over to the metal countertop on the other side of the room, shuffling through a drawer—just under the security camera.

"Were you watching the security feed?" she asked.

He threw a smile over his shoulder. "Clever kitten."

"Don't call me that."

Warren handed her two items: a passport and a driving licence. "Look at these."

She didn't have to look for long.

Graves

Mr William Daniel

Swallowing, she gazed at the photograph next to the name. *Daniel.* There was no mistaking him. Kate opened the passport, coming to the same conclusion.

Warren lifted her chin, holding firm against her attempts to jerk out of his grip. "You told me once that you met him on a dating app. That he disappeared after you'd slept with him."

"Yes," she whispered, recalling the miserable loss of her virginity. The hollow feeling when she realised he'd disappeared. The hopeful messages she'd sent, only to swiftly realise he'd blocked her. The hurt of abandonment. The loss of something that could have been.

Warren shoved his phone into her hands. "Look at this."

Kate nearly choked on her gasp when she realised what it was. She recognised the video at once; her bedroom at home. Her miserable bedroom with fading blue curtains and threadbare carpet. In the video, Daniel covered her, twisting her nipple. Kate winced, remembering the unexpected pain. "You've watched this?"

"It was on Graves's phone," Warren explained.

Graves. Not Daniel. "I don't understand," she said numbly.

"Your father mentioned Graves blackmailing him. He mentioned a recording specifically. There's business records of prostitutes operating out of your father's club, but no money was ever paid to him. I assumed Graves had something illegal on your father, but it was this recording."

Kate's eyes went so wide they hurt. "You mean my father has seen this?"

"It doesn't matter, kitten. Because you're *innocent*." He cupped her face. "I saw the recording. I thought you'd been fucking him whilst we were together. I thought it was you who'd poisoned me. I thought the baby was his. It never occurred to me that Daniel and Graves were the same person until you saw the body, until you said *Daniel*." Pressing their foreheads together, he sighed, before looking over to Brax. "I'm sorry I dismissed your concerns, Brax."

Brax? Was Brax really the person who deserved an apology here? Irritation prickled within her; a growing sensation. It was a chasm from which fissures began to shoot in all directions. "Concerns?"

Brax, who had exhibited a statuesque stillness in the corner since Warren's appearance, finally spoke up. "Part of that video has been muted. It's half a second at most, but your lips move. Because of the angle, you can't read them, but I suspected that it had been muted intentionally."

Humiliation fired in her cheeks, until it was all she could do not to vomit. "You've seen the video too?" Her throat tightened at the indignity.

"It doesn't matter," Warren threw an arm around her shoulder. "Come on, let's get out of here. We can talk properly upstairs." He seized the driving licence and passport from her hands, casually chucking them over to the metal counter.

Kate let herself be led upstairs, not taking a second look back at Graves's body. Relief spread through her the minute the lift doors closed, sealing the cellar off once more. She'd be perfectly happy to never see it again.

When the lift doors opened into the living room, Kate could breathe again. Her brain began to fire into action with the ramifications of their conversation in the cellar. "You're not going to have me imprisoned on false charges?"

He frowned, as though the mere suggestion was outlandish. "Of course not."

"You're not going to have my child—my *daughter*—taken away from me?" She gritted her teeth against her rising anger.

"I shouldn't have said that, I—"

"I need an answer, Warren."

"No, kitten. *We* are going to raise our daughter together."

For the second time that day, a whirlpool of emotions swirled around her. This time, however, it comprised neither melancholy nor suicidal tendencies.

It was rage. An icy fury that she finally let loose.

"Our?" she whispered, deadly quiet. Venom gathered in her, ready to strike.

"Look at it from my perspective, I th—"

"No, Warren, look at it from *mine*." Kate heard her voice harden into a snarl. "I've thought of nothing else since then. I've dreamt of nothing else since then. An endless nightmare of having my child ripped from my arms. Only to wake and realise that it isn't a nightmare; that *it's actually going to happen*." She narrowed her eyes. "All because I was too stupid to give her a better father."

The insult struck true, and Warren flinched.

"You would have subjected *our daughter* to the same upbringing you were blessed with," she spat. "The children's homes rife with abuse, foster parents with wandering hands." Kate's sneer creased her nose. "You know first-hand what those places are like, Warren—particularly what they're like for young girls."

"*I* was going to ad—"

"A father is supposed to protect his daughter from the world, Warren, and you tried to feed her to the lions before she was even born." He tried to take her hand, but she slapped away his touch. "I will be damned if my daughter knows what a failure her father is. She deserves better than *you.*"

"I will do anything, *anything,* to make this up to you," Warren swore, his expression as earnest as Kate had ever seen. "To make this up to her."

"Anything?" Kate smiled then, the relief washing over her like a balm. "Do you promise?"

"On my life."

"Good." She lifted her chin. "Then you'll agree to give up your parental rights over *my* daughter. The daughter you denied. The daughter you *literally* treated like shit on your shoe."

Warren began to protest, like a condemned man facing the gallows, but she spoke over him.

"How would you feel if a man treated *my* daughter the way you've treated me?"

He reared back slightly. "Kitten… That's not fair. I love you. I love you both."

Kate just shrugged. The words meant nothing to her. "And I'll never love you again," she spat, almost believing it. "You've made sure of that."

Kate had never lived alone before.

Perhaps that was why, when she heard that Sarah and Mattie were looking for a place of their own, she suggested they get somewhere together. Admittedly, she might have gone a *bit* overboard with renting a property. Did she really need a Victorian house with ten acres in the Surrey Hills? Absolutely not.

But it was *so* pretty. And it even had a games room for Mattie!

Plus Warren was footing the bill. So why not try and bankrupt him?

An unexpected benefit of her suggestion had been that, for the first time in her life, she had a maternal figure. A maternal figure providing advice and support in what was arguably the most vulnerable time in a woman's life: pregnancy.

"Hold still, sweetheart," Sarah murmured, dabbing antiseptic onto Kate's stitches with a shaky hand. She placed the dark bottle onto the kitchen countertop, screwing the lid back on. "You need to remember to eat today."

"I know. It just came on so suddenly." One minute she had been coming out of the shower, and the next thing she knew she was lying flat on her back with Sarah looming over her, on the phone to an ambulance. She'd promptly received four stitches to the gash above her eyebrow, had an emergency ultrasound to check the baby was okay, and been sent on her way.

From the way Sarah's phone had blown up with messages whilst they were in hospital, Kate knew who was on the other end.

That was the disadvantage of her current arrangement. It was hard to have nothing to do with Warren when she was living with his mother and brother. It was especially difficult to refuse his gifts. The strange cot he'd bought that, as best she could work out, would vibrate and hum the baby to sleep by itself. The belly band that he'd bought her in three different colours. Acid reflux tablets. The expensive massage gun. The compression socks. An entire wardrobe full of babygrows and sleepsuits, all with zips instead of poppers. A memory foam pregnancy pillow.

The memory foam pregnancy pillow had quickly become her best friend, but Kate would never tell him that.

"All done," Sarah leant back against the kitchen countertop, observing her handiwork. "It looks much better than it did yesterday."

"Thank you," Kate replied. She idly scrolled through her phone. A notification pinged up at the top of the screen; her weekly pregnancy update app. "The baby is the size of a cabbage now," she read out to Sarah, tilting the phone slightly to avoid the reflection of the late autumn sun coming through the vast kitchen skylights. "And apparently at thirty weeks she's starting to put on a layer of fat."

Sarah's adoring gaze landed on her bump.

"Apparently," Kate continued, "she's forty centimetres long and weighs more than a kilo." Kate snorted. "And yet I've put on two-and-a-half stone."

"Tch," Sarah chided, waving away Kate's complaint. "You're growing an entire human in your stomach. You're allowed to put on as much weight as you want."

"Ooh," Kate sucked in a breath, her hand going to her stomach.

"Are you okay?"

Kate nodded. "She's in a kicking mood lately. I can only assume her aim is to deprive me of any sleep whatsoever."

"Babies tend to do that," Sarah grinned, fiddling with her headscarf.

"And this is just the beginning." The gentle chiding of the doorbell rang through the house. Leo, who had been snoozing peacefully in a customised dog bed in the corner, jumped up, barking incessantly. "That should be Rhys and Alison."

It was.

Walking through the duck-egg blue front door, Rhys crowded Kate in an enormous bear hug in the entrance hallway. "Hello, darling. What have you done to your eye?"

"Fainted," she exclaimed, hugging Alison in turn and leading the two of them towards the living room. A bright, airy space furnished with plush sofas, complete with a view out into the vast garden, currently bathed in golden autumnal light. "But I'm fine. Apparently it's normal."

Alison frowned. "Have you been eating?"

Sharing an amused look with Kate, Sarah answered. "I've been on her case about that, don't you worry."

The conversation was largely baby-focused, but Kate remained silent unless spoken to, perfectly happy with listening. Leo jumped up onto her chair, settling in against her stomach. His favourite place to sit. "Who's my good boy?" she whispered, stroking his face. His little white tail whipped against her leg, but even its steady beat couldn't stop her eyes from drooping.

The next time she opened her eyes, darkness had fallen. Someone had placed a thin blanket over her, but Leo had jumped ship. She sat up from her slumped position, attempting to regain her bearings. Laughter from the dining room told her that Alison, at least, was still here.

She sniffed.

Had she really been lured into consciousness by the smell of fish and chips?

Kate had no sooner identified its source when Rhys slinked through the door. "Ah," he said, smiling. He held a familiar box emblazoned with the name of the local chippy. "You're awake. I was jus—"

"Is that my cheesy chips?" she blurted out.

Rhys surrendered it to her grabbing hands.

She did a giddy little wiggle when she opened the box to find a steaming array of chips drowning in cheese. "Oh my god, I love you. Baby needs cheesy chips." Snatching the fork from Rhys, she frantically stabbed her meal.

"Don't let Warren hear you say that."

"Warren can go and fuck himself," she said idly, moaning at her first bite and immediately going in for a second. "I've been thinking about this all day."

"Not the joy of impending motherhood?" Rhys suggested with a cheeky smile.

"Nope," she said thickly, her cheeks bulging.

Rhys simply shook his head. "You know, before I saw you eat, I would have said you were a normal human being like the rest of us. And yet you turn into this savage monster as soon as you smell food."

"You're not allowed to insult a pregnant woman. I'm pretty sure it's illegal."

"You were like this before you got pregnant. It doesn't count."

His hand came dangerously close to stealing a chip, and she swatted him away. "If you try that again, I swear to god I will bite you."

His lips pressed together. "See this is the kind of stuff I'm talking about."

"Only an idiot would try and steal food from a pregnant woman." She paused. "Have you had any luck in finding her yet?" Kate asked—because if she kept him talking, hopefully he wouldn't try and steal her food again.

"Saffron? No. We found the house she was staying in, but it was empty."

Gritting her teeth, Kate chewed away some of her anger. "I'm surprise Warren hasn't dragged her back here by her hair."

"Why do you hate her so much? I thought she was your friend."

Kate was incredulous. "Why *don't* you hate her? She fucking poisoned Warren!"

"Saffron was raped by Graves from the age of fourteen, and poisoned Warren to try and free her sister from the same fate. I'd have done the same in her position, no question. Am I slightly miffed that she didn't trust us enough to try and help her? Maybe." Rhys shrugged. "But you hate Warren too. Why do you care if he was poisoned?"

"I didn't hate him at the time."

"I'm wondering if you don't hate him at all."

Kate narrowed her eyes to slits to disguise the unease bubbling within. "He threatened to frame me and have my daughter forcibly removed from my care." And then there was the video…

The knowledge that countless people had seen her intimately. If it wasn't the baby keeping her awake, then it was that. True, Warren had paid a company to scour the internet for the video. They hadn't found it, but people *had* seen it.

Warren. *Her father.* Warren's guards. Brax. God knows how many of Graves's men.

It made her ill some days, to the point that Warren had paid for her to have therapy sessions.

The therapy had helped. She was better than she had been, but the knowledge remained.

Rhys stared at her for a moment, a frown weighing down his brow. "He told me that you want him to give up his paternal rights?"

She nodded.

He pulled his phone out of his trousers, fiddling with it until Kate heard her new phone ping. "Then I'm sure you'll want to speak to a solicitor. I've sent you the details of the law firm I use. I'll set up an appointment with them for you."

"You aren't going to fight me on it? Or try and change my mind?"

"Nope," he chirped, standing to his full height just as she finished the last of her chips. Rhys waited until he reached the door before speaking again. "Warren's here by the way; I brought him. I think he's with Mattie at the moment."

Kate's jaw dropped, and she flung a manky chip at his head. "You bloody judas!" It missed, leaving a damp patch on the wall where it had splattered. She stared hatefully in the direction of Rhys's retreating footsteps.

Struggling to her feet, Kate stormed upstairs, thankful that Warren was nowhere to be found. With any luck, he'd stay with Mattie over in the games room. Her room, she was pleased to report, was at the other end of the house.

Even so, she had barely closed her bedroom door before dissolving into tears against it. "Shh, shh, shh," she gasped to the squirming baby in her belly. "I'm sorry, bub. Did I wake you up?"

She whispered to her bump through her tears, softly cradling it and murmuring soothing words. It was comforting to focus on something other than her own feelings. Or the fact that her daughter's father was under the same roof.

Worry had done its best to consume her over the last couple of months. Was she doing the right thing? Keeping her baby away from her father? Kate changed into her pyjamas and crawled into bed, snuggling up to the pregnancy pillow.

Her bedroom was full of baby gear—most of which Warren had purchased and sent over. She'd sent the first couple back, unwilling to accept his gifts. But the more gifts that arrived, the more useful they became.

Especially the pregnancy pillow. Over her dead body would she be separated from that gem.

She smiled as her daughter moved again. A small shift, as though she too was trying to get comfy. "Are you enjoying the chips I sent down?" Kate asked her quietly, eyes closing. "They're not particularly healthy, but I think you'll like them." She chewed her lip, wiping away a final tear. "Just like your daddy's not behaved particularly well, but I think you'd like him too."

Kate snoozed into the early hours, phasing in and out of sleep, letting it carry her away like the tide. Her dreams were filled with her daughter to begin with. Who she would be. What she would look like. Would she take after Warren? Would she have his emerald eyes? Eyes that Kate could drown in…

And then her dreams took a turn, changing from an ethereal hopefulness into a darker, more sensual vista that had her moaning in her sleep. When she finally woke, needy and aching, Kate cursed her timing. With just a few moments more, she would have climaxed.

She opened her eyes and stared at the darkened ceiling. Alison had asked earlier what pregnancy symptoms she'd had. The truth was that Kate hadn't had that many. What Kate hadn't said was that her libido had gone into overdrive, and that she regularly woke in the night, desperate for relief.

Settling into what had become her usual routine, Kate reached into her bedside table for her vibrator. A rubbery, purple device that had become her closest friend in recent weeks.

Kicking off both her pyjama bottoms and the bedcovers, Kate sighed with relief at the gentle buzz against her clit. She nudged it further down, letting the pleasure dance across her aching skin. Whilst she would never admit it, the only fantasies that got her over the finish line involved Warren.

Kate lost herself in them, inching closer and closer to the end.

Until her finger slipped over the button, changing the setting from a gentle buzz to strong, jarring jolts that shook her teeth. The sudden shocks pulled an involuntary cry from her chest just as quickly as Kate pulled the vibrator away.

Barely ten seconds later, the door burst open.

Dressed only in pyjama bottoms, Warren stood there, coming to an abrupt halt at the sight of the juncture between her thighs.

Squealing with indignity, Kate threw the covers back over herself. "What the fuck, Warren? What are you doing here?"

He picked his jaw up off the ground. "Sarah invited me to stay. I'm staying in the room opposite. I… I heard you cry out. She said you'd fainted yesterday. I thought you'd hurt yourself, kitten."

He was staying overnight in the room opposite her, was he? How convenient. *Sarah, you are not being at all inconspicuous with your meddling.* "Close the door."

With a tilt of his head, he stepped inside and followed her order.

"That is not what I meant and you know it," Kate hissed.

He merely shrugged. "And yet—" Warren spread his arms, and Kate tried not to notice what it did to his tattooed chest "—here I am."

Yes. Here he was. The very man she'd been fantasising about, half naked in her bedroom.

She was going to hate herself for this in the morning, but fuck it.

"Are you going to carry on staring or are you going to come and help me?"

The carnal growl of satisfaction that left Warren's throat had her thighs squeezing together. "Fuck yes," he snarled, darting forwards and flicking the covers back in one strangely alluring movement. "Open your legs, kitten. I need to taste you."

Kate bit her lip. How could she refuse such a request?

He descended upon her like a starving man, his tongue going straight to her clit. Kate threw a hand over her mouth to muffle her moan, her eyes rolling back in her head with pleasure.

Warren had no qualms about being quiet. His groan sent ecstatic vibrations into her sensitive flesh. "I've missed you." His lips moved against her. "I've missed you so fucking much, kitten."

"Stop talking," she hissed, digging her hand into his hair. She yanked him back against her clit, gasping when he lashed his tongue against her. "Just make me come."

He had her at the edge quicker than she could have done it herself. Warren's long fingers curled inside her as he sucked her clit. With a muffled cry, she came on his tongue, her toes curling into his shoulders. Warren kept up with her movements, the blissful undulations of her hips that moved in time with the riotous pleasure storming through her body.

Until she fell back against the bed, utterly exhausted.

"Kate…"

The sound of his voice chased every ounce of contentment from her body, until shame nipped at her heels. Kate opened her eyes reluctantly.

Warren sat on his haunches between her legs, his thumbs hooked into the waistband of his pyjama bottoms, as though he'd paused midway through taking them off. His attention had been snared, it appeared, by the movement in her stomach. His hand hovered over it, not quite touching. "Is that the baby?" he asked in hushed tones.

She nodded, pressing herself into the bed.

He laughed then. A small, happy sound that spread a smile across his face. "Can I feel her?"

For the first time since he'd entered the room, he was close enough for her to realise that shadows hung below his eyes, and black bruises of restlessness had sharpened his face.

"No," Kate said, shoving his hand away from her bump. She pulled the bedcovers up like a shield. "Get out."

The disappointment on Warren's face was so palpable she might have called it grief. "But I thought we…"

She cuddled into the pregnancy pillow, her hands fisting the memory foam. "You thought wrong."

"I love you," he said weakly. One final offering. "I love her. From the moment I saw her heartbe—"

"And I hate you. Now get out. You've served your purpose."

16

Kate

Rhys lowered his voice, sitting next to her on the sofa in the solicitor's waiting room. "Do you want me to come in with you?"

Kate gave him a dismissive shake of her head. "I'll be fine." She rested her hand over her growing bump. With every step she'd taken towards the solicitor's office, she'd felt a sense of *wrongness* creeping up on her.

I love you. I love her.

"Would you forgive him?" she asked quietly, Warren's voice circling her brain like a pack of hounds cornering a fox.

He didn't have to ask who she was talking about. She saw it in his face. Rhys crossed his arms, deep in thought. "I don't want to upset you—"

She barely refrained from rolling her eyes. "So yes, then."

"Why did you ask the question if you don't want to hear my answer?" Rhys bit out.

That shut her up.

"If I'm being honest, Kate, I grew up without a fathe—"

"Miss Charlton?" A blonde solicitor called from across the room, standing in an office doorway. "I'm Jennifer, your solicitor."

With Rhys's help, she struggled to her feet, approaching Jennifer's office with a tired, bogged down waddle.

"Please sit," Jennifer said kindly, gesturing to a plush seat in front of a sweeping grey desk. "Can I get you anything? Tea? Coffee?"

"I'm fine, thank you."

At that, the blonde woman sat, shuffling through the papers in front of her. "Rhys tells me you're here to discuss the legal arrangements for your child, is that correct?"

Kate nodded. Between Jennifer's perfectly coifed hair, impeccable nails, and designer shoes, it was easy to see she was paid well. No wonder the car park behind the building was full of Range Rovers and Audis. "Correct," Kate said politely, trying not to think of the rumbling in her stomach.

Baby needs cheesy chips.

And baby also knew it was takeaway night tonight.

Which was a good thing, but Kate couldn't deny she was slightly ashamed of herself. Not because of the food she'd been eating, but because of her behaviour last week.

Because judging by what Sarah had said to Kate before she left for the solicitor's appointment, Sarah was once again inviting Warren over—both for dinner and to stay the night. And given that Mattie had changed the sheets in the bedroom opposite Kate's, Warren would once again be sleeping across the hallway.

"So I've read the details of the file. Warren Stone is not the biological father but wishes to adopt the child anyway," she recited, reading from the papers in front of her.

Kate blinked. "When was that, sorry?" Had the files gotten mixed up with another case?

The solicitor scanned the notes. "Four months ago. It mentions here you were waiting for DNA test results to come back, but Mr Stone believed that he wasn't the father. There was also the possibility of you being incarcerated, but him still wanting to adopt the child."

Swallowing her way into a nod, Kate replied. "Apologies, things have been a little bit hectic over the last few months."

"I can imagine."

But had Warren not mentioned having her child put into the foster care system? Kate would remember that until the day she died. "He mentioned still wanting to adopt even though he believed he wasn't the father?"

Jennifer's smile faltered somewhat. "Was that not something you were aware of?"

"No, it was," Kate lied. "Things have moved on since then, however."

"In what way?"

She winced slightly as the baby kicked her increasingly small bladder. "I'm not going to be incarcerated. I never did anything wrong. And Warren was always the child's biological father. But after his behaviour I don't want him to have anything to do with the baby. Can I still do that? Keep him away?"

"You can. In fact, if you were wanting to raise the baby alone then it would put you in a stronger position by not putting him on the birth certificate. Has he been reluctant to support the child in the months since?"

"Um… well, no. He pays for the house his family and I live in, actually."

The solicitor's eyes narrowed somewhat, as though she was trying to puzzle the situation out. Was that a hint of judgement she saw there? Or was that only what Kate expected to see? "Well even if he isn't on the birth certificate, you would still be able to claim financial support from him. The onus would then be on him to prove that he isn't the child's father."

"I don't have any intention of…" Kate trailed off. She had been going to say, *I don't have any intention of claiming financial support from him*, but she had to, didn't she? It wasn't like she'd be able to support her daughter by herself. Not in the way she deserved.

That thought was depressing in and of itself.

Jennifer gave Kate a moment to think before she spoke again. "Even if you don't list him on the child's birth certificate, however, he would be able to apply for parental responsibility. Either in an agreement with yourself or through a court order. And even if he was granted that, it doesn't necessarily give him the right to spend time with the child."

"It doesn't? So even if the father pays for everything and has parental responsibility, he may not even get to meet his child?" Kate said incredulously. How was that fair?

"It's important to remember that these rules apply to a wide variety of situations, including domestic abuse cases. It's not simply a case of the mother wanting to keep the father away out of spite. Sometimes it's to ensure the safety of the mother and child both," the solicitor said, her voice gentle.

"Sorry," Kate replied, duly chided. "I wasn't thinking."

"No need to apologise. I suppose out of context it does seem harsh."

Perhaps too harsh for mine. Especially if...

"But Warren definitely discussed the legalities of adopting her even when he believed she wasn't his?"

"He did, yes. He filled out the necessary forms, in fact, but a day or two after that we received instructions to halt the proceedings." The solicitor's lips thinned somewhat. "Does that change things?"

"I..." Kate's speech faded into nothing.

What was it he'd said in her bedroom that night? He'd loved her from the beginning. And yet that couldn't be further from his behaviour, from him treading her scan photo into the carpet like she meant nothing to him.

"Do you mind if I make another appointment at a later date?" Kate asked, after her silence had become deafening even to her. "I need time to consider the next steps."

"Of course," the solicitor said, getting to her feet. "I'll give you our business card, or you can ask Rhys to get in touch. I'm sure he won't mind."

The manner in which the solicitor spoke of Rhys indicated some measure of informality. "Is he a friend of yours?"

Jennifer opened the door for Kate. "I actually went to university with Aldous. He was one of my housemates." Sighting Rhys in the reception, she shook Kate's hand. "I look forward to hearing from you."

"Thank you for your help."

"It was a pleasure, and congratulations on your upcoming arrival."

Kate thanked her again, letting Rhys lead her out of the building with idle chit-chat that lapsed into silence on the drive home. At least until—

"Did you know Warren wanted to adopt her, even when he thought she was Graves's biological daughter?"

Rhys took the sharpness of her question in stride. "Yes."

"Did you know he told me he was going to have her placed in the care system against my will?"

He sighed, flicking his indicator on as they joined the motorway. "What someone says in anger and what they actually mean are often two—"

"Not when it comes to stealing someone's fucking baby, Rhys!" Another suspicion occurred to her. "Did you take me to that precise solicitor's firm because Warren had gone there regarding adopting her?"

A side-eyed glance. "Maybe." At her jaw drop, he threw all pretence out of the window. "Would you have believed me if I'd told you? No. Was Warren a dickhead? Yes. Obviously. Was he saying things to hurt you? Yes. Was he out of line? Massively. Did he intend to adopt her and love her as his own, even when he thought she was the daughter of the man who'd destroyed his life? Yes."

Kate huffed, repositioning the seatbelt over her stomach, but Rhys wasn't finished.

"Are you now punishing him by threatening to keep him from the daughter he would love to the ends of the earth? Jesus fucking Christ, Kate, do you know how much of a mess he is right now? He's sold his house and moved back in with me because he couldn't bear the thought of being there without you. He's up at all hours of the day and night, reading fucking baby books and buying anything that you might want." Rhys hit the steering wheel. "If you want my advice, stop trying to punish him and start thinking about what's best for your daughter."

Kate said nothing, because what was there to say? Was that what she was doing? Was that her *intention*? And he'd sold his house? When had that happened?

The thought of Warren staying up into the small hours for a baby that would never know him damn near broke her heart.

By the time Rhys pulled into the driveway of their new house, he'd calmed down a bit. "I'm sorry I shouted." Helping her out of the raised SUV, he hugged her. "It's just... a sore subject for me." He let out a heavy breath. "I'll see you in a bit, okay?"

"With Warren?"

"Yes," he opened the duck-egg blue front door for her. "With Warren."

Kate bade him goodbye, feeling overwhelming sadness—and a sudden craving for cheese. Mozzarella, specifically. She rushed to the kitchen like a panda on the hunt, ungracefully closing in on her prey: the fridge. She swung it open, sighing with relief at the grated packet of mozzarella in her sight.

Was it the best mozzarella that money could buy? No.

But was it *exactly* what she wanted in that moment? Oh yes.

Shifting from foot to foot in her excitement, Kate shook out a decent portion into a bowl before digging in, settling into a seat on the breakfast bar.

She was on her second bowl when Mattie entered the kitchen, quickly followed by Leo. "Ah," he said, smiling. "You're back. How did it go?"

"It was… enlightening," she said miserably. "Whilst you're over there, could you get me a can of Coke? And the rest of the packet of grated mozzarella?"

Grinning, he delivered her food. "You still wanting cheese?"

"Literally every chance I get. I can't wait until Rhys comes back with the food. The thought of warm mozzarella makes me want to swoon."

Mattie chuckled, pointing to the microwave next to her. "Why don't you put the bowl in there for a few seconds? That'd soften this up."

Her stomach grumbled its acquiescence. "Oh my god, Mattie, you're a genius." She pushed the bowl in, setting the timer for ten seconds. "Have you heard back from your interview yet?"

"I did actually." His smile lit up the room. "I got the job."

"Aah, well done!" she cried excitedly. "I'd give you a hug if I wasn't all cheesy." Trying her first handful of warmed mozzarella, she groaned. "Oh, this is so good. But when do you start? This is the one you really wanted, right?"

"Right," Mattie slid onto a seat on the other side of the breakfast bar. "It's an independent shop, and quite a lot of their stock is model trains as well as *Warhammer* stuff, but I'm excited."

"Good, I'm glad."

He smiled, giving her belly a quick glance. "Uncle Mattie can save up to get his niece a little model army of her own." He glanced down, seeing Leo waiting patiently at her feet. Probably for some cheese. "*Space Wolves*, perhaps? After Leo?"

Kate caved and sprinkled some cheese on the floor. "I wouldn't do that for just anyone, you know?" she assured the little dog. "I'm sure Leo will keep them in check. Won't you, puppy?"

"He's seven."

"That doesn't matter," Kate picked Leo up—albeit with difficulty—his stubby front legs poking outwards. "You'll still be the cutest little puppy even when you're twice that age."

A laugh of disbelief echoed through the kitchen. Both Mattie and Kate looked over to the doorway to find Sarah with her hands on her hips, one of them clasping a letter. "We're having dinner in a minute."

Kate scrunched her lips to one side, offering what had quickly become her only defence. "Baby needed cheese?"

Mattie had something else on his mind. "Is that Dad's handwriting?"

"Err…" With a small sigh, Sarah placed the letter on the breakfast bar. "It is, yes. Dad and I are getting divorced, sweetheart. This is the first step." She took Mattie's hand, but Mattie pulled her into a hug.

"I'm sorry, Mum."

Sarah's shrug was that of a woman who had long since accepted her marriage was over. "Did you know they warned me about it after I was diagnosed?"

"Who? And warned you about what?" Kate asked.

"The Macmillan nurses who work in the cancer care team. They warned me about divorce. The fact that twenty percent of men whose wives are diagnosed with cancer divorce them."

"Wait," Kate abandoned her precious cheese. "Seriously?"

"Seriously." Sarah gave a sad little laugh. "They even gave me a leaflet about it."

As if getting diagnosed with cancer wasn't bad enough…"What's the rate of women divorcing husbands diagnosed with cancer?"

Sarah paused for a moment. "Something like two to three percent, the leaflet said. It's awful when you think about it."

Shaking her head, Kate looked away in anger. The situation had struck a nerve she didn't know she had; she had cared for her father all those years and he'd abandoned her in a heartbeat. "I guess *in sickness and in health* doesn't mean jack shit when it's the men who have to care for the women instead of the other way around." And here she was pushing away a man who was desperate to care for her. A man who, by all accounts, would love her and their baby to the ends of the earth.

"The meetings that I've been going to on Wednesdays, the cancer support meetings that Warren takes me to, myself and some of the women there have a little WhatsApp group and I'm not the only one it's happened to. There's about twenty of us in total, and four marriages have broken down so far." Sarah clocked her jaw to the side. "Andy was apparently the quickest to ask for a divorce though. I didn't even start chemo before he jumped ship. Literally." Sarah looked to Mattie suddenly. "I'm sorry, sweetheart. I shouldn't be talking about your dad that way in front of you, I kn—"

"Yes, you should, Mum," Mattie said forcefully. "Dad's a coward, and I'm not a child. I know what he is. You don't have to protect the name of a man who abandoned you when you needed him most. Besides," he smiled, patting Kate's shoulder, "we have a new family now."

Kate positively beamed at the inclusion. "And we're here for you. No matter what."

The doorbell rang, quickly followed by Leo's deep yaps.

"I'll get it," Mattie offered, moving towards the corridor that led to the front door. "It should be Warren with the food."

Whilst her heart leapt at the mention of Warren, her stomach panged at the mere mention of food. The sudden need for cheesy chips was so powerful it almost had her doubling over. "Oh my god, I'm so hungry."

"Your little girl is telling you what she needs," Sarah grinned.

"I'm so glad she chose cheese and not something disgusting like olives or fish—"

Sarah gave a gasp of outrage. "Do you not like fish?! Even fish and chips?"

"She never has done," Warren's voice came from the arched doorway. He stood, weighed down by bags of takeaway. Rhys and Alison followed him into the room, the former also bearing bags of food.

"Darling," Sarah cried happily, sweeping him into her arms.

Kate watched them both, feeling slightly like an outsider. She remained silent as the food was dished out, unable to take her eyes off Warren. Unable to think about anything except the fact that he would have adopted the baby even if she wasn't his. Unable to see anything except the dark circles under his eyes or the newfound sharpness under his cheekbones. Unable to stop visualising him in her mind's eye, wandering around his house, alone and grief-stricken.

When they eventually migrated to the living room, Kate found herself taking the seat next to him on the sofa. Sarah and Alison dominated the conversation, sharing memories of raising sons and the mischief they found themselves in. Kate laughed when it was necessary, but she couldn't help keeping an eye on Warren. On his stiffness. On the strain packed onto his shoulders.

Halfway through the meal, he spoke to her. Quietly, he pulled two unopened takeaway trays from the bag at his feet. "We passed an Indian on the way here," he explained. "I thought you might want these."

A smile curved her lips when she finally deciphered the scribbles on top. *Gulab jamun.* And the other one—

Salt and pepper chips.

"Like we had when we were kids?"

Warren nodded. "Like you used to steal from me when we were kids."

Glancing around to see if anyone was listening, she found Rhys watching them like a hawk, but he quickly looked away. *Nosy.* "Thank you," she whispered.

Uncertainty was clear on his face. "There's something I have to tell you."

"It's okay, Rhys already told me you sold your house."

A sigh clipped the back of Warren's throat. "It isn't that… It's your father."

Spine straightening, she bit out a reply. "Is he dead?"

"I handed him over to the police. Or at least I've arranged for him to be handed over, as well as all the evidence I had on Graves. It won't happen for a few weeks yet, but there's enough evidence to have him put away for the rest of his life. The CCTV footage from his club alone…" Warren hissed in disgust. "Prison is where he belongs. It's where he's always belonged."

"I know," she said truthfully. She poked the tray of salt and pepper chips with her fork. "Do you want to share?"

He nodded, letting a companionable silence fall between them as they ate. Their forks clashed occasionally, fighting over a particularly tasty-looking chip, but Kate noted that he always let her win. Between the two of them, the gulab jamun didn't last long either.

When they'd finally finished eating, with the rest of them migrating to the dining room to play crochet poker, Kate held Warren back. "Come upstairs."

Warren's head shot around to face her. Hope overflowed in his eyes, but his brows drew down. "Are you going to kick me out when you're done like last week?"

"Would you still come if I said yes?"

Warren's exhale was long and steady, as though he had already accepted disappointment. "If it's the only way I can have you, then yes."

He followed her upstairs, a silent shadow trailing in her wake. As soon as she closed the door, however, he struck, clasping her face with both hands and claiming her in a lustful kiss that drew whimpers from her lungs. "Wait," she breathed.

Shaking his head, he replied. "Just let me hold you. Please. Just give me a moment. Something to remember."

That gave her pause. "Okay," she nodded. She'd never seen him like this. Emotion hit her as he clutched her in his arms, squeezing tightly and burying his nose in her neck.

"*Kitten*." His voice was muffled in her hair, warming the skin beneath it.

The baby kicked between them, as though she was furious at being squashed.

Warren lurched back, croaking slightly. "Was that her?"

"It was." She took his hand and placed it against her bump for the first time. "Our daughter."

17

Warren

*O*ur daughter.

Warren was infused with a love so strong it nearly felled him. His other hand came up to her belly, feeling the movements beneath. "She's so strong," he murmured, joy warring with loss inside him, strangling his voice.

"She is. Alison told me that it's possible for babies to bruise their mothers when kicking."

"Has she bruised you?"

She shook her head, never taking her eyes away from him. "No."

"Good," he said sincerely, bending down to address her bump. "I'd have to have words with you if you were beating your mummy up, you know," Warren whispered. He grinned as their daughter gave him a nudge in response to his voice. "Hello, baby girl," he murmured.

His attention shifted when Kate pressed her hand against his cheek. But when he looked up, he realised she was crying. Rising, he pulled her close. "Kitten? What's wrong?"

"I'm sorry," she sniffed. "Pregnancy has me bursting into tears constantly these days. Do you know I cried at a Dog's Trust advert on telly the other day? I just thought of Leo in that situation and I had to hug him for ages afterwards…" She laughed tearfully, wiping her cheeks dry. "I went to the solicitors today."

"I know." He swallowed, half expecting her to hand him an agreement that would award her sole custody. "Rhys told me he'd sorted it out."

Kate looked at him then. A long, hard look. "He told the solicitor I was there to continue discussing your adoption of the baby. Something you'd apparently started after mistakenly assuming she wasn't yours." He went to step back, but she grabbed him. "After you told me you were going to have her put in the care system."

Warren looked away, finding it easier to focus on her bump.

Kate, however, continued. "You lied to me. You let me hate you all this time for something you never intended to do."

"I wanted to hurt you," he admitted, caressing her stomach. His voice was a mess of emotion, but he persisted. "But from the moment I saw her on the scan, I loved her. It didn't matter if she was my biological child. I had proof that you and Graves were an item, but she... she was innocent. She was my daughter, no matter what."

"You were going to raise the daughter of the man you hated most in the world?"

His answer was swift. "Yes."

"You were going to raise the daughter of the man you tortured to death?"

"Yes."

Kate drew closer to him then, her belly once more pressing against him. There was no anger on her face, no hatred. Her eyes flicked to his lips, and Warren seized the opportunity presented to him.

Just as before, he gripped both sides of her face, taking full control of the kiss. In contrast to before, however, his lips were gentle. It wasn't lustful, or aggressive; it was the apology he couldn't put into words, a declaration that he would never again wrong her, a promise that he would love her and their daughter until his last breath.

Kate pulled back. "It was never about what you were going to do to me, you know?"

"What?"

"You were going to have me put in prison."

Her words shamed him. "The video of you and Graves…"

"Exactly. You had what you thought was proof. I can forgive that. I wish you'd talked to me instead of flying off the handle like a complete fucking idiot, but I can forgive that. It was you saying you were going to put her into the care system that I couldn't forgive."

He cottoned on to what she was saying. "Except I never intended to…"

A small smile spread across her face then. "Exactly," she said again. "You love her just as much as I do. You would have loved her even if she was Graves's daughter."

Warren gave a shake of his head. "She was always mine. I loved her from the first. Just like I loved you. And I'm sorry for what I put you through. I'm sorry for everything."

"Good," Kate said, with the air of someone completing a long-dreaded task. "Because she's going to need her daddy, you know."

Sucking in air like he was taking the breath of life, Warren choked out a reply. "You're going to let me see her?"

"I should hope so, if you're going to help me raise her."

Were Kate not pregnant, he would have swept her into an ungainly circle. Instead, Kate's giggles filled the room as he pecked a thousand kisses onto her head. "I love you," he said repeatedly, almost light-headed.

She stilled him with a hand to his chest. "I hope you know that means waking in the night to a screaming baby. And changing dirty nappies. And helping me recover from the birth."

"I'll do them all," he vowed, finally moving down to her lips. She met him eagerly, and he groaned into the kiss, laving his tongue against hers. "You won't have to lift a finger."

Her eyebrow cocked. "I'll remember that."

"Do," he insisted. "Keep me on my toes."

At once, her expression changed into something altogether different. "I'd rather keep you on your knees, if I'm honest."

Warren's nostrils flared; a predator catching the scent of his favourite prey. "Are you going to throw me out again?"

"No." Kate backed away, her knees meeting the edge of her bed. Warren trailed her all the way. "You live here now. I've made the decision."

His lip curled at the irony. "You're kidnapping me and holding me hostage in your bedroom?"

"I may have been inspired by a certain someone, I admit." She gave him a knowing smile.

He inclined his head towards the mirror on the wall. "I don't suppose there's a room on the other side of that from which you're going to spy on me when I get changed."

"Oh no, I'm going to have a front row seat, thank you very much. And do you know why?"

Her heavy-lidded eyes gave him some idea. "Tell me," he said, his hands still roaming her body, unable to believe she was here in front of him.

"Because I lied when I told Alison my pregnancy symptoms were minimal."

He paused in the act of taking her dress off. "Oh?"

"I've been so fucking horny it feels like my skin is crawling. All day. Every day," she whimpered as he wrenched her dress apart, splitting it down a seam until it sagged open to reveal her heavy breasts and engorged stomach.

"Oh kitten, *look* at you," Warren whispered, shrugging the ruined dress off her shoulders until it fell to the floor. He cupped a bare breast, satisfaction zinging through him at her moan. "No bra?"

Her eyes closed when he moved to her nipple. "Too sensitive."

Warren paused. "Too sensitive for me to touch?"

"God no," she bit her lip. "Too sensitive because the fabric rubs and it turns me on and that's really not what I need when talking to your family. Touch me, please."

He yanked his shirt over his head and slid his arms around her, guiding her onto the bed. "Fuck," he whispered, unable to resist running his hands over her bump as he descended. "You're the most beautiful thing I've ever seen."

"Even with my very large, very attractive maternity pants on?" Kate said, her face disappearing behind her baby bump as he knelt.

Warren hooked his fingers underneath them, inching them down slowly, building her anticipation. He kissed her bump, resting his forehead against it. In relief. In adoration. In excitement. "I happen to like your maternity pants."

But when he took them off her...

"*Christ*, kitten," he groaned hoarsely, spreading her thighs. "Pretty and pink and perfect."

Kate wasn't having it, gyrating her hips towards him. "Stop looking and touch me. *Please.*"

He snarled. "God, I love hearing you beg."

And then he pounced.

Kate's triumphant *yes* spread through the room like a shockwave.

He laughed into her pussy, sucking her clit and lashing it with his tongue. He'd intended to savour this, to bask in her taste, but now he was here he couldn't hold back, curling his fingers inside her until she was balancing on the edge and crying out for more.

"Right there, right there, right there!" she panted.

He gave it to her. Eagerly.

"*Ohhhh*," Kate shrieked, falling into ecstasy above him. She was rabid in her pleasure; fists tightening, toes curling, voice breaking, thighs squeezing, pussy clenching, until Warren became slightly jealous of how long her climax lasted.

"Stop," she rasped finally, her thighs falling back to the bed in a heap. Rising to his feet, Warren watched her sigh. "Oh god."

He bent over her, slinking his hand into her hair and tightening. "That isn't my name, kitten."

"Warren," she said, grinning lazily.

"Good girl."

Kate raised an eyebrow, glancing down at her bump. "Can I be a good girl again? Or are you going to treat me as though I'm made of glass just because I'm pregnant?"

"I'll give you what you need when you need it. If you need a back massage because you're in pain, I'll do that." He gripped her throat, tightening slightly. "And if you need to be punished, if you need to be spanked until you're crying out for mercy, or you need to be forced to swallow every drop of my cum, then you can be damn sure I'll do that too." Warren finished with a gentle kiss. "What do you need, kitten? The former, or the latter?"

"The latter," she said hungrily.

His softness withered. "Sit on the edge of the bed and spread your legs."

Watching her position herself, Warren undid his belt, freeing it from the belt loops on his trousers until he could wind it around his hand. "I didn't use bondage before, did I?"

She shook her head, lips parting slightly.

The form popped into his head. The one he'd asked her to fill out whilst he was in New York, listing all of the things she wanted to try. "You're fine with it, as I remember."

Those wide eyes couldn't hide her excitement.

"Arms behind your back, kitten." She sprang to follow his order, and he locked his belt around her wrists like handcuffs. Task accomplished, he stood back to observe his work, his cock rock solid beneath his fly. With a quick zip, he freed his erection, letting it hang heavy before her.

"Open your mouth," he commanded her, aiming his cock at her with one hand and fisting her hair with the other. "You kick me if you want me to stop, understand?"

Kate didn't answer. She simply leant forward and fixed her mouth over his cock. He groaned at her sudden heat, driving into her mouth, addicted to the suction she created.

"I'm going to fuck your mouth. You're going to swallow every drop of my cum, and you're going to thank me for it. Aren't you?"

Her noise of acquisition was muffled around his cock, its vibrations clenching his jaw.

He didn't wait then, seizing her head with both hands to plunge inside her. Her cheeks hollowed out whenever he drew away, urging him to sink back in. With every movement, Warren felt more confident, giving her more, until he could feel the back of her throat.

Pleasure was a savage sneer on his face, roughening his voice and his touch, pushing her limits with every stroke until he could feel the end approaching, until he could concentrate on nothing but seizing it and holding on with both hands.

"Every drop," he reminded her, his balls pulled tight underneath his cock. He exploded with a roar, emptying himself down her throat. True to her word, she swallowed him, adding to his mountain of pleasure, turning the world to rights until it was all he could do to stay standing.

Breathing heavily, Warren pulled out, releasing Kate from her bondage and guiding her to lay back down. "What do you say?" he asked, swiping a bit of spillage from the corner of her mouth and returning it to her tongue.

She licked at it eagerly. "Thank you."

He bent, knee thudding into the carpet.

Struggling onto her elbows, she gave him a quizzical look. "What are you doing?"

He spread her thighs, exposing her slickness. "My cock may need a moment, but my tongue is ready for more."

Giggling slightly, she flopped back onto the bed. "Do your worst, then."

He intended to do his best. Warren gathered her wetness on his tongue, eagerly swallowing everything he could find, enjoying her chorus of sighs. "Oh kitten, I'm just getting started."

"*Enough!*" Kate cried, pushing his head away.

Warren rose, licking his lips. His fierce erection had likely stabbed through the mattress by now, but he was in no hurry to put it to good use. "Never," he whispered, kissing her bump. "It'll never be enough. I need you too much."

"Then take me. I'm yours."

He rose to kneel between her legs, his hands landing on his thighs. "I don't want to hurt you."

Lips pursed, she grinned. "Yes, you do. I believe you said something along the lines of it making you hard."

"I don't want to *really* hurt you." His hand skimmed her bump—and the child beneath it. "Or her. My girls." They were everything to him, and the past couple of months had been abject hell. The sleepless nights. The *pointlessness* of everything.

"You literally had me choking on your dick half an hour ago."

"Your mouth is *very* far away from our daughter." He stretched his body out over her, careful of her stomach. "Kate, I am nothing without you. I *have* nothing."

Her expression finally sobered. "I'm allowed to have sex, Warren. The midwife says it's fine. If it hurts, then I'll tell you to stop."

He knew. He'd read so many books on pregnancy and childcare that he could have likely repeated what the midwife said word-for-word. Even so...

There was the hypothetical, and then there was reality.

"I love you," Kate's soft voice came. He groaned when her hands settled around his neck, pulling him down further, until her lips were at his ear. Their bodies came together, his hips angling towards hers. "So make love to me. Show me what we've been missing."

He was lost.

Warren slid inside her, drawing moans from them both. Rough and smooth, a melody that was uniquely theirs.

"Sing for me, kitten," he rasped, setting a slow, steady pace. "Let it out. I want to hear it. I *need* to hear it."

He leant back on his haunches, his thrusts coming harder and faster. "I love watching my cock disappear into you," he grunted. "I love seeing you spread beneath me. All mine. Say it. You're all mine."

"I'm yours, Warren—*oh!*" Kate cried out when he tilted his hips. "There, there, *there*. Don't stop."

Warren kept up his steady pace, sheathing himself inside her, letting his ferocity loose. "You're perfect, kitten. So fucking perfect. This is how we were meant to be, you and I. Together. Locked tight. I was never right without you, boy or man. Every day separated from you was a lifetime. But you… you're my home, Kate. Always."

"And you're mine," she panted, interspersing her words with moans.

Her thighs hugged him, squeezing his hips. Pain registered on his forearms, and he smirked when he realised his kitten's claws were sinking into his skin. "That's it—*oh,* fuck, I can feel you squeezing my cock. Come for me, kitten. Come for me."

Kate's body broke, her spine bending with the sheer force of her climax. Her moan of ecstasy was a high, rasping wail, but her little claws never released him.

That was what took him over the edge.

His body curled into hers, taking her lips and groaning into their kiss, cock pulsing into her as she drained him of his seed. "Mine," he bit out. "You're mine, kitten. *Mine.*"

She bit right back. "I always was."

18

K ate deposited the final box into the room, rubbing the side of her—admittedly enormous—stomach. Leo trotted in behind her, hopping up onto the armchair to survey his new kingdom: the nursery.

God knows he was in for a shock when their baby arrived.

She eyed the hospital bag in the corner, chewing her lip. The pain had woken her up this morning, long after Warren had left for his meeting at Stone Holdings in London.

The last meeting he'd attend before taking his paternity leave.

She glanced around the nursery, still feeling that itch to do *something.* The baby wouldn't be needing these books for months yet. Even so, Kate organised them on the bookshelf, currently mostly occupied by black-and-white books with large, easy-to-see writing.

Padding around the room, Kate reasoned with herself. The baby would be staying in their bedroom for months yet. The nursery didn't *need* to be perfect.

And yet…

She eyed the boxes of baby wipes and nappies in the corner with a twitch of her lip. That could be organised.

With some difficulty—and a handful of ungainliness—Kate knelt and got to work, stacking the baby wipes in the bottom drawer of the changing table. All the right way up and facing the same way, of course. Four boxes of baby wipes later, she was satisfied.

Then she started on the nappies, organising them by size from left to right, side eyeing Leo hopping down from the armchair and toddling from the room, abandoning her to her work. She should really have bought little separating boards like she'd done with the wardrobe, where she could easily tell newborn clothes from three to—

A sigh from behind made her jump. "I told you I'd do that," Warren grumbled, his hands slinking underneath her arms. "Come on. You're thirty-eight weeks' pregnant. You should be laying on a sun lounge being fanned and fed grapes."

"I mean, it's literally snowing outside." Kate allowed herself to be helped up, leaning back against Warren's firm chest. He still wore a suit, but his tie had been loosened. The top two buttons of his shirt had also been undone, exposing the faintest hint of the tattoos and chest hair that lay beneath. "But then why do you not come bearing grapes?"

She twisted around in time to see the faintest hint of nerves on his face. "Well," he said, "it's not grapes, but I do come bearing gifts."

"Oh?"

He pulled a long, flat jewellery box from his pocket. A familiar one. "This isn't so much a gift as something I found when I was unloading the boxes from the old house. I was worried it had gotten a bit banged up, but it survived."

Kate opened it. "My mother's locket," she whispered, running her thumb over the faded heart. Her other hand drifted down to her stomach. "I've been thinking about her a lot lately."

He lifted it gently from the box to place around her neck, pulling her closer to clasp it. "You're missing her?"

"Is it silly to miss something you've never had?"

Warren pulled back to hold her gaze. "I think that's when you miss it most of all."

Her breathing was a jumpy mess, not helped by the soreness across her stomach, but she ploughed through. "She must have done this with me, you know. Prepared clothes and nappies and muslin cloths and breast pumps and dummies. Written out a birth plan. Read baby name books until their covers fell off. Gone through her hospital bag twice a day, just in case anything had made a break for it." Kate took his hand, looking at the floor. "And then I came home from the hospital, and she didn't…"

A firm hand lifted her chin until Kate stared into Warren's intense eyes. "You're not going to die," he said, as though he could ensure it by sheer force of will. "The midwives are aware that your mother haemorrhaged, kitten. They're going to be on high alert for that eventuality. Medicine has advanced since you were born. You're going to be fine."

Kate let herself be pulled into his arms—as much as she could be with her belly in the way. She fiddled with the locket as she did so, stilling when she felt something moving around inside it. Reluctantly stepping back from Warren's embrace, Kate paused. "I think the glass in here might have been broken in the house move."

But when she opened the little heart, it wasn't just the glass that fell out.

The tattered old photograph of her pregnant mother, her father, and Aaron fluttered to the floor. The closest thing Kate would ever come to a family portrait.

Followed by a microSD card.

Warren bent to pick the glass, photograph, and the little memory card up. "Did you know the SD card was in here?"

She shook her head, rubbing the sore spot on her stomach. "Do you think it could be family photographs?" she asked hopefully. "Photographs of my mother."

"I don't know if microSD cards had been invented back then," Warren mused, pulling his phone out of his pocket and depressing the memory card slot. It popped out. Warren slid the microSD card into place with a grim expression. "Perhaps I should see this first. Some of the videos from your father's club were horrif—"

Kate began to protest, stepping onto her tip toes to see Warren's phone screen. "It might be more photos of my mother. Why else would it be in her locket?"

She watched as Warren opened a video file, but then the blood drained from his face.

And when her father's voice sounded on the video, so did hers. "Put him in the driver's seat," her father's pained grunt came.

Warren's own voice was next. It was higher than he sounded now, but identical to her childhood memories. Except Kate had never heard him sound so terrified. "Please, Paul. Don't do this! *Please!*"

Kate snatched the phone away from the frozen man in front of her, catching a glimpse of Graves backhanding Warren round the face on the screen. She paused it, trying not to look too hard. It was CCTV footage, with the flashing blue lights of a police car illuminating the mangled car in front. Her father's old Mondeo. Nor did she look at the still figure slung across the road. The one wearing Aaron's favourite hoodie.

The worst was Warren. A young, broken boy clutching what remained of his leg and pleading for help.

She put the phone on the changing table, pressing her hand into her hip. His screensaver flashed up; the most recent scan of their baby.

When she turned, she found Warren leaning against the windowsill, his jaw clenched tight. Kate joined him, pressing her face against his shoulder. Down on the snow-covered gardens, Mattie and Sarah used plastic ball-throwers to launch balls for Leo, who legged it down the garden, tail wagging. Little trails in the snow marked his progress.

"I love you," Kate whispered quietly. "And I'm sorry."

He said nothing, simply lifting his arm and pulling her underneath it. Shivers ran up her spine when his lips found her neck, just as his hands delved around her bump. Her own came up to join them. "And I love you."

The weight of her father's crimes was heavy on her shoulders, but the video offered an opportunity. "We can send the video to the police. Anonymously, obviously. You say he'll be handed over soon?"

Warren began to rub the sore spot on her back, pulling a groan from deep in her chest—just like he had when he'd massaged her to sleep last night. "The end of this month," he confirmed.

"Then add this to the evidence he'll be handed over with." An idea struck her, one she'd been thinking about since she'd discovered evidence of her father's crimes. "I don't want us to be associated with him. I don't want the baby to be associated with him. I don't want his name."

"If you don't want his name," his hands left her suddenly, and Kate turned to find him kneeling on the floor, "then take mine."

Her brain seemed to work in slow motion, directing her gaze from his face to the little box he held up. A ring sparkled within, presenting a diamond set between two emeralds. "Warren," she whispered, lost for words.

"The other gift I mentioned," Warren grinned. His soft smile was as bewitching as it had been a decade ago. A smile that she would have followed anywhere, come what may. "Marry me, kitten."

Kate wanted to accept—she really did—but her answer was swept away by a gasp of pain. A band of pressure had settled around her navel, squeezing the very life out of her. It gathered in intensity, rolling over her like thunder. Strong hands came around her, guiding her to the armchair, but she could do nothing but hold her breath and wait for it to abate.

"Breathe," he whispered, brushing her hair out of her eyes. "Just breathe. I'm here."

It was an age until she could follow Warren's instructions, until her breaths came freely once more. "Oh, god," she panted, her head laying against the cushy armchair. Swallowing, she gave him a tentative grin, finding that her own excitement was mirrored on his face.

Warren's palm cradled her cheek, whilst the other found her bump. "Is it time to get the hospital bag?"

She nodded, giving a nervous laugh. "I think so. I don't want to get there too late and find out I've missed the window for an epidural."

His lips conquered hers in a swift movement, pressing the engagement ring box into her hand. "And is this a yes or a no, by the way?"

Kate's eyebrow quirked as she flicked it open, sighing at the ring inside, her insides gooey with happiness. "Depends on how much grief your daughter gives me on her way out."

"Kitten…" Warren warned, the edge of his lip curling.

"It's a yes," she said simply. "I've told you—I was always yours."

"And I was always yours." He slid the ring onto her finger, leaning their foreheads together. "Now let's go meet our baby girl."

Want to meet the daughter that Warren would love to the ends of the earth? Or do you want even more steamy action? **Download your free bonus scene from steviesparks.com.**

Want to learn what kind of absolute *filth* Jensen got up to in New York? Don't worry. We'll pick up right where we left off. **Read *A Stone's Throw* on Amazon.**

Want to pre-order Aldous's book? It'll be an enemies-to-lovers, arranged marriage, why choose romance. And yes, there will be MM action. Can you guess who with? ☒

Also by Stevie Sparks

DAD'S BEST FRIEND | SECRET BABY | AGE GAP | COLLEGE STUDENT HEROINE | SCOTTISH HERO | SECOND CHANCE | VIRGIN HEROINE | HIGHEST BIDDER

I paid to have her once. Now, I'll risk it all to have her forever.

The first time I saw her, she was an innocent. An untouched beauty offering herself up to the highest bidder.

I told myself I was only bidding to keep her safe. To protect her from men who would shatter her innocence without a second thought.

If I'd had any idea who she was, any idea what defiling her would mean for my future, I might have walked away without ever touching her.

But I didn't. And now the secrets we've kept threaten to unravel both of our lives.

Having her the first time cost me nothing but money. Keeping her... could cost me everything.

.

Click here to read now!

VALENTINE'S DADDY VIBES | 'GOOD GIRL' | AGE GAP | PLUS SIZE HEROINE | TATTOOED MMC | BILLIONAIRE HERO| PIERCED HERO | PIERCED PEEN | SURPRISE BOSS | BOSS TO LOVER | DOMINANT HERO | IDIOT CAT

.

When Skye walks in on her boyfriend sleeping with her sister on Valentine's Day, she does what any woman would do. She breaks up with him, grabs her cat, and high tails it out of his life. Dressed in her sexiest outfit and out on the town, she meets Silas.

When billionaire Silas Silver heads to the bar after a hectic day at work, he never expected to meet someone like her. Captivated from the moment she walks in, he watches from the shadows until he sees a man follow her to the bathroom.

But if her curves catch his attention, her personality holds it. Their chemistry sizzles, and before long the two of them end up back at his penthouse for a very *climactic* Valentine's evening. Bad dating experiences made him focus on his career, but maybe his happy ever after isn't so far away after all...

In Silver Fox, a spicy Valentine's Day novella, the worst day of Skye's life turns into anything but as she and Silas find themselves entwined in desire and passion. Their connection soon proves that, on Valentine's Day, love really can be found where you least expect it.

Click here to read now!

LATE HUSBAND'S BROTHER | AGE GAP ROMANCE| HE FALLS IN LOVE FIRST| ONLY ONE BED|

HAPPY EVER AFTER

His brother's wife. He loved his brother's wife.

After losing his heart to Emmeline, the one woman he could never have, Michael committed himself to a life in the army, fighting for King and country in the Great War.

...Until his brother died, and Michael returned to Scarlett Castle as the Duke of Foxcotte.

Fed up with her lack of grandchildren, Michael's mother hatches a plan to bring Michael and Emmeline together in a marriage of convenience. However, whilst Michael agrees to court Emmeline, they both secretly long for something more passionate than a business arrangement. But Michael could have never imagined that hidden trauma lurked beneath Emmeline's emerald eyes.

Michael and Emmeline soon ignite a flame that threatens to consume them both as they learn that all relationships come with risks both wanted and unwanted. Will their marriage of convenience be successful? Or will Emmeline's traumatic past catch up to her and sweep her away?

Click here to read now!

ENEMIES TO LOVERS | SECOND CHANCE | ONLY ONE BED | FORCED PROXIMITY | HAPPY EVER AFTER

Sixteen years ago, Lady Annabelle Fraser broke him.

Kit, the Duke of Aylesbourne, has been running from his demons ever since, be it journeying into the heart of the Antarctic or narrowly avoiding death in an avalanche on Mount Everest.

He would have rather faced death than Annabelle.

But when he finds her in bed with one of his old friends, he snaps.

Because sixteen years ago, Annabelle promised to wait for him. And this time he isn't going to let her escape.

Sixteen years ago, Kit abandoned her when she needed him most.

Some might call her a spinster. Annabelle prefers to think of herself as an independent woman. When Kit discovers her affair, however, he does what she never expected him to do again.

He ruins her.

Disgraced in the eyes of society, if Kit thinks Annabelle is going down without a fight, he's got another thing coming.

.

Click here to read now!

Talia

Attempting to scrub the gritty feeling from her eyes, Talia finally abandoned her textbook. She was nestled on the mezzanine level of the reading room, surveying the students diligently working below.

Nerves pulled her focus to the window, through which Low Memorial Library lurked. That had been the photograph on the welcome leaflet she'd received alongside her acceptance letter to Columbia University; smiling students lounging on Low's sun-kissed steps.

Once, that image had filled her with excitement. She'd let out a shriek in the living room, thrusting the letter at Dad and Darcy, unable to believe she'd been accepted into Columbia—on their *premedical* track. It had been the first step on the road to being a doctor, to accomplishing everything she'd worked towards.

Today, a look at Low had her digestive tract tying itself into a gnarled lump.

Talia didn't even need to look at the clock. She'd checked her phone five times in the last two minutes. Her appointment was 57 minutes away.

An hour until I lose my scholarship.

She shook her head, ridding her brain of the thought. Her situation must happen all the time, surely. Students' progress would go up and down. They'd give her time to get her grades back up. They wouldn't pull the rug out from under her at the first sign of failure. Universities would be devoid of students if that were true.

A thin fissure of doubt ran through her mind.

Back home, that may be true.

But this was America.

Talia bit her lip. It seemed simple enough, on the surface. America and England were similar countries; the former derived from the latter, so of course there would be similarities.

She just hadn't expected how *different* it would be. On her first day in America, she'd nearly been mowed down by a taxi because she looked right when crossing the road instead of left. And then a bad-tempered police officer had threatened her with a ticket for jaywalking.

A year later, her dream of studying medicine at one of the best universities in the world was in danger of caving in on itself.

Because if she lost her scholarship, she may as well head straight to the airport.

Her face twisted into a grimace. Dad would be so disappointed. During her school years, he'd assisted with every assignment, every essay, every project. He'd helped her make countless flash cards and brainstorms and revision questionnaires.

All because her dream was to become a doctor like Mum. To live up to her memory.

Talia looked up at the clouds brewing over the autumnal day. Would Mum be proud of what she'd accomplished?

"I don't know how he hasn't been kicked out yet," a conspiratorial whisper came from the level below. "Quinn *and* the girl who sold herself. Talk about lowering the freaking standard."

Talia poked her nose over the end of her graffitied desk. It abutted a balcony, over which she could see the rest of the reading room below. On the other side of the room, a lone student sat at the desk nearest the door, his pencil steadily moving across the paper, his dark hair falling over his forehead. There was no one else in sight. Was that the Quinn they were talking about? She caught his eye just as he looked up, quickly averting her gaze.

Another whisper came, sounding as if they were directly below her. "A hundred grand is worth it to some people, I guess."

The first one snorted just as her blonde bob edged into view. "Would you sleep with some rich guy for a hundred grand?"

"I'd rather eat this textbook page by page. And to think he facilitated the entire thing at that sex club he works at. He's no better than a pimp, and she's no better than the prostitutes swarming Roosevelt Avenue."

Talia stared at her phone, lost in thought. A hundred grand for sleeping with some rich guy? At least she wasn't the only girl at Columbia feeling the bite of desperation. Her lips contorted at not only the thought of *some rich guy* thrusting atop her, but that being her first experience of sex.

When she lost her virginity, she wanted it to be with someone she loved. She knew that for certain.

She let her attention wander as the girls below her drifted onto another topic of conversation. Her phone flashed on, and Talia felt herself smile for the first time all day.

Her sister Darcy had sent a selfie of herself and Dad, smiling over a table brimming with afternoon tea. Talia recognised where they were immediately—the café near the family home in Covent Garden, with its familiar floral decorations and expertly made cakes.

Homesickness hit her like a freight train.

A second message popped up as Talia gazed wistfully at the photo.

Darcy: We shared a strawberry tart in your honour. Miss you x

The sight of Darcy and Dad steadied her somewhat. *They* were why she was doing this. She was fascinated by the human body, of course. Ultimately, her ambition came down to wanting to help people, but she also wanted to make her father proud. He had been a nurse for years before going into property development with the money from Mum's life insurance payout, and as a child Talia had been obsessive in wanting to know about the people he'd helped during his workday.

He'd never been prouder of her than the day she announced she'd been accepted into Columbia University—just like her mother.

She couldn't let him down. She couldn't let Darcy down. Her little sister had always looked up to her, and Talia going abroad for university was the first time they'd really been separated. Darcy had been excited for her, but Talia knew the separation hadn't been easy. There wasn't a day that went by without them texting and calling each other.

Her heart clenched at the thought of home. She could be in that café in Covent Garden with them both, and instead...

Talia shook away her maudlin thoughts and pulled her laptop towards her. She wasn't going to go into that scholarship office meeting unprepared. A quick look at the clock told her she still had 44 minutes left. Plenty of time to gather her thoughts, prepare an argument in her favour, and fight her case.

Half an hour later, Talia gathered her things into her bag, confidence and nerves swirling together in her stomach, before slinging it over her shoulder. The walk across the South Lawn to Low was short, and Talia trailed her hand over the squat hedge lining the path.

She climbed Low's steps, slipping between the imposing columns lining the front of the building. In her opinion, its proud exterior was no match for what lay within. In a few years, this would be where her graduation ceremony was held—and the cavernous rotunda was certainly well-equipped for the job, complete with sleek columns of its own.

For now, she headed towards the scholarship office with a singular goal in mind, her prepared speech fresh in her mind.

The building's interior was a maze of marble, but Talia knew the way by now. At her first visit during orientation week, she had quickly become lost, wandering deeper and deeper within. Had an older student not come to her rescue, she suspected she would still be lost in its depths.

Today, the Financial Aid Office was a bustling hub of activity. Its dark wood walls were obscured by shelves bursting with binders full of paperwork. Yet more paperwork could be found stacked on the employees' desks, alongside the steady tapping of keyboards and the low whir of computer cooling fans hard at work.

Talia sat on the row of seats at the Office's entrance, waiting for her name to be called. She swallowed, smiling politely when she accidentally caught the eye of the man pushing the mail trolley into the room.

Attempting to keep her breakfast in her stomach, she watched the clock on the wall with rapt attention. The minutes ticked by. Three o'clock. Five past. Ten past. *Quarter* past. Until—

"Natalia Llewellyn?"

Talia honed in on the caller, an older woman whose bright orange blouse glowed against her dark skin. She sat down on the opposite side of the desk, her polite expression looking more like a rictus grin. "Good afternoon."

"Good afternoon. How can I help, Miss Llewellyn?" Brianna—according to her nametag—said, sweeping a handful of her locs over her shoulder.

"I've come to discuss my fees."

Brianna's fingers tapped the keyboard, eyeing the monitor in front of her. A frown pulled at her forehead. "I can see you were awarded a merit-based scholarship for your freshman year. Is that correct?"

Talia nodded stiffly, feeling shame cover her like a shadow. "It is, but—"

"And the fees for your sophomore year are almost due."

"I haven't… I haven't met the scholarship's eligibility requirements for this year." Talia lowered her voice. "My GPA is too low, but they recommended that I speak to yourselves to see what assistance would be available."

The flash of incredulity in Brianna's eyes was like a dagger over her head. "Have you been affected by any extenuating circumstances during the past year?"

Talia paused. Somehow she didn't think crippling homesickness would qualify. "No."

Brianna turned her attention back to her computer, her fingers flying across the keyboard. "I can see you've already retaken Calculus and Organic Chemistry."

"That's correct." Those modules had nearly been the death of her. She seemed to have left the straight-A student she'd once been on the runway at Heathrow.

"And you weren't able to improve your grade?"

"Maths and chemistry aren't my strong point," she admitted. "Can I try again? If I can bump up my grades there—"

"Students are only permitted a single retake."

Oh. "Can I retake some of my other modules? My Physics I grade wasn't brilliant, perhaps if I—"

"But you *did* pass. If you received a passing grade, you're not eligible for a retake."

Panic began to set in. "Are there any other scholarships available?"

Brianna pulled out a binder from the nearest shelf, flicking through its pages. "The deadline for most scholarships have passed. Only one is still accepting applications. Here."

Talia took the proffered leaflet, but her heart sunk at its title. *Needs-Based Aid.* She placed the leaflet on the desk, bowing her head slightly. There was no point even opening it. "I won't be eligible for this. My father is…"

A multimillionaire.

"… wealthy," she finished quietly.

There was a pause before Brianna answered, and Talia could see the compassion drying up before her eyes. She briefly looked at her computer screen, her eyes flicking from one line to another. "I can see your fees are due in the next seven days."

"Is there no other option?" Talia whispered, her hand coming up to her mouth.

"I'm afraid not. If this payment isn't made in seven days, your account will be formally referred to the university's agents for debt collection and possible legal action regarding the fees already incurred for your sophomore year. Your enrolment on the premedical program would also lapse, and you would be unable to rejoin."

A start of fear bolted through her spine. "*Legal action?*"

"The account details you'll need for the payment are on the email you received this morning. Thank you for coming in, Miss Llewellyn." Brianna raised a firm hand signalling towards the door, but her tone wasn't unkind.

Talia didn't remember leaving the Financial Aid Office, nor did she remember the winding route out of Low. All at once, she found herself sitting on those famous steps, hugging her knees like her life depended on it. She ignored the cold seeping through her jeans, attempting to quieten her swirling thoughts.

For the first time in her life, Talia was glad her mother wasn't there to see her now. *She never knew what a failure I was.*

Her eyes burned as she realised she was going to have to tell her father and sister. All of the support they'd given her over the years was going to be for nothing. She was doing this for them—Dad, Darcy, and Mum's memory. And what exactly had she achieved?

The image of her acceptance letter floated through her mind.

And here she sat. On those stupid fucking steps, her life in ruins. Not only was she going to arrive at home with her tail between her legs, the debt collectors and legal action were going to be biting at her heels.

A hundred thousand dollars. That was what her freshman year scholarship had been worth.

Could Dad pay it? This year, perhaps. But this was the *first* adult thing she'd done in her life. Talia imagined making the phone call to Dad, her dignity crumbling further with every word. She couldn't be a failure. She didn't want to use her family's money to get ahead.

When her parents were young, *they* didn't come from money. They'd stood on their own two feet. They'd been adults. It'd been hard, but they'd found a way.

Talia just had to find *her* way.

She blinked, her eyes suddenly refocusing—on Butler Library opposite her.

"Would you sleep with some rich guy for a hundred grand?"

Wasn't that what the gossiping student had said earlier? She swallowed away her spiralling panic, standing so quickly her head spun. Quinn. That had been his name, the dark-haired student studying in the corner. The one who'd apparently facilitated the arrangement.

A hundred grand.

Talia had never slept with anyone before. How bad could it possibly be? Even if it *was* bad, it wouldn't last long. A few hours at most. The alternative—telling Dad and Darcy of her failure—would be far worse.

Was she really considering this? Her first time with a complete stranger?

Maybe she had more in common with that other desperate student than she realised.

A lifetime of humiliation in exchange for a couple of hours of misery.

That was all there was to it. Once her first time was over and done with, maybe she could learn to enjoy herself with other partners. Maybe this would be a new start for her, both academically and sexually.

A curious calm settled over her as she took that first step, and every subsequent step came easier.

Quinn. She needed to talk to Quinn.

Talia

T alia glanced around the dorm room, her nerves grating with every breath. She wasn't quite sure what to expect when Quinn had welcomed her in. He worked in a sex club, after all. Somehow, the image she'd conjured in her mind had included explicit photos and expensive furnishings.

But no. Nothing in Quinn's dorm gave her any hint that he worked in a sex club. There was a stack of posters on the desk—identical to the one she'd used to find him—offering a wide range of tutoring sessions in the reading room she'd been in earlier. Next to those, she saw the familiar letterheaded paper of the scholarship team. The furnishings were minimal, and even the bedding looked like the cheapest money could buy.

The only hint of Quinn's personality lay on the shelf on the wall. Books like *The Basics of Bitcoins and Blockchains* and *Rich Dad, Poor Dad* weighed the shelf down. She eyed the Bitcoin book. Her dad had said one of his friends had got lucky with Bitcoin, but he didn't have anything good to say about the cryptocurrency as a whole.

Either the books left Quinn's shelf on a regular basis or he was particularly fastidious in his cleaning, because Talia couldn't see a single speck of dust.

Unlike my own bookshelf, she thought, her conscience giving her a surreptitious kick.

Quinn himself leant against his desk, his hands gripping its edge. "So what subject was it you needed tutoring in?"

"I, um," Talia stalled, twisting her hands together. "It's more of a referral I'm looking for, rather than tutoring."

Dark, windswept hair covered his forehead, until it met brows that seemed to be permanently frowning. Or at least Talia *hoped* they were permanently frowning—it was either that or he really didn't like her. "A referral to who?"

Deep breath, Talia.

"I've heard that you work at a club," she said tentatively, hoping he would fill in the gaps in her knowledge. When he didn't, she threw caution to the wind. "An adult club."

Eyes so dark they were nearly black glared back at her. "Who told you this?"

"People were talking about it in the library earlier today. I overheard." She'd never given much thought to sex before, but now it was potentially on the table it was all she could think of. Would her buyer have the same kind of untidy hair he did? Would they be good in bed? Was *Quinn* good in bed? Would her buyer be as handsome as him?

Stop it, she hissed at her thoughts.

Quinn pushed himself away from the desk, stepping around a neatly-stacked tower of dumbbells to sit on the bed. He leant forward, his elbows on his knees. "What's your name?"

"Talia. Natalia, but everyone calls me Talia." Except for Dad. He called her Nattie.

"Talia…?" Quinn slowly looked her up and down, his gaze tracking every curl in her hair.

"Llewellyn," she answered, trying not to squirm with discomfort.

"And how old are you, Talia Llewellyn?" Her name was a caress on the soft curve of his lips.

What did that have to do with anything? "Eighteen. I'll be nineteen later this month."

He paused, as if in thought. "What's your body count?"

Talia reared back, bewildered. "I've never…" She dropped her voice. "I've never *killed* anyone." Jesus, what kind of club did he work at?

A bright laugh lifted Quinn's expression, his eyes shining with the first smidgen of warmth she'd seen in the man. His grin was almost fond as he looked up at her. "I mean, how many people have you slept with?"

"Oh." A red tinge came to her cheeks. "My body count is the same for both meanings, I guess. None."

Quinn smirked up at her. "Good. I can work with that."

The duality of emotions that burst through her veins was almost shocking. The relief of being one step closer to paying her tuition fees and the utter panic of *holy-shit-am-I-actually-really-doing-this*.

He didn't give her a moment to process either. "But it'll need to be soon." He looked at the calendar on the wall. "When's your birthday?"

"That's fine," she nodded, trying not to seem desperate when her brain was screaming *the sooner, the better*. "The second of October. Sunday after next."

Quinn made an indistinct noise. "Are you doing this for the money or the thrill?"

Her eyes flicked between his. It hadn't escaped her notice that neither of them had explicitly stated what they were discussing. "And by *this*, you mean?"

"Selling your virginity to men who are willing to buy it," he supplied, his eyebrow cocking up. "I assume that's what you're wanting."

There was a pause before she nodded. "It's for the money," she replied quietly.

His expression wasn't unsympathetic. "Then, like I said, it'll need to be soon. You'll fetch the highest price as an eighteen-year-old virgin. That's the lowest they'll go."

Legally, she thought uncomfortably.

"They'll want to interview you first. Then there are several rounds of testing you'll need to undergo, and they'll need your medical records. You good with that?"

Talia nodded again, feeling slightly queasy. "I'm good."

About the Author

Stevie Sparks is a British author and long-time copy editor from Windsor, England (where Windsor Castle is).

She suffers from a terrible medical condition that has left her incapable of reading books without smut. When it comes to books, she prefers the phrase 'full steam ahead.'

Stevie writes dark romance and historical romance. She can be found on Goodreads, BookBub, TikTok, Instagram, Facebook, and Twitter.